tota
fine´

Life . . . Series

Life . . . On a High

Life . . . With No Breaks

Cornerstone Series

The Cornerstone

Wordsmith (The Cornerstone Book 2)

totally fine

nick spalding

LAKE UNION
PUBLISHING

Published by Lake Union Publishing, Seattle

www.apub.com

Amazon, the Amazon logo, and Lake Union Publishing are trademarks of Amazon.com, Inc., or its affiliates.

EU Product Safety contact:
Amazon Publishing, Amazon Media EU S.à r.l.
38, avenue John F. Kennedy, L-1855 Luxembourg
amazonpublishing-gpsr@amazon.com

ISBN-13: 9781662520013
eISBN: 9781662520006

Cover design by Emma Rogers
Cover images: © Gannvector © janista © Artst0ry © SalmaStocks / Shutterstock

Printed in the United States of America

To everyone who knows that sometimes it's okay if you're not totally fine.

So much to do. So many people to see. So many plans to put into action!

The phrase 'busier than a one-legged man in an arse-kicking competition' doesn't really apply to me, because I'd be far too busy to even get to the competition in the first place.

'Busier than a one-legged man, who'd like to attend the arse-kicking competition, but just cannot spare the time between meetings' is a more accurate idiom – but nowhere near as catchy.

I have Zenith Games at 10.30 a.m. to talk about the event they'd like to hold for the launch of their first PC adventure. Then at 2 p.m., I'm back over to Howling at the Moon to go through the finer points of their first gig back together for sixteen years. And then I have to fit in poor Elaine and the poodles at some point, as well. The pet expo, which is only three weeks away now, has told her she needs to reduce her floor size by ten square metres, which is going to be problematic, to say the least. Those poodles enjoy their space.

My brain is buzzing with a whole series of disparate jobs that I wish I could manage over the course of the next few weeks . . . but here I am in the perfect storm of them all needing to be sorted out today.

And then there's little Teddy's birthday party!

Okay, that probably shouldn't take precedence over the stuff I've got to do for actual, proper work – but I promised my new girlfriend, Annie, that her nephew's birthday was going to be one for the ages, and

I don't want to let her down – not this early in our relationship. It'd set a very bad precedent, wouldn't it?

I don't want to let Teddy down, either. Poor kid's been through the wringer with his parents' divorce, according to Annie. So, showing him a good time for his eighth year on this planet is the least I can do.

But first, it's the appointment with Zenith Games – and trust them to have a development studio out here in the sticks, rather than in the centre of town, like anyone with a sensible grasp on logistics. This is a beautiful part of the country, what with its rolling hills, quaint villages and at least one very picturesque little church I wouldn't mind attending a special occasion in, but it's a pain in the arse to drive through, on a day where I could really do without the extra journey time.

Or being stuck behind this tractor. 10.30 is going to rapidly become 10.40, and even 10.50, if I don't get a wiggle on. And I hate being late for meetings. When you're the guy being paid to co-ordinate events, it doesn't do much for your reputation to be late. Sets up a precedent in the client's mind that you're unreliable. Which doesn't help my stress levels in the short term, or my bank balance in the long term.

Thankfully, the tractor turns off onto farmland after I've only been stuck behind it for about five minutes, so it could have been worse. My face is only a mild shade of pink, instead of the bright puce it would no doubt have been if I'd been behind the bloody thing all the way to the studio.

Maybe I won't be late, after all!

My stress levels reduce somewhat – enough for me to start singing along to the radio again. It's all fine. I'm going to be fine. I can get through this meeting with no problems, and I have plenty of time to spare before I see the craggy-faced, leather-clad monsters of rock that Howling at the Moon most definitely still are. They may need a little help getting up and down the stairs to the stage these days, but they can still rock out with the best of them, once they're on it.

Getting that out the way as well should leave me the evening free to pop over to Elaine's to see about the claustrophobic poodles.

Then after that maybe I'll get ten minutes to have a chat on the phone with Annie, when I can promise her that I'll get to Teddy's birthday party arrangements tomorrow. It's still a good few weeks off anyway, but I like to get these things sorted out way ahead of time, to make sure that any changes or problems can be dealt with.

I don't think I'd be able to do this job if I didn't know how to forward plan properly. Especially not as a freelancer. I am my own secretary – and can't exactly fire myself if I do a bad job.

Ring ring.

I nearly jump out of my skin as the noise from my phone bounces around the car's interior.

Well, well. Speak of the devil! It's Maurice from Mega Lanes – the bowling alley Teddy apparently loves more than any other place in the world. Maurice is probably ringing about my plans to theme the alley with a metric shit tonne of Jurassic Park *memorabilia for the birthday party. According to Annie, Teddy is a huge fan of that film series, and I want dinosaurs everywhere. Absolutely bloody everywhere. Not a square inch will be dinosaur free. They'll be rammed in. The poodles would have a heart attack.*

Best not take the call now, though. Not with my brain as busy as it is. I'll have to get back to him later today.

I have to concentrate on Zenith Games for the moment. My bank account demands it.

But it's fine. I have loads of time to think about Teddy's birthday, and how I'm going to impress the hell out of Annie with what I've got planned. No point in stressing myself out today more than I need to.

Best to just keep my head down, get through the rest of today – and then I can take a breather.

Everything is fine.

Everything is totally

Chapter One

HUMPS

'You do realise they look like plucked chickens, don't you?'

I give my girlfriend a look. 'They're dinosaurs.'

'Yes. I can see that, but you can't deny their resemblance to barnyard fowl, which have very unfortunately been standing in a force 10 hurricane.'

I roll my eyes.

Having a stand-up comedian for a girlfriend has its benefits, but it also very much has its *drawbacks*. Annie has a way with words that gets right to the heart of the matter – in the most amusing way possible. To her, anyway. I've discovered this over the three months we've been seeing each other now.

I look down at the selection of Compsognathus models I've hired for the party (and try saying that fast after you've had a couple). They do indeed look like chickens. I should have checked the size properly before I ordered them from Prop World. They looked impressive in the photos, but they also looked like they were six feet tall. They are most resolutely *not* six feet tall. They barely come up to my knee. I'll have to send a friendly email to

Prop World to expound on the virtues of including measurements in their adverts.

I asked for the dinosaurs to be placed close to the lanes that we have hired for Teddy's birthday, figuring they'd look dead scary and cool.

But the only scary thing about them is that they are a trip hazard.

Still, the animatronic velociraptor over in the corner has worked out much better – as have the *Jurassic Park*-themed bunting, the film music being piped through the PA system and the two poor jobbing actors both dressed up as a T-Rex.

This is the most Jurassic Park a place has looked since they were *filming Jurassic Park*. Steven Spielberg would feel right at home.

All of this has been made possible thanks to the fact that four years ago I got Mega Lanes back on its feet with a marketing campaign and series of free experience days that I'm still extremely proud of.

Maurice owed me big time. This is the repayment.

. . . I just wish it didn't involve chickens masquerading as dinosaurs.

'Don't make that face,' Annie says. 'He'll love everything you've done.'

I point down at the nearest dinochicken. 'Yeah, but . . .'

'Yeah, but nothing. One little cock-up doesn't matter at all. You need to stop being such a perfectionist.'

'But I wanted everything to be *perfect*.'

'Everything *is* perfect,' she replies, giving me a hug. 'You've done brilliantly. Thank you.'

I smile and give her a kiss. This still feels like such a privilege to do in a public place.

I know she's right. I'm sure Teddy will have a lovely time.

But . . . those dinochickens will plague me for the rest of the day, until the guy from Prop World comes to collect them later, along with all the other stuff I've hired.

'Didn't know they had chickens in the Jurassic era,' a voice says from behind us. I turn to see Maurice waddling over from the reception counter, surveying all of my efforts at turning this corner of the bowling alley into something Jeff Goldblum could be proud of.

I roll my eyes. 'They're Compgonarthus,' I tell him sagely – and incorrectly.

'Bless you,' he responds, and looks about himself. 'Great job you've done here, Charlie. As always.'

'Thank you,' I reply, deliberately not looking down at the dinochickens.

Maurice looks at his watch. 'So, I can give you two hours with the music playing, but I'll have to go back to the regular stuff after that.' He makes a face as he says this. Maurice is forty-seven years old and about two concession-stand hot dogs away from a coronary. Pop music designed to appeal to 'the youth' is not his thing. But endless Oasis and Ned's Atomic Dustbin would no doubt drive the customers away, so he has to put up with it.

'No trouble,' I say. 'Annie's nephew and the rest of the guests will be here in about five or ten minutes, and I'm sure most of the actual bowling with be done after two hours. No problems if not, though. We won't need the music any longer.' I fix Maurice with a look a drill sergeant would be proud of. 'As long as things are the way I've asked them to be when Teddy comes in, that's the main thing. First impressions are the best impressions!'

'Alright, alright,' Annie chides me gently. 'Leave poor Maurice alone. Teddy is an eight-year-old boy, not the CEO of a company. You're not at work now.'

Maurice laughs. 'Isn't he? This place is almost as decked out as it was when he did the relaunch.'

'There are less Marvel superheroes this time around,' I point out.

I themed that event around the always popular characters of Marvel Comics. They certainly brought in the crowds the way I hoped they would. Iron Man pretty much saved Maurice's bacon that day – which is something Robert Downey Jr would probably be as proud of as Jeff Goldblum would be about what I've done here today.

'But there are a lot more plucked chickens,' Annie says, unable to resist getting the joke in. I feel like if we have a future together, this will be the story of my life.

And I do so *want* that to be the story of my life . . .

Maurice laughs again, before patting me on the back – and going off to busy himself with something that's no doubt very important to the continued efficient functioning of the bowling alley.

I look at my watch. It's 3.54 p.m. People should be arriving right about now.

. . . and would you look at that! Here is Annie's sister, Jude – with a very excited-looking Teddy in tow. He's practically pulling his mother through the bowling alley entrance.

I wonder if I have time to hide the dinochickens before they get over here?

I did not have time. But it didn't seem to matter, anyway.

Teddy was absolutely delighted with everything, which made my heart sing. His little blond mop of unruly hair bounced around happily as he jumped between the different elements I'd brought together to turn Mega Lanes into a tiny slice of a Steven Spielberg movie. A movie that Teddy has now watched about forty times, I'm led to believe.

He was particularly enamoured with the two guys in the giant, bulgy inflatable T-Rex costumes. Which I knew he would be. They look altogether far too ridiculous not to be of supreme entertainment value to an eight-year-old boy.

Jude and Annie had to prise him away from them both, just so he could go and say hello to the other guests as they arrived at the party.

I am delighted to see how Annie lights up when her nephew is happy, and I'm just as pleased that Jude seems to have taken a liking to me as well, thanks to all of my efforts. A sister's approval can be very important for a new relationship.

With Jude's say-so, I'd invited a total of nine other couples to the event, including the parents of many of Teddy's friends from school – as well as my best friend's kid, who Teddy has got to know because they coincidentally go to the same school. Having Jack at the party, with his ball of energy Tyler, is a nice little confidence boost for me. It's great to have someone here I know well.

To my surprise, Jack has dragged my other best friend, Leo, along with him, who we've both known since college. It's lovely to see Leo out and about, to be honest. It's something of a rarity these days.

They make a right pair together, my best friends. One looks like he's just come out of a mosh pit, and the other couldn't do scruffy if you put a gun to his head.

'You look knackered,' Jack remarks with a grin as he watches Tyler run over to start harassing one of the T-Rexes with Teddy. 'As usual.'

'Sod off,' I say with good-natured derision, keeping my voice down. Swearing and small children really shouldn't mix.

'Charming,' Jack says, before hooking a thumb in Leo's direction. 'I managed to drag him out once. Something of a miracle.'

Leo gives me a slightly unsure smile. 'He pretty much bullied me into it.'

'No, I didn't,' Jack snorts. 'And it's nice to see you out and about in public. Isn't it, Charlie?'

I nod and smile. 'Yep, it certainly is.'

'I hope it's okay, mate,' Jack says. 'I know you're still in full-on "making a good impression mode" with your new squeeze, and having your dumb-arse mates here could put a dampener on that.'

I wave a hand. 'Nah. You're fine. Just don't start telling her any stories about what we got up to at university.' I make a face. 'She does not need to know about Marita the Maniac.'

My friends' eyes go wide with recognition.

'No. She really doesn't need to know about that,' Leo says with a smile.

Jack looks over at where the crowd is gathered around the four bowling lanes Maurice has provided me with for today's entertainment. 'Good set-up as usual, Charlie,' he remarks.

'Thanks very much.' I always feel incredibly proud of myself when Jack approves of something I've done.

But then his brow knits, and I know what he's going to say before it comes out of his mouth. 'But why are there a load of bloody plucked chickens over there? Are they food for the dinosaurs?'

The next two hours of my life are pretty much par for the course at events like this. I've been to so many of them now, I think I could co-ordinate them in my sleep.

I can never say that I particularly enjoy them myself, but as long as everybody else does, I'm more than happy. I get to have fun when it's all over, when I can have a drink somewhere warm and quiet.

You'd think there wouldn't be all that much to actually organise at this event, now that everyone is ensconced in their respective bowling lanes, having got the business of the hellos out of the way. But in my experience, any time you get a dozen or more human beings together in one place and time, there's always going to be something that needs arranging, fixing or changing. No matter how well organised you've been beforehand.

For instance, who exactly should go in each team to make sure things are fair and balanced for everyone? Or when exactly is the right time for Teddy to open his presents? When should Maurice get the guys over in the café to bring out the food? What drink orders do people have? How long should everyone have to eat? Are the vegetarians properly catered for? Are the people with allergies?

The list inevitably goes on, and on, and on. But it's fine, because that's what I'm here for. That's always what I'm here for.

I am the man who organises. It's something I feel like I've turned into an art form over the years.

'Are you planning on actually bowling a ball at this bowling alley party?' Annie asks me as she takes a bite of her third prawn vol-au-vent. I'm constantly surprised and delighted at how relaxed she is around me. It's like she's known me for years. I wish I was the same with her.

I shrug my shoulders. 'Eh, I'm not that fussed,' I say as I write down the third drinks order I've taken today.

She frowns. 'No, you don't seem it.' She gives me a gentle poke. 'It's okay for you to actually take part in stuff like this, you know. You don't have to treat the whole thing like you are at work.'

It's clear that she *hasn't* actually known me for years, with a statement like that.

'I'm fine. Honestly,' I reply.

11

Annie gives me a look. 'Alright,' she replies. 'Just try to take a few minutes out at some point to at least eat something, okay?'

'I will. I promise.'

. . . but only after I've got this drinks order in over at the café . . . and made sure that Teddy's cake is ready to come out in ten minutes, when we all sing 'Happy Birthday' . . . and then tell Maurice he's okay to put the pop music back on the tannoy . . . and make sure the actors in the T-Rex costumes are okay . . . and check that the animatronic velociraptor isn't covered in too many sticky children's hand prints . . . and—

A prawn vol-au-vent appears in my field of vision. It wobbles slightly.

'Eat,' my girlfriend commands, breaking into my reverie.

I roll my eyes, take the vol-au-vent from her hand and pop it in my mouth. 'There you go,' I say, around the pastry.

'Well done. Make sure you get something more substantial in you, before it all gets hoovered up by the gremloids.'

If this relationship does work out, I'm not 100 per cent sure Annie and I will ever be having children. Not unless I can persuade her not to call them gremloids, anyway.

A bolt of pain suddenly shoots through the back of my neck, and I have to hide the wince on my face from Annie. I don't do a very good job of it, as she looks suddenly concerned. 'You okay?'

'Yeah, I'm fine,' I tell her. 'Just always get a little tense when I'm at wor— when I'm doing stuff like this.'

'Sounds like you could do with a massage,' she says, her eyebrows waggling ever so slightly.

The implicit invitation in this makes me smile broadly – and forget the pain in my neck.

'Maybe we could discuss that later,' I say.

Annie smiles with an arched eyebrow and starts to answer, but my attention is then drawn by the loud sound of crying.

I look over to the bowling lanes to see that little Piper has fallen over again. Quite why her parents, Lindsay and Claire, thought it appropriate to let their delicate little girl try bowling is beyond me. The balls are heavier than she is.

'Oops. Gremloid down,' Annie remarks, pointing at Piper with a satay stick taken from her plate.

'I'd better go and see if they need another plaster,' I sigh.

An event co-ordinator's job is never done – even when he's not technically at work.

I kiss Annie on the cheek – again marvelling that I can do this – and march over to where Lindsay has propped his daughter up on a chair, and is inspecting the fresh graze on her left knee. It will no doubt match the one on her right very soon.

As I do this, I pass Teddy, Tyler and two other boys giggling their heads off at Teddy's new dinosaur mask, which makes loud roaring noises whenever he opens his mouth. I knew that would go down well. It's just the type of obnoxiously noisy toy that boys of Teddy's age adore above all other things.

Excellent. The birthday boy is happy. And that's all that matters.

I can eat later. Right around the time I have that drink in a warm, quiet place.

Piper doesn't need a plaster, thankfully – just a lot of sympathy from her mother and father. I leave them to their ministrations, and make my way over to where Leo is stood at the back of the party near the bowling ball racks, nursing a Coke in one hand.

'How are you doing?' I ask him.

'I'm okay,' he says with a quick smile. 'Everyone seems to be having a good time.'

Possibly with the exception of you, my friend. You look like you're about to jump out of your skin at any moment.

'You gonna play pool with Jack over in the amusement arcade?' I ask him.

'Yeah, in a minute.' Leo doesn't look entirely happy about it. Jack tends to get far too competitive in such situations.

'Okay, cool. Maurice had new tables put in a few weeks ago, so they should run well.'

'You gonna play too?' he asks.

'Yeah. Hopefully. When everything's been taken care of.'

. . . which probably means I won't, if I'm being honest with myself. Everything being taken care of is a scenario I have yet to encounter in my life.

'Great. You're likely to give him a better run for his money than I can.'

I doubt that. Jack is better at pool than either of us. I think we only play so much as it's something to do while we talk and drink beer.

I'd like to spend a little more time with Leo, as I can tell he's not happy.

I have no idea why, but I know he's not. Hasn't been for a while now, either.

Jack's sensed it too – hence why he invited Leo today. Our friend has become increasingly unwilling to come out with us over the last couple of years, and both of us would really like to know why. Leo's always been the quiet one out of the three of us. And he's certainly been silent on what's troubling him.

I can't do any more about it now, though, as I've just spotted Maurice fussing around, over in the café with a couple of his staff. He must be talking to them about the cake. It's almost time for it to come out. God, I hope there's nothing wrong with it!

'Go on,' Leo says, noticing my look of worry as I stare over at the bowling alley's manager. 'Looks like you've got something important to sort out.'

I give my friend a tight grin, and hurry over to Maurice.

Please don't let there be anything too badly wrong with the cake. Everything has gone so well, so far. Everything has been under control. The last thing I need is a cake-shaped spanner in the works!

Thankfully, Maurice informs me that there is absolutely nothing wrong with the birthday cake. Other than the fact it's so loaded with E numbers that every child who eats a bit will be bouncing off the ceiling in about half an hour.

'So, you're ready with the routine we practised?' I ask him. He looks at me like I've just shot his dog.

'Yes, Charlie.' His face is a picture. A badly painted one, made by someone with chronic depression. 'But are you sure it's what Teddy would like?'

I nod enthusiastically. 'Oh yes. I'm sure he'll like it,' I say, trying my very hardest to ignore the look of dismay on Maurice's face.

It's right about now that he's probably wishing he didn't owe me so much of a favour for getting his bowling alley back on track.

I glance at my watch. '5 p.m. on the dot, then?'

Maurice nods like a man going to the gallows.

As do his two staff members.

They don't owe me a favour, but they do have a boss who does.

'We'll go and get . . . *changed*,' Maurice tells me, his face downcast.

'Thanks, mate,' I reply, with an encouraging grin, watching the three of them disappear into a nearby staffroom.

Excellent. Everything is proceeding as scheduled. Now all I have to do is make sure the T-Rexes are ready with their part of the upcoming show, and then I can sit back and watch as—

Oh, good God almighty, has Piper fallen over *again*? Has that girl got rubber bands for legs, or something?

15

Sorting poor old Piper out for the third time, along with actually having a go at the bowling myself, keeps me occupied until 5 p.m. When – on the dot as agreed – the *Jurassic Park* theme swells over the tannoy system, and from over by the café we all turn to see Maurice and his two staff members appear. The female of the two is dressed like Laura Dern from the movie, in khaki shorts and a pink shirt. The other one is wearing the closest approximation to Sam Neill's big hat that I could find, along with his baggy blue shirt and red cravat.

Maurice is dressed like Jeff Goldblum.

Well, he would be if he was a good two or three stone lighter.

As it stands, Maurice is dressed as Jeff Goldblum, if Jeff Goldblum had suffered severe bloating from a wheat allergy. I couldn't find a black jacket big enough for the poor guy, so the bowling alley manager looks like I've wrapped him in a thick bin liner with arm holes. The black trousers are similarly stretched, and the wraparound black sunglasses are also several sizes too small for Maurice's head.

I will apologise to him (again) at length later on, but for now, he's more or less achieving the desired effect, so I'm more than happy.

Maurice Goldblum is carrying Teddy's E-number-loaded birthday cake (which is in the shape of a T-Rex head) and he and his staff are being pursued by the two T-Rexes, as they all come over to the lanes we are using.

The T-Rexes are doing a very good job of trying to look menacing and angry. A job made easier by the fact that it rather looks like they're chasing after someone who's decapitated one of their loved ones – and shoved its head on an over-sized plate.

Teddy is beside himself with joy at all of this, as I knew he would be.

So are the rest of the kids, who know a big pile of lovely E numbers when they see it coming towards them – carried by a somewhat overweight Jeff Goldblum.

I'm very appreciative of the look of mock horror on Maurice's face as he arrives at our lanes with the cake – although this is quite possibly a look of absolutely *genuine* horror at the fact he's had to dress up like this in front of several dozen bowling alley customers this afternoon. He may never live it down. But, you know, as The Goldblum once said, life finds a way . . . so it might work out alright for him, after all.

The cake goes down onto a trestle table set up in front of the party's lanes, and the birthday boy is called over to blow out the eight candles on top of it. Which he does with great gusto, and enough spittle to guarantee that I won't be partaking in any of the cake myself.

We all sing 'Happy Birthday' – which is made slightly awkward by the fact the *Jurassic Park* theme is still playing loudly over the speaker system. The two competing tunes do not sound good together. I should have thought of that beforehand, *damn it*. Both that and the dinochickens are things that will put a crimp in my day, no matter how well everything else goes.

But other than that extra cock-up, the ceremony goes without a hitch, and very soon all children have been sent off to spread cake crumbs all over the bowling alley.

'Well done,' I say gratefully to Maurice, and pat him on the back.

'Thanks, Charlie,' he replies, trying his best to smile.

Jack has no problem doing that. 'Don't feel too bad, mate,' he says to Maurice. 'This bastard once convinced me to climb Ben Nevis in a mankini. He said it was for charity, but I've never been entirely convinced by that excuse. I'm pretty sure it was just to embarrass me for the rest of my natural life.'

'Did it work?' I ask.

Jack thinks for a moment, before taking a bite of the piece of cake he's holding. 'Not really.'

'Would you do it again?' Maurice asks him, now smiling a bit more genuinely. Jack has that effect on people.

Jack's face clouds for a moment. 'No. But not because of this idiot. My mountain climbing days are over.'

'Too old?' Maurice asks.

'Something like that,' Jack says in a noncommittal tone.

I know what he's talking about – but I very much doubt Maurice needs to.

'Anyway, thanks for making Teddy's party so damned good,' I say to him, to get things back to a positive place again.

'My pleasure.' Maurice tugs at a tight jacket sleeve. 'Now, if you don't mind, I'm going to go away and take this costume off.'

'Go right ahead,' I tell him, and chuckle as I watch him and the other cast members of Spielberg's dinosaur spectacular walk off across the bowling alley floor at a hurried pace.

Jack regards me with a look. 'You're a monster, King. That poor man.'

I wave a hand. 'Aah . . . he loved it. The same way you did in that mankini.'

His eyes narrow. 'An absolute monster,' he says, and pops the last of the birthday cake into his mouth.

'Would you like this monster to smash you to pieces at bowling?' I reply, knowing full well that I will not smash him to pieces at all, but equally knowing that it'll make Jack happy to prove that.

'You're on,' he says, pointing a finger at me. 'Leo!' he calls over to our friend – who is still stood slightly apart from everyone else, with a disconcerted look on his face. 'Can you come and be referee for a game with me and him? I don't trust him as far as I can throw him!'

'Hey!' I protest. But not all that much, if I'm honest. I did once cheat at a game of *Mario Kart* when we were kids, and Jack's never forgiven me for it.

As the three of us head over to an empty lane, I can feel myself relaxing a little. The hard stuff is all over with now, thank God. Teddy's birthday has gone without a hitch so far, and he's had a great time. I can take my foot off the accelerator a little, and have a halfway decent time myself. I'll still keep an eye on everyone to make sure they're still having fun in the last hour or so that we are here, but my job is more or less done for the day. The tension that suffuses my entire body in the run-up to any event I'm organising has started to unwind. Even my neck is aching a lot less than it was. I won't need to take any more painkillers today.

The *Jurassic Park* theme gives way to the more typical pop music that Maurice plays over the speaker system, which is something of a relief as well. John Williams is an extremely good composer, but his music does tend to either make you feel either anxious or rambunctious. Neither of which are emotions I particularly wish to feel right now.

I'm frankly happier with a bit of Taylor Swift and Beyoncé.

Jack absolutely destroys me in our impromptu bowling match, which I am not surprised about in the slightest. To be honest I kind of let him win, as I'd much rather put a smile on his face than work myself into a lather trying to beat him.

Besides, Annie comes over to commiserate with me with a rather lovely kiss, so who's to say I don't win anyway?

'There's no point in you taking your last go,' Jack informs me, with his chest puffed out. 'I have vanquished you upon this day, sir. My point score far outweighs your own tally!'

Quite why he feels the need to become a lordling from the sixteenth century when he's winning is quite beyond me. Some sort of past-life regression, possibly.

'Actually, if he bowls three strikes, he still can,' Leo points out, earning him a dark look from Lord Jack of Winning Town.

I will not bowl three strikes. I very much doubt I can bowl one. I am tired – no, actually, I am *exhausted*. Arranging and hosting an event like this always does that to me. I would just like to have a lie down.

So, I'll complete Jack's victory for him by failing to bowl three strikes, and go and have a nice drink somewhere dark and child free.

'Go get 'em!' Annie encourages, which I'm grateful for, even though I'm too exhausted to put up much of a fight. I should probably be more worried about proving my manhood to her, but I'll just have to ride on the success of today's event rather than my prowess at bowling to do that.

As the Black Eyed Peas start to tell me all about their humps over the sound system – in a song I've never really understood the import of, if I'm honest – I take up position at the head of the lane.

Jack now tries to put me off by singing along to the song.

Sort of.

'*Yeah, yeah, yeah. Your humps! My humps! You've got a big, fat hump!*' he sings at the top of his voice. '*Humps humps humps!*'

I'm not even going to describe what he's doing to poor Leo while he's singing. It doesn't bear thinking about. And certainly doesn't bear describing. I try not to look at the expression on Annie's face. Maybe Jack was right about not having my dumb-arse friends here today . . .

I try to ignore my idiotic mate, and look back down the lane. I have to shake my head as my eyesight has gone a little blurred. I really am tired. My heart rate is right up as well. I guess the competition with Jack has got me going more than I thought it would. Maybe I do have something to prove to my new girlfriend, after all.

Setting myself, I walk forward and pitch the bowling ball, in what I hope is an accurate shot.

As I watch the ball fly down the lane, my heart rate feels like it spikes even higher. I must really want to win this match.

Sadly, the ball strikes the pins off to the left, and only six go down.

'Hah!' Jack crows. '*You humped it! You lumped it! Humps humps humps humps!*'

I try to smile back at his antics, but for some reason, I'm now finding it quite hard to breathe. I need to sit down.

'Charlie? Are you okay?' Annie asks, rising from her seat.

I wave a hand. 'Yeah, yeah. I'm just knackered is all. Need to sit . . . sit . . . I need to . . .'

Oh *God*.

Someone has dumped a bucket of cold water over my head. At least that's what it feels like. My heart is pounding out of my chest and my legs have suddenly gone very weak.

Christ, what's happening to me?

Then, the worst thing of all happens. I start to feel faint.

The edges of my vision start to turn black, and I can't take a breath.

I'm dying!

I'm dying right here in this bowling alley! my mind screams at me.

Well, that'll ruin Teddy's birthday party, won't it? Annie won't be impressed with me *at all*.

As I drop to my knees, though, she is by my side. As is Jack. All humour has disappeared from his face.

'Charlie? Mate? Are you okay?' he says, his voice full of heightened concern.

'Charlie?!' Annie cries, causing everyone to look over at what's going on with us.

And what's going on is that I'm collapsing onto the floor of a bowling alley, with my heart pounding out of my chest, a feeling of utter and abject doom rising from the depths of my soul, my vision completely blurred by what I can only assume are tears, and the blackness of death about to envelop me in its horrifying embrace.

'Charlie!' Annie almost screams.

Oh God. How utterly and completely *embarrassing*.

I try to hold up one arm to pat her in a reassuring way, but I can barely lift it.

In fact, I can barely do anything. I just feel like I'm going to—

'Charlie! Charlie! Can you hear me?' Jack's voice has a tremulous, terrified quality to it I can't remember ever hearing before.

. . . well, except for maybe once. Right after he was found, and I went to see him in the hospital.

'Yeah, yeah,' I reply, my voice thick. 'I'm okay.'

'You're clearly not, buddy,' he argues. 'We've got you in the recovery position, so don't try to move. An ambulance is coming.'

Oh God, no. I don't need an ambulance!

The last thing I want all these kids to see is me being lifted out of here on a stretcher. Not to mention Annie. We've only been dating for *three months*!

'No, no. I'm okay,' I insist, trying to sit up.

Jack attempts to hold me down for a moment, but I can feel the strength returning to my body now. I manage to successfully push against him, and sit up against the back of the seats.

'Charlie, are you okay?' Annie says, and I can see tears in her eyes. That won't do at all. I reach out and take her hand. It feels freezing cold.

'Yes, I'm okay,' I try to reassure her. 'I don't know what that was, but I think I'm coming out of it now.'

What that was is the scariest thing that's ever happened to me.

I genuinely thought I was dying.

What the hell happened?

'Don't try to move too much,' Jack insists. 'You might be feeling better, but I still want the paramedics to give you a once-over.'

I don't argue. I know that tone.

At least the kids won't have to watch me stretchered out – I don't think.

Speaking of whom, they are all crowded around me with their parents. How deeply humiliating. Is this going to ruin their memories of the party? Is this all they're going to think about after it's over? Oh God, *no*.

With them stands Maurice, now in his regular clothes, along with the two T-Rexes, who are leaning over me in quite a disconcerting manner. I now have a strong inkling what it must have felt like to be a small, plump, tasty dinosaur from the Jurassic era.

I lift a hand that still shakes a little a bit. 'Don't worry, everyone, I'm perfectly okay. Just had a tumble on the slippery floor, I think.'

That still sounds highly embarrassing, but not quite as strange or terrifying.

'Can you help me sit up on the seat properly?' I ask Annie and Jack, who dutifully help me up into a position that looks a little less stricken.

Annie is still pale of face and cold of hand, but she looks a little less distressed now, thank goodness. I really hope this isn't going to put her off me!

I don't know how long I was unconscious for, but 'My Humps' by the Black Eyed Peas is still playing over the sound system, so it can't have been that long.

'Can I have a drink?' I ask.

'I'll get it,' Leo says, who I now notice is standing just behind me. If anything, he looks more distressed than my girlfriend.

I spend a few minutes continuing to reassure everyone that I am, in fact, okay and not about to die. I am terrified this weird episode is going to ruin everyone's experience, so the more assurances I can give that I'm okay, the better.

By the time the paramedics arrive, I think I've even managed to convince myself.

But as one of them slips a blood pressure monitor on my arm, I can't help but think back to that hideous feeling of doom, and the edges of my vision turning black.

There's something very wrong with me, I just know it.

I confess as much to the paramedic quietly, so Annie doesn't hear.

He gives me a sympathetic look and shakes his head. 'I don't think so, Mr King. All of your vital signs appear to be normal. I'm not detecting anything out of the ordinary anywhere. We'll stay with you for a while longer, but I think you're going to be okay.'

I want to be relieved by this, but how can he think that after what happened?

'It felt pretty serious while it was happening,' I counter. 'Never had anything like that happen to me before.'

'No, I'm sure. Serious panic attacks are rare, but when they happen, they feel like the worst thing in the world.'

I blink a couple of times in surprise. 'A panic attack?'

'Yeah, most probably. All your symptoms indicate that. It's rare for someone to faint during one, but it does happen, if it's bad enough.'

'But I'm not panicked about anything.'

And that's the truth. I'm not. In fact, I was feeling the best I have all week, knowing Teddy's birthday party had gone off without a hitch. I knew I was losing to Jack at bowling, so I certainly wasn't panicked about that. Everything has been perfectly under control. Perfectly okay. It's been *perfect* . . . aside from the dinochickens.

The paramedic shrugs. 'Our minds don't always work the way we want them to. Try not to worry about it, though. These things happen, and you don't seem to have suffered any ill effects. How are you feeling now?'

My turn to shrug. 'I'm fine,' I tell him. And again, I'm telling the truth. Physically I feel perfectly alright.

Mentally, though – that's a different story. He may be able to convincingly tell me there's nothing to worry about, but that sense of overwhelming doom just will not leave me.

Why the hell did this happen? And if my body is fine, then what's going on in my head?

By the time my friendly paramedic and his colleague are done with me, most of the children and their parents have left the party. Even Teddy has been taken away by Annie's sister. This leaves just me, Annie, my two best friends and Jack's son with me as I climb to my feet, and am happy to see that my legs hold me up just fine.

'Well . . . that was weird,' I say, underplaying it for all I'm worth.

'Yes, it was,' Annie concurs. 'You should go home so you can rest.'

I start to put up an argument – and then stop, because I really don't have one. I do feel exhausted. I would do after all of today's organisation anyway, but with the panic attack piled on top, I would like to sleep for a couple of centuries.

The fact I have a 6.30 start tomorrow morning proves that Annie's idea is a very good one. An evening of rest and relaxation is the best thing for me right now, before getting back into my hectic lifestyle tomorrow. I guess that massage will have to wait, though. I can't tell you how deeply disappointed I am by that.

I manage a semi-hearty goodbye to both Jack and Leo. I don't want them going home worrying about me. It's a little hard to fake the cheeriness I most certainly don't feel, but this kind of thing comes quite naturally to me most of the time, so I think I get away with it.

They still both have concerned looks on their faces as they leave the bowling alley, though.

By the time Annie and I get to her Clio, my legs have gone a little shaky again, and I have to confess I fall asleep in the car on the twenty-minute drive back to my apartment. I'm pretty ashamed of that, but there's nothing I could have done about it.

Annie seems reluctant to leave me on my own when she drops me off, but I'm fine with it. I don't want her to see me in this vulnerable state, if I'm honest. Better she pops off home, and lets me sleep it off. I truly, truly hope this episode doesn't put her off me in any way.

The kiss she gives me at my door before she leaves seems to indicate that it hasn't, which is something of a relief.

I try my hardest to get some rest and relaxation during the evening, but it is tempered by flashbacks to the panic attack that I can't stop thinking about.

Why?

Why did that happen to me?

I am worried. I can't deny it. I guess I have to take the paramedic's word for it when he told me I haven't got anything seriously wrong with me, but that doesn't in any way explain such a visceral and strange occurrence.

My sleep that night is far more fitful than I'd like.

Not least because I have 'My bloody Humps' by the Black Eyed Peas stuck in my head as I look up at the darkened ceiling of my bedroom, trying to fathom the events of the day.

The only way I manage to get off to sleep is by repeatedly convincing myself that it was just a one-off incident. I should treat it as such, and try and move on from it.

But what if it happens again? At work this time? What the hell do I do then?

The idea of not being in full control of my own body fills me with an existential dread that means that when 6.30 comes tomorrow morning, it will be a fitful and anxious Charlie King that greets it.

What the hell is going on?

Chapter Two

IT'S A BOY/GIRL! (DELETE AS APPROPRIATE)

Let's just get through this, eh?

Hold it together, and we can be out of here in three hours, maximum.

. . . and drink more of that Red Bull. It'll keep us going.

I drain the sickly-sweet liquid from the bottom of the can, and open the car door. I do this with towering reluctance.

The headache that has settled in over both eyes is hardly going to react well to a noisy party involving a large number of excited middle-class people.

Eloise and Conrad have invited approximately seven thousand of their closest friends to this shindig, and all of them are likely to be speaking at the top of their voices.

That's what being influencers, and the friends of influencers, gets you – endless attempts to be the centre of attention.

I really should have cried off the job, and handed it to one of my competitors, but the kudos of handling Eloise and Conrad's gender-reveal party for their first baby was just too large an opportunity to pass up.

They have *two million* followers on their travel channel. Two million people who could be potential customers for King Promotions, if my ebullient clients put out a few social media posts about how wonderfully I arranged their important day – as they have promised to do.

So, I have to suck up the fact I've had about two hours' sleep, get in there and be the absolute best Charlie King I can possibly be.

'There' being the expansive four-storey terrace in a pocket of north-west London that I couldn't afford to live in, even if I arranged gender-reveal parties for every influencer on Instagram for the next several centuries.

Mind you, I should be fine. I got a deep and restful *three* hours' sleep the night before last, so I should be perfectly okay to handle this event, yes? Five hours' sleep in two days is more than enough to function at 100 per cent capacity.

Christ on a bike.

'Do you think you should go and see a doctor?' Annie asked me this morning. She's been staying over at mine more and more, and has really noticed the decline in my sleep patterns over the last month. 'This has been going on for a while now.'

I cringed with embarrassment. I thought I'd been doing a good job of hiding my tiredness and general lack of oomph from Annie, but quite clearly not. My girlfriend is very perceptive.

'No. I'm absolutely fine, I promise,' I told her, with as broad a grin as I could muster. 'I just need a decent night's sleep. I don't need to trouble a doctor with it, when that's all I really need. I have the sleeping pills I bought in the chemist. I'll take them tonight.'

Annie would no doubt have tried to convince me more, had I not looked at my watch and leapt up from her kitchen table, citing that I had to be at Eloise and Conrad's place in an hour.

This was a lie. I had plenty of time. Two hours, in fact. But I didn't want the conversation with Annie to continue any longer. Which is something I never thought I'd say.

But I don't need to see a doctor. I don't *want* to see a doctor. I'm perfectly okay. I just need *some sleep*.

What I most assuredly do not need is a cacophonously loud doorbell that plays Taylor Swift's 'Blank Space' in a hideous two-tone chime that makes my head ache all the more.

Novelty doorbells died out among the working class a good thirty years ago, only to be resurrected by the middle class – but louder, more digital and programmable on your iPhone.

I'm hoping against hope it's Conrad who comes to let me in. He is enthusiastic about life – but he's also German, so still maintains some reserve, which makes him easier to deal with, when you're not feeling at your best.

'Aaaah! Charlieeeeee!'

The door is not answered by Conrad. It is answered by a World War II air-raid siren in a kaftan.

Otherwise known as Eloise – who is the walking, talking answer to the question, 'What would happen if you gave electricity a face?'

'How are you?!' she exclaims at the top of everyone's lungs, and hugs me in the kind of embrace usually reserved for the climax of a professional wrestling match.

'I'm very well!' I attempt to exclaim back, which isn't easy when a five-foot-seven-inch blonde maniac is squeezing the very life out of you.

. . . I'm being grossly unfair to my client here, to be honest. My lack of sleep is making me extremely intolerant. Eloise is a lovely human being. She just has all the dials turned up to eleven all the time, and today my cold, tired soul is burning in her overwhelming presence.

She should probably be careful not to hug me too hard, as the heir to the Travels With El & C empire is currently gestating in her womb. Don't want the poor little girl to come out with a flat head, do we?

'Your people have done a *wonderful* job with all the decorations, Charlie!' Eloise screams at me as we walk along the expansive corridor of their house.

She's right. I picked out several 'tasteful' items based on a theme of international travel, along with a few more kitsch pieces themed around newborn babies. I'm particularly proud of the bespoke prams with wings I had put together by Roselle and the team at her design studio. They're pretty silly – but mesh well with the fantastically bright and colourful depictions of various international landmarks. I thought the flying passports were a nice touch as well.

The whole effect is a lot more garish and in your face than something I'd choose for a celebratory event like this of my own, but this is what Eloise and Conrad wanted, so this is what they've got. Always keep the client happy.

'Glad to see it's all up and ready to go,' I reply, stifling a yawn. Thank God I can rely on Aisha and the guys from Golden Apple events to do all the legwork for me. I feel comprehensively terrible today, and if I had to be the main co-ordinator I think I'd drop dead of an aneurism before the party was half over. I'm so glad I took the precaution of hiring more of Golden Apple's staff, predicting I still wouldn't have got over this hideous spell of insomnia I'm fighting.

I really couldn't do my job without some of the people I employ, and I'm very proud of the relationships I've built up over the years with them.

'Would you like a cocktail?' Eloise bellows.

Oh God. It's 10.30 in the morning. She's insane.

'No, thanks. But I'll take a coffee, if you have one?'

'Of course! I'll get one of your catering boys to make one for you. They've been wonderful with my chai tea soup so far this morning!'

Chai tea soup? What the bloody hell is that?

Best I not try to understand these things. It'll only make my head hurt more.

I smile at Eloise as she bustles off into the kitchen, where there should be three caterers from Flavours of the World. They are exorbitantly expensive, but Eloise doesn't like to see the hard numbers when there's a guarantee of strange and wonderful delicacies from far-flung corners of the map being waved under her nose.

I spot the aforementioned Aisha, and head off to talk to her. She's standing by the ridiculously expensive reveal cake I had the lovely folks at the Red Velvet Patisserie whip up for me. On the surface, it is a very elegant white frosting job, with a few artistic question marks in pastel blues and pinks artfully piped onto its surface. Inside, it is bright pink, and somehow has swirls of white baked into the delicate sponge. I have no idea how this was accomplished, but people are going to be delighted when they receive a slice of it. It's a level of cake-related sorcery I can't even begin to understand.

That would probably be it for a bog-standard gender-reveal party.

Mum and dad would cut the cake, and that would be the time everyone would find out what the baby is. This is an influencer's party we're talking about, though, so beyond where Aisha is standing fussing over a tablecloth is the back garden of Eloise and Conrad's glorious home, where you will find a large glitter cannon. If you go poking around the undergrowth, you'll also find a whole collection of exterior spotlights that will all light up at once in a pink splash of colour when the cannon goes off.

And then there's the PA system that will blast an extremely annoying dance track called 'You My Baby Girl' at a hideous volume, to accompany everything else I've organised.

Yes, it does all sound comprehensively *awful* – but Eloise and Conrad will love it. They've left me carte blanche with all the arrangements, and I pride myself on knowing just what my clients want.

And young, twenty-something, gorgeous influencers want gaudy, large and Instagrammable. This will be all of those things, and then some.

'Are you okay, Charlie?' Aisha says.

'Yes, I'm fine.'

Aisha looks unconvinced. 'Only you've been staring out into the garden with a horrified look on your face for a good thirty seconds.'

'Have I?'

'Yes.'

'Sorry, I'm just a bit tired this morning. How's everything going?'

She smiles. 'All good. We're pretty much done here for now. I'm just putting a few finishing touches on things, and then I'll have the team vacate in time for the party to start. We'll stand off to the side and make sure we're there to assist any of the guests if they need it.'

'Thank you, Aisha, you've done a wonderful job, as always.'

She looks around the room at her four staff as they straighten decorations and fuss around cleaning up after themselves. 'It was a strange one, Charlie,' she says. 'But your clients have definitely got what they wanted.'

'They're quite strange themselves,' I say, in what I hope is a quiet enough whisper.

Aisha laughs at this, and returns her attention to the tablecloth.

I resist the urge to stare out into the back garden again, and instead head for the kitchen. I really need that coffee.

Inside, it's a maelstrom of activity, as all kitchens are in the run-up to an event of this nature.

Eloise is standing over a rather scared-looking young man as he finishes off my coffee. She's smiling at him in a very friendly manner, but I gather that's what sharks do before they attack, so I can't say I blame him for his anxieties.

I spot Conrad for the first time, standing with head chef, Pixie – who is to novelty food items what Eloise is to a high decibel level.

'These look very good,' Conrad tells her in his clipped German accent as he looks down at one of the platters Pixie and her team have prepared.

'They do,' agrees Pixie, who nods her head, setting her various piercings jangling.

Pixie is the perfect caterer for my clients. She has her own extensive social media following, and the kind of multi-coloured hair that is roundly approved of by the influencers of the world.

She also knows how to bake a marvellous Guatemalan *polvorosa*, and an equally tasty Latvian *bubert*.

Both of which are on the extensive menu I worked out with Pixie for today.

'Coffeeeeeeeee!' Eloise exclaims, using more vowels than is healthy for anyone with a grip on their sanity, and hands me a rather silky-looking flat white, which I take gratefully and have a long sip of.

'Thank you so much,' I tell her, and nod thankfully at Pixie's teammate, who gives me a relieved look, and bustles back over to the far side of the kitchen – as far away as possible from the maniacal pregnant woman.

'Everything is proceeding according to plan, yes?' Conrad asks me in his Teutonic manner. You'd think his more reserved demeanour would make him ill-suited to social media influencing, but his calmness acts in necessary counterpoint to his wife's over-excitable personality. It all works very well – if you're into that sort of thing.

I nod, and have to resist the urge to snap off a salute. Conrad's a good ten years younger than me, but demands respect. Probably something to do with being six foot four and having the kind of chin people write stories about – and possibly construct municipal building foundations from.

'Yes. It's all coming together nicely,' I say, and instantly have to stifle another yawn.

Conrad's brow furrows. 'Are you okay, Charles?'

Nobody calls me Charles. But I let Conrad get away with it, because of that chin.

'Yes, yes. Just a little tired, is all.'

'Ooh!' Eloise cries and puts her arms upon my shoulders. 'You poor thing! We've made you do so much, haven't we?' She looks aghast.

'I'm fine, El,' I tell her. 'More than happy to do whatever I can to make sure your special day goes off without a hitch.'

. . . just please remember to send a few posts out on the socials over what a good job I've done. And maybe speak a little quieter? Not much of what you're saying is going in, because my brain is putting up a large defensive barrier.

'Ooh! Thank you so much, Charlie! It means the world to us that you've done such an amazing job. He'll be so pleased with everything!'

'It's my absolute pleasure,' I reiterate, and take another much-needed sip of coffee.

On any other day, I'd be able to cope with Eloise's enthusiasm with considered ease, but today is not that kind of day. Today is the kind of day that requires several more of these coffees, and some peace and quiet.

Just cope with it all for three hours.

Four at most.

'Shall we go and take a proper look at the things we've set up outside in the garden?' I ask my clients, affecting an enthusiastic expression. 'I know we've been through it all a hundred times, but I want to make sure you're happy with the placement of everything.'

'Ah yes, that is a very good idea,' Conrad says with a curt nod.

Eloise squeals, because of course she does.

Heading back through to the dining room, I see that Aisha and her team have vacated, leaving everything looking just right.

Excellent.

'Here's the cannon,' I remark, when we step outside and walk up to it. 'You'll want to make sure you're both standing on these white markers when it goes off.'

'Will there be a lot of glitter?' Conrad asks.

'Oh, I do hope so!' Eloise cries happily.

'There is indeed a lot of glitter,' I tell them confidently.

So much, in fact, that I'm going to make sure I'm as far away as possible when it goes off. I don't think my brain can survive that loud a noise today. Or being covered in several million pieces of glittery pink paper.

. . . all of it 100 per cent biodegradable, of course. Eloise and Conrad may think nothing of racking up thousands of miles in business class, but present them with anything made of plastic and they have a collective apoplectic fit.

'That's wonderful!' Eloise exclaims, and gives me another bone-crushing hug. How can anything this tiny be so bloody strong?

And oh, my God . . . her head is right by my left ear. If she says anything else at her usual volume, it's likely to spark off that aneurism.

'He'll be absolutely amazed when he sees it!' she says, obliterating my cochlea. 'We will have plenty of people recording everything, won't we?' she continues, still right in my ear, but looking at her husband.

'Of course. Four cameras, as agreed.'

I'm eternally grateful for the fact that Conrad is the one who's organised that part of this morning's entertainment. Not having to wrangle a bunch of cameramen on top of everything else has been a great relief. To my stress levels, if not my wallet. I wish I could have taken on that aspect of the event as well, because it would have bumped my pay up even more, but I just couldn't cope with it.

By the time I've walked the two of them around the placement of the light display, it's nearly 11 a.m. I let them go off to stand by their front door so they can welcome their guests.

I hang back – as I always do at these kinds of shindigs. I delight in organising them (usually), but I don't want to be the centre of attention at them, ever. It's not professional.

I grimace as I think back to the weird panic attack I had at Teddy's birthday party a month ago. I certainly became the centre of bloody attention that day, didn't I?

And ever since that day, it's been rare for me to get anything more than six hours' sleep a night at most.

My bloody *humps*, indeed.

Stop it.

You're fine.

Just stressed with the amount of work you have on at the moment. Nothing else.

I drain the last of my flat white and breathe deeply.

Everything is *okay*. It's just a question of sitting back and watching this party unfold . . . and then getting out of here as swiftly as possible, before Eloise has the chance to destroy my other cochlea, and render me completely deaf.

I hear that awful two-tone version of 'Blank Space' again, indicating that the first of the guests have indeed arrived. There's a lot of screaming coming from all quarters, suggesting that these arrivals are the same level of extrovert as Eloise. How delightful.

I should have brought some earplugs.

I go and hide myself under a Japanese maple tree at one side of the garden, slightly away from the double doors, and hope that this will be enough to avoid having to do a meet and greet, along with being far enough away from the cannon for what remains of my ears to survive when it goes off.

This hidden position works to keep me away from the arriving guests.

Partially.

There's a hairy moment about five or so minutes later, when a person of indeterminate sex, but very determinate woollen clothing, comes over to ask me if I'm the gardener. This is a fair assumption to make, given how I'm trying to disappear behind the leaves of the Japanese maple as much as is humanly possible.

Mind you, from that kind of cursory assessment, I could also conclude that this person is a wool salesperson. They are covered in the stuff. Wool hat, wool coat, wool trousers, wool sandals and probably wool underpants. None of it is the same colour. And none of those colours are subtle.

I assume this person is some sort of wool influencer, if such a thing exists.

It probably does. You can be an influencer for anything these days. I saw one the other day advertising suppositories. Her toilet seat was covered in sequins.

Other than this one strange person, though, I manage to remain alone, and deeply unobtrusive – and thus am spared any more encounters with the increasingly bizarre series of human beings that are attending this gender-reveal party.

Eloise and Conrad's little girl is going to have to grow up in an environment where keeping her feet on the ground is going to be about as impossible as if someone has tied a thousand helium balloons to her feet. Poor little thing.

Still, at least none of the flamboyant extrovert looneys are looking over at me. I'm far too dull and sensibly dressed to draw any attention. I look like what I am – one of the staff.

I brave a move into the kitchen twenty minutes into the party to secure myself another coffee. My brain has taken on a hazy, dreamlike quality that is not commensurate with watching over an event you're meant to be co-ordinating, and should be taking careful note of, to make sure that everything is going well.

Other than this one venture, I make no other moves for pretty much an entire hour, as the partygoers settle themselves in for the duration.

It's only as we get closer to midday that Conrad comes over to me.

'So, we are ready, I think, for the big moment,' he tells me, indicating towards the three separate cameramen he has set up at various locations.

'Excellent,' I reply. 'Well, as we discussed, then, all you and Eloise have to do is press the big red button next to the cannon, and everything is timed to go off at that moment. Once the initial surprise is over, you can move into the lounge to cut the cake, and the caterers will take that as their cue to start bringing the rest of the food out.'

It's not quite what you'd call military precision, but it is all very well thought out – even if I do say so myself. *Keep it simple, stupid* is a motto I try to live by as much as possible. People don't want over-complicated, even if it sounds like they do. What they want is effective, memorable and exciting. They just *think* that means over-complicated. But it really doesn't.

Eloise and Conrad extremely experienced at dealing with crowds, and being the centre of attention, so I can leave the ceremonies to them. I rib them a fair bit for their jobs as influencers, but having a client who's comfortable with being a big part of the event in a constant, upfront capacity is always a great help. It's the quiet or inexperienced people that can make things difficult. You have to do a lot more of the heavy lifting publicly yourself, in those circumstances. I don't mind being the *hostess with the mostess* at these kinds of events, but I prefer not to do it if I can get away with it.

I can certainly get away with it today, given who I'm working for.

'Everybody!' squeals Eloise with delight. 'It's time for the big reveal!'

Several stunned pigeons fall out of a nearby tree thanks to the high-pitched sonic wave she generates. I wonder if the Navy could harness her power for warfare purposes?

Needless to say, this announcement captures everyone's attention. Up to and including the residents of the graveyard a few streets away.

Conrad bids the throng of happy partygoers gather on the patio that leads from the house's bifold doors. We've been through this several times in previous days, and Conrad plays his part beautifully. Everyone has a good view of the cannon. But at a safe enough distance, so that none of them are in the blast radius. I spent several hours researching the best and safest glitter cannon that can be handled by a layman, and this was the one that came out on top in every review I managed to find.

I shake my head to clear the slightly blurry vision that's afflicted me all morning. I have to pay attention here. This is the moment of truth, and I need to make sure that my clients are stood where they should be.

And indeed they are, God bless their little Instagrammable hearts.

Provided there are no technical issues with the big red button, everything should go off without a hitch. There will be bright lights and obnoxious music to accompany all the glitter in the world.

And there bloody *shouldn't* be any problems, because I spent about as much time researching the electrical system I'm using as I did the cannon. Those sleepless nights have come in handy for something.

Eloise can barely contain her excitement. 'Thank you all for coming today!' she tells her bizarre collection of guests. 'This is such an important moment for Conrad and me and we wanted to share it with the people we love most in the world!'

And the people who will share the content the most on social media, no doubt.

'Yes, indeed,' Conrad continues. 'This is our first child, and revealing their gender to all of you in this manner is the perfect way for us to celebrate our good fortune.' He gestures over at me, which makes me blink in surprise. 'And we have our friend Charles to thank for this celebration. He has done a wonderful job putting it all together for us.'

The influencer gang all look over at me in the manner of people who have just realised there's a moth in the room with them.

I return this sudden attention with a sheepish smile that feels very strange on my lips. I'm not usually this socially awkward. Must be the lack of sleep.

'And now it's finally time!' Eloise exclaims, and I'm delighted that she does. Attention is immediately drawn away from me again, in the same manner attention would be drawn away from a small fluttery moth to a nuclear warning alarm going off.

'We are both incredibly proud . . .' she continues.

'And incredibly grateful . . .' Conrad adds.

'To be able to tell all of you . . .' Eloise says.

'Our wonderful friends, both old and new . . .' Conrad carries on.

They've clearly rehearsed this a great deal. I'm sure it's supposed to be charming and inventive, but to me it sounds like they're a pair of malfunctioning robots. I know AI is taking over everything online these days, but I didn't realise it bled out into the real world quite so badly.

'That we are going to have . . .' Eloise cries, the excitement on her face at its most extreme, and her body vibrating so much it could result in friction burns, if she's not very careful.

'That we are going to have!' Conrad repeats at the top of his voice.

They look lovingly at each other. Conrad takes Eloise's hand in his, and they both press the big red button at the rear of the glitter cannon at the same time.

The boom is louder than even I'd anticipated. So much so that I hope I'm not going to have some of my fee docked for repairs to the bifold door glass.

Shiny pink glitter bursts forth from the cannon in a spreading plume that flies a good ten feet into the air, and straight at the partygoers. The lights snap on around the edges of the garden, suffusing absolutely everything in a garish pink light that I wish I'd brought sunglasses for.

The song 'You My Baby Girl' bursts into life, the thumping bass beat and electronic vocals doing to my ears what the lights are doing to my eyes.

This is quite literally the worst thing that can happen to somebody who's had two hours' sleep. I have to shut my eyes tight for a moment against the glare.

Still, at least it should be big enough and loud enough for Eloise and Conrad to be delighted by its ostentatiousness. After all, these are the people who do a regular Instagram update on Mardi Gras every March. It's a very popular thing for them. Gets millions of likes.

I open my eyes again, expecting to see Eloise jumping up and down like Tigger on a kilo of cocaine.

But instead, she is frozen like a statue.

Odd.

All her friends are whooping and cheering the reveal of her baby girl. You'd think she'd be beside herself.

But no. She's just stood there, a slack-jawed expression on her face, and her eyes as wide as saucers.

Maybe I went a bit too far with the reveal. Maybe it was all a bit too much for her, and something has short-circuited.

Conrad is equally silent, but his face has gone bright red. He is also staring at me with eyes that burn with a German intensity possibly not seen since the Allied forces crossed the Rhine.

'Vot have you done?!!' he exclaims over the loud music, the anger really bringing out his accent.

'What?' I reply, suddenly understanding that he is extremely mad at me for some reason. 'What do you mean?'

'Vhy vould you do this?!' he rages.

'Do what?' For the first time today, I have a completely clear mind, but for all the wrong reasons. The adrenaline dump that's suffusing my entire being is sending me into a fairly extreme fight-or-flight response.

I've done something very wrong here.

'Vhy vould you say we are having ze girl?!!'

The partygoers have realised that something is not quite as it should be – not least because the usually animated Eloise has suddenly decided to do her impression of a gobsmacked statue. They are looking between me and Conrad with no small degree of confusion. Glitter is still falling from the sky, like pink radioactive ash. Someone somewhere with some common sense has flicked off the horrific music.

It'd be a little hard to hear it anyway, because a bomb has obviously just gone off, and I appear to be the one responsible.

'Because you are!' I say, and for some reason I point at Eloise's belly as I do this. 'There's a girl in there,' I insist.

'No zere is not!' Conrad demands, his hands becoming fists. 'We are having a boy!!'

I look at him dumbfounded for a moment.

'No, you're not,' I tell him. 'You're having a girl.'

'No ve are not!'

I nod my head. 'Yes, you are. You most definitely *are*.'

I am insistent, because I know I'm right.

There is no way I would get such a fundamental thing wrong about today. I spent *hours* making sure the big red button worked properly. I wouldn't get the gender of the baby wrong, now would I?

Conrad must be mistaken.

This is obviously an epically stupid position to take, but I've had two hours' sleep, and my addled brain cannot comprehend the horror of what I've clearly done. The father of the child is just a little bit more likely to know what gender it is than me, after all.

Suddenly, Eloise lets out a braying wail that makes me want to call in the emergency services.

Enormous, photogenic tears start to flow down her cheeks, as if on cue.

She hugs her belly protectively.

'He thinks my baby Zaxxel is a girl!!' she screams to the heavens.

'That's because she is!' I reply, with almost the equivalent level of dismay in my voice.

'Zaxxel iz not a girl's name!' Conrad insists.

Which is something I cannot argue with, given that Zaxxel is not a bloody name for anything – save a defunct Eastern European electronics firm from the 1980s.

'But your email said you were having a girl!' I tell him, pulling out my mobile phone. 'Here, I'll prove it to you!'

In approximately thirty seconds from now, my world is going to come to a swift and disastrous end. So, let's just bask in this half-minute we have left – where I still have a career, and some sense of self-worth – shall we?

. . . aah. *Lovely.*

Got anything nice planned for the rest of the year? Holiday? Maybe a little light renovation of the house? Perhaps you would like to start a new job as a freelance events co-ordinator? I hear there's a very definite opening coming up in the sector in about five, four, three, two

The blood drains from my face as I read the email Conrad sent me about their full requirements. There's quite a lot in the message – Germans are very thorough people, after all. And everything else I understood and acted upon correctly. All except one tiny detail, that Conrad mentioned just in passing towards the top of the email.

It reads thusly:

> *We are very delighted to be having our first baby, and we want to be able to celebrate this with a fun and exciting gender-reveal party, where we can tell all our friends about our new little boy. Eloise is a girl who loves a big moment (as I'm sure you can tell from our Instagram!) so we really want this to be a very memorable occasion. You have been recommended to us, as you have a reputation for making these kinds of events happen in an effective and enjoyable manner for all concerned.*

The truth is there for all to see, in black and white. He did write that they were having a boy! But why did he have to refer to his wife as *a girl* a mere four words later??

She's a fully grown woman, Conrad!

What are you? Some kind of misogynist who can't accept that women play a valuable and necessary role in our world, and that they should not be described as merely being 'girls'?

Yes, yes! This is all Conrad's fault!

He's the reason why an entire crowd of multi-coloured lunatics are looking at me like I just told them to stop posing for the camera for five seconds, and get out of my bloody way.

Aaaargh.

'I'm so . . . so sorry,' I stammer, attempting to back away, but being rendered unable to do so by the sturdy Japanese maple. 'I could have sworn . . . I thought that . . . I really didn't . . .'

'He thinks Zaxxel is a girl!!!' Eloise once again wails, underlining the point in what I feel is a frankly unnecessary manner.

My mind races for ways to get myself out of this hole.

I could point out that it's now 2025, and gender is seen as an out-of-date construct. There's a fluidity to it that people like Eloise, Conrad and their friends should probably be able to appreciate, damn them.

What's wrong with you, Eloise? Why are you being so old-fashioned? You spent several Instagram stories telling everyone about how plastic pollution is killing our oceans, but where's your progressivism now, huh?

Maybe little Zaxxel *wants* to be a girl? Have you even thought of that, Eloise? *Have you?*

My internal attempts to shift the blame to someone – anyone – else are as pathetic as they are pointless. I might as well point at the woolly creature and blame the whole thing on them.

I do not make mistakes.

I never make mistakes.

Especially ones as astoundingly huge as this one.

And it's not just transposing two words across one short paragraph that I'm guilty of.

I never followed up with them in person.

In my cocksure way, I simply told them they didn't have to worry about anything. They could leave it all to me. I thought I knew everything. And I did.

. . . almost.

Aaaargh.

'Honestly, I don't think he's a girl!' I exclaim at Eloise, my hands held out. 'I honestly thought you were *having a girl!* I read your email wrong! I'm so sorry!'

'You read the email *wrong?*' Conrad spits, now fully swimming in the waters of indignancy. 'There was nothing wrong with it!'

Apart from your grotesque old-fashioned views of women, Conrad! Would you like to join in with your wife about her post-war, backwards beliefs regarding gender as well?

Stop it! This is all your fault and there's nothing you can do about that!

'I'm so very, very sorry,' I repeat. 'I've been very tired of late. I haven't been sleeping well at all, and I must have misread. I must have misunderstood . . .'

'Zis is your excuse?' Conrad demands.

'Yes!' I wail. 'You see it all started with "My Humps" by the Black Eyed Peas – which I still don't really understand.'

'I love that song,' the woolly creature pipes up, earning a chorus of approving nods from their fellow lunatics.

'But it gave me a panic attack, you see, for some reason,' I continue to explain, 'and I haven't been sleeping since, so then I haven't been all that focused, and—'

'Zaxxel is a boy!!' Eloise screeches. My hideous error appears to have rendered her unable to speak in sentences of more than a few words, which must all, of course, be uttered at ear-splitting volume.

A stabbing pain shoots through my head above my right eye.

'I'll . . . I'll refund everything you've paid,' I stammer.

'Yes, you vill!' Conrad agrees.

'And . . . I'll get someone to change the lights to blue.'

'Vot about ze cake?!' Conrad's accent has now fully developed into camp Kommandant. This is the first and last time in my life I'm going to feel like Steve McQueen in *The Great Escape*.

What I wouldn't give to be able to make one of those right now . . .

'Er . . . er . . . there's not much I can do about that! It's pink inside!'

There's an audible intake of breath from the influencers.

'It still tastes very nice, though!' I say, trying for all I'm worth to soften the disappointment.

'I don't want pink!!' Eloise tells me in terms that really do brook no argument.

'Oh God, I'm so sorry!'

There's nothing else I can say at this point. I've already promised a full refund (which is going to cripple me financially for this month). I simply don't have anything else in my usually full repertoire of charming responses. I am bereft.

That's because nothing in your repertoire is about you apologising for screwing something up so badly.

I don't make these kinds of mistakes!

You do now, idiot! And we bloody well know why, don't we?

Yes, we absolutely do. It all started at a bowling alley.

Maybe Annie is right. Maybe I do need to see someone?

It's one thing for a lack of sleep to make you a bit cranky, it's another thing when it starts to threaten your livelihood.

'I zink you should leave,' Conrad tells me. 'Eloise is very upset by your presence.'

My eyes go wide.

This is humiliation beyond anything I've ever experienced before. It's the kind of thing you're only supposed to experience in anxiety dreams – but here it is, happening right here in the real world.

I stare at Conrad for another couple of seconds, before lowering my head and scuttling away as fast as possible, through the crowd standing around the bifold doors. I can see a few of them recording all of this on their phones. God help me if this gets out on social media.

. . . *as if that's* not *going to happen.*

'Dickhead gets gender wrong at reveal party' is the kind of top-drawer entertainment that nails you at least a million views on TikTok. I'm going to be ruined.

Once I'm out of the house completely and stumbling back to my car, I can feel wetness on my cheeks in the cool breeze. Oh God, now I'm crying. Partly from the sheer, unadulterated humiliation . . . but probably also because I'm so bloody tired.

Annie is right. I must see someone about this.

But does it have to be a doctor?

That's going a bit far, isn't it?

I consider this carefully as I snap the seat belt into position and fire up the car's engine.

Yes. A doctor at this stage would be *ridiculous.*

I'm not actually sick. There's nothing really wrong with me that a good night's sleep wouldn't fix. I don't need to be bothering a doctor with any of it.

I'm *fine.*

Just out of sorts enough to screw up a gender-reveal party, that's all.

Yes.

That's what I am . . .

Out of sorts.

Nothing more.

I'll sort myself out, get a decent night's sleep, think up a winning strategy to apologise to Conrad and Eloise, and move on from this torrid, embarrassing affair as quickly as I possibly can.

I relax a little in the car seat as I very slowly make my way home. At least I feel like I have some sort of plan to move forward.

That's more the Charlie King everyone is used to. The Charlie King *I'm* used to. That's the Charlie King I want Annie to be around.

The man with the plan.

Even when things go comprehensively wrong, he always knows a way to dig himself out!

I can repair the damage I've done here today to my reputation. I know I can.

I can work out why I can't get a decent night's sleep, as well.

And why I can't get the stupid lyrics of that song out of my head.

Everything is going to be alright.

Everything is going to be totally *fine*.

I continue to feel that way until about an hour after I get home, and I start to see notifications spring up on my phone.

You see, not only have all of Conrad and Eloise's influencer friends decided to share my humiliation on TikTok, they've also decided to tag me in their posts. Because what's the point of destroying somebody's life if you don't make sure they know all about it, eh?

@KingPromotionsUK is absolutely inundated with notifications over the course of the evening. It becomes such a social media nightmare that I have to cancel my evening with Annie so I can deal with the fallout.

Still, it's the highest amount of engagement I've ever had on TikTok, so it can't be all bad, can it?

What do they say? All publicity is good publicity!

Sadly, I think the only people who ever actually say this are serial killers, CEOs and marketing executives.

What on earth am I going to do?

. . . about *all* of this?

Chapter Three

THE WRONG ROAD

'A medium?'

'Yes.'

'That sounds a little . . . *out there*, Charlie, I'm not going to lie.'

'You think? Zitana uses her skills to help a great deal of people with their issues.'

'By reading tea leaves, and telling you how much your great-great-grandmother approves of your new haircut?'

My eyes narrow. 'Zitana isn't like that.'

Annie crosses her arms. 'Isn't she?'

'No.'

My girlfriend gives me a quizzical look. 'Didn't you arrange that tour for her? I remember you showing me pictures, not long after we got together?'

'I did, yep.'

'Wasn't it called "Zitana Joins with the Spirits"?'

'It was.'

Annie expression changes from quizzical to extremely doubtful.

I think it's the first time I've ever seen that look on her face in relation to me, and it causes something cold and rather horrible to bloom into life inside my chest.

She picks at a thread coming out of her duvet. 'I think it might be better if you saw a doctor, Charlie. Don't you?'

I shake my head vociferously. 'No, I don't. Nothing is really that wrong with me . . . honestly. I'm just not sleeping that well, for some reason. Zitana does this kind of thing all the time. She can help me. It's only one session. I want to see how it goes.'

Annie looks away from me. 'I'm not sure it's the right thing to do.'

Oh God. I hate seeing Annie like this. But what can I do?

I need to do things my way, and I just can't let her think I'm so far gone that I need proper, professional help from a man in a white coat. I'm just not sleeping. That's all. And someone like Zitana can help with that. Without the need for me to have anything go on my medical record, or have my girlfriend thinking there's something seriously wrong with me.

'It's fine!' I insist again. 'I know Zitana well. And I know how to work with my clients. The free holiday I managed to get from Europe Unpacked for Conrad and Eloise certainly worked out well, didn't it?'

I say this with no small degree of pride. The damage I did to my relationship with the influencers was mended quite effectively, thanks to the week in Santorini I scored for them from the independent travel firm I worked with a couple of years ago. Both parties got something out of it, and I got to apologise again for my grotesque error. I did it all in the space of a week. Even with little to no sleep.

It's not helped the fact that the steady influx of new clients I used to have has completely dried up, thanks to all those ever so lovely social media posts about my huge cock-up – but at least I've mended fences with the people at the centre of it. That must count for something.

'That's a very different thing, Charlie,' Annie says. 'You sorting things out with the Instagram nutcases is not the same as dealing with your own health issues.' There's now an adamant tone to Annie's voice I've not heard before.

'But I don't have any health issues!' I say in a voice that sounds falsely cheery, and genuinely brittle.

Annie gives me a look that cuts right through this façade. She's very good at that kind of thing, I'm learning. Annie is so damned perceptive about me that I find it slightly scary.

She's doubting me. Doubting whether I know what I'm doing or not.

I can't have that. I can't have her thinking I'm not
in control
doing something positive and useful.

'Look, why don't you come with me?' I say. 'You can see how useful the session is, *and* you can make sure I'm honest with Zitana about everything. You can see what happens, so I can't pretend everything's okay, if it isn't.'

Annie thinks about this for a moment. 'Alright, Charlie. That sounds like a good compromise. I'll come with you.'

'Thank you.'

'But if it doesn't work . . . If Madame Tea Leaves is as big a crank as I think she's going to be, then it's off to the doctor with you, okay?'

'Okay,' I agree . . . quite hesitantly. There's that adamance again.

I have *some* degree of confidence in Zitana's skills – but have to confess that when I did arrange and promote her tour, I got a very good insight into what she does for a living.

And there's a lot of *oogie woogie* going on.

Bagfuls of oogie woogie. A mountain of the stuff.

But on her website there are testimonials from many very happy people, who appear to have turned their lives around thanks to Zitana's assistance, so that must stand for something, right?

Let the poor overworked doctors deal with people with actual, real problems. Folks like me, who just need to find out why they can't sleep properly and have song lyrics stuck in their head, can easily be helped by a woman who speaks to the *other side*.

I mean . . . if anyone knows how to get a good rest, it's dead people, isn't it?

◆　◆　◆

Dead people are also extremely profitable, it appears, because Zitana lives in a very nice, very *large* house, on a road that only has houses on one side, and a super view of the countryside on the other. You know you're doing well for yourself when you don't have to look at your bloody neighbours when you stare out of the window.

Zitana holds her personal, face-to-face sessions (you can Zoom with her if you like, for half the price. Though quite how the spirits are going to help you over a broadband connection is beyond me) in a stylised wooden tent in the garden of her house. It's called her 'Place of Healing and Connection'.

'Stylised wooden tent?' Annie scoffs. 'What you mean is, she works out of a bloody wigwam, Charlie.'

'I'm sure she doesn't call it that,' I protest.

'She can call it what she likes. I know a wigwam when I see one' – she points towards the thing as we pull up onto Zitana's drive – 'and that's a bloody wigwam.'

It's kind of hard to argue, I have to admit.

The structure is much more than just a bunch of cloth and sticks in the shape of a cone. It's made of a very glossy, dark hard wood, and has several windows around the sides of it. It looks like the type of executive office that people with money love to slap down at the back of their gardens to make it feel like they actually have to go out to work in the morning.

Except the fact that it is, undeniably, wigwam-shaped. It even has the sticky-up bits of wood appearing from out the top – though whether they are structural or purely decorative is anyone's guess.

The wigwam is also covered in several bright illustrations of dream catchers. There's a few zodiac signs stuck on there too. And for some reason, a surprised goat. I guess I'd be quite surprised if I was a goat that had been drawn next to a bunch of *oogie woogie* stuff for no apparent reason, so I can't really blame it.

'I can't believe we're actually doing this in a wigwam,' Annie says, staring at it. 'Sorry, I mean . . . the "Place of Healing and Connection".'

'Yep. It'll be great,' I reply firmly. 'Her reviews are excellent.'

'Are they from experts in the wigwam field? Because I honestly can't see how anyone in their right mind could give her five stars otherwise.'

I sigh. 'Please just give it a chance.'

Annie can see the look of slight desperation on my face that I'm trying very hard to hide.

She reaches out and pats my hand, which is still resting on the gear stick. 'Okay. Sorry. Let's go and find out if this woman can help you or not.'

'Thank you.'

Annie leans over and kisses me lightly, which feels extraordinarily nice. A tension I didn't know I had between my shoulder blades loosens a little. The world is a much better place after Annie kisses me. It's like a magic trick.

Sadly, the tension returns in an instant when my phone rings. We both jump.

Ring ring.

'Bloody hell,' I mutter, and pull the damned thing out of my pocket. I press the button to let the call go to my answer service.

'You're not going to answer it?' Annie asks. 'It could be work?'

'No,' I reply, a pulse of pain spreading across my left eye. 'Not the right time at all. It'll keep.'

She nods and squeezes my shoulder sympathetically.

'Let's go, shall we?' I say, ramming the phone back into my jeans.

We both climb out of the car, and then make our way along a winding concrete path that snakes its way towards the wigwam. At the edges of the path are strategically placed tiny statues of what look like fairies. One is doing something with a trumpet that I'm not sure is entirely legal.

As we approach the wigwam, a series of lights around the entrance start to emit a rather lovely warm glow.

Ah, yes. Zitana does like her light shows. I remember that from the tour.

She would have appreciated the display of pink at Conrad and Eloise's house – even if they bloody didn't.

'*Oooooh*,' Annie moans in a spooky fashion, waggling her fingers around.

I give her a look.

From the door set into the side of the wigwam, a shape appears.

Zitana has not changed much from the last time I saw her, three or so years ago. She's still a statuesque woman, whose sharp features are unmistakable, even in this relative low light.

The outfit hasn't changed much, either.

It would be tempting to expect some sort of riff on a Gypsy fortune teller, but that would expose some prejudices and misconceptions that I don't have time to go into here.

No.

Zitana is dressed in an elegant, but very formal purple suit. The white shirt underneath has many, many frills. The black pointed high heels are shined to the point of unreasonableness, and her hair is scraped back into a high ponytail, giving her a somewhat austere expression.

Look, there's no getting around it. She looks like Prince.

Or Symbol. Or whatever the poor chap's name was before he died.

I'm about to have my fortune told – and possibly my issues laid bare – by someone who looks more like they should be telling everyone about how she's going to party like it's 1999.

I have no idea whether the homage is deliberate or not, but I never quite felt comfortable enough with Zitana to ask.

'Charlie,' she says in a melodious voice. 'So nice to see you again.' Zitana walks forward with a grace that you just can't teach, and takes my hand in hers.

Annie lets out a small squeak from beside me. This is somewhat understandable. Zitana is a *presence*, of that there is no doubt. And my girlfriend may be as quick with her tongue as she is perceptive, but she's also quick to compare herself unfavourably with other people, I've noticed. She has absolutely no need to, she's beautiful and amazing – but I can understand the little dismayed exclamation that escapes her mouth when faced with something like Zitana.

'Hi Zitana,' I say. 'This is Annie, my girlfriend.'

Zitana turns her megawatt smile on Annie. 'So lovely to meet you. Charlie is a very lucky man.'

'Thank you,' Annie says. 'Nice wigw— I mean . . . nice building you have here.'

Zitana nods. 'It is rather lovely, isn't it? A place of sanctuary and harmony in a world full of the opposite.' She holds out her hand. 'Would you both like to come in? I have camomile tea.'

We do as we are bid, and once inside we see that the interior of the wigwam is very much congruent with the outside. The walls are covered with pictures of dream catchers again. And there are several large real ones hanging around the edges of the circular room. The zodiac signs are drawn across the walls in here as well. But no sign of the goat.

At some point I'd really like to ask about the goat.

The room is bathed in a warm, soft glow by the single small chandelier that hangs from the centre of the cone-shaped ceiling. The chandelier itself is cut glass – and features a load of frolicking fairies. They are all naked. And they are all doing things fairies really shouldn't. Especially if they are the type of fairies that you'd find at the bottom of your average child's garden. It's enough to send anyone into therapy for many years.

Beneath the sexy fairy chandelier (oh God) is a round table, with two relatively ordinary chairs on one side, and an enormous, high-backed, throne-like chair on the other. This is covered in plush purple velvet.

Stamped in silver on the back of the chair's headrest is an eight-pointed star with an eyeball at its centre. This looks tremendously disconcerting. The eyeball is staring at me. Possibly judging me for the way I looked at the shagging fairies.

'Pray, sit,' Zitana intones, before languidly heading over a small table at the rear of the room, upon which sits a white bone-china tea set and a metal water urn.

As Annie and I take our places, Zitana pours us both a camomile tea and brings them over. She does not pour herself a drink.

Kind of the same way Dracula acts in the novel, when Jonathan Harker pops round for a nice chat.

Zitana sits down in her throne, and a portal to hell immediately opens above her head.

No. Of course this does not actually happen, but you'd be forgiven for thinking that it could.

'Now what brings you to me today, Charlie?' she asks. 'Your email sounded quite distraught.'

'Did it?' I thought it sounded about as bland as your average email always does. Not sure how she could interpret being distraught from 'kind regards'.

Zitana nods. 'Yes. What troubles you, my friend?'

I wave a hand. 'Oh, it's not really that much, honestly,' I say in a light voice. I am instantly embarrassed by the question.

Annie turns and looks at me.

'Oh, alright. It's fairly *bad*,' I admit. 'I'm not sleeping, Zitana. Not sleeping *at all*.'

Her hands rest lightly on the arms of the chair. 'Explain, please.'

And I do so, over the course of the next ten minutes, with helpful interjections from Annie on a frequent basis. By the time I am done, Zitana knows all about my funny turn at the bowling alley, my disgraceful performance at Conrad and Eloise's house, my disdain for 'My Humps' by the Black Eyed Peas, and the fact that some dinosaurs look like plucked chickens.

'I see. Very troubling,' Zitana says, regarding me carefully. 'Something is obviously hurting you deep within your many soul.'

I blink. 'My what?'

'Your *many soul*,' Zitana repeats. 'We are all made up of multiple creatures, Charlie. All housed within a single earthly vessel. Each one vying for supremacy in an eternal struggle. Our inner space reflects the complexities of outer space. Many heavenly bodies both attracting and repelling each other. We are in a dance with ourselves, at all times. And that dance continues on, even after our mortal frames have fallen to entropy. They cry out for acknowledgement and connection. And they can see the many soul in others. That is why I can help you, Charlie.'

I stare at her for a moment.

I stare at her for a moment longer.

. . . I kind of wish she'd just started singing 'Raspberry Beret', to be honest.

'Ah. I see,' I tell her.

I most assuredly don't.

I also make a very special point of not looking at Annie. There will only be one of two expressions on her face, and neither will help matters.

Zitana smiles in a knowing fashion. 'Do not worry, both of you. You do not need to understand the intricacies of the many soul to receive my help and assistance. Just know that it is the truth, and be at peace.'

'Er . . . fair enough,' I reply.

I'm very glad I don't need to understand the intricacies. That might lead me into knowing too much about the shagging fairies and the goat, and I'm not sure I'm in the right head space for that kind of illumination.

'All I would ask is that you both relax, and allow me to do my work,' Zitana says.

'That's it?' Annie asks. 'No . . . you know . . . *boards*? Or . . . *cards*? Or . . .'

Oh *no* . . .

'. . . crystal balls?'

Again, Zitana supplies a languid smile, which indicates she's very probably heard all this before. 'No. Others who commune require physical vessels through which they make communication. I do *not*.'

She says this with a finality that almost makes me jump. No wonder this woman has made so much bloody cash with this malarky. She's extremely convincing, and equally as sure of her own abilities.

'All I require from you, Charlie, is to sit calmly, and allow your many soul to the surface.'

'O . . . *kay*. And how do I do that exactly?'

Zitana changes her posture slightly so that she is sat taller in the chair. She briefly closes her eyes and rolls her head slowly on her neck. There's something quite sensual about this act, and I feel my face flushing.

Oh boy.

Annie lets out another squeak.

'You just have to allow me in,' Zitana says.

'Allow you in,' I repeat.

'Indeed. Allow me inside so that I may know your many soul, and create a link to those I speak to. That way, we might glean what afflicts you.'

'Okay. Gotcha. Let you inside. Right.'

My levels of awkwardness are peaking. Not least because I'm sat next to my girlfriend, while a statuesque, sensual woman dressed as famed sex connoisseur Prince is asking to get inside me.

Is it hot in here?

It's hot in here, isn't it? Definitely quite *hot.*

'Pray be silent, so that I may begin,' Zitana asks, and I immediately do as I'm told.

She closes her eyes again, and raises her head so her face is bathed in the light of the shagging-fairy chandelier.

In seeming response to this, the light itself slowly starts to dim. Simultaneously, around the edges of the wigwam, a purple glow begins to emanate from some effectively hidden lighting. It's all very ethereal.

And probably cost a good couple of thousand for the electrician to install.

I know full well what's going on here, but Zitana sells the whole thing so well, it's hard not to get caught up in it.

'My humps,' Zitana says. Her voice has taken on a somewhat raspy quality. 'My humps,' she repeats, in an even more breathy tone. 'My lovely humpy lumps.'

It should be completely impossible to make those lyrics sound anything other than extremely silly in this context . . . but Zitana manages to make them sound intolerably spooky and horrific.

Maybe because I've had them running around in my head for so long – usually at 3 a.m., when I can't sleep.

Annie lets out another squeak, this one sounding like a laugh cut off before it can get going. Which is understandable.

Zitana ignores this and starts to breathe heavily. This requires that her chest move up and down in a way that the staff of Charlie's trouser department finds more than a little interesting – even though that is completely inappropriate and should require a meeting with HR.

'I feel you, Charlie,' she moans.

Good lord.

'I feel your pain. I feel your uncertainty. I feel your confusion.'

Please stop saying you feel me. I'm having uncomfortables.

'The song. The words. The story. I can feel your many soul reacting. Reaching out for comfort. Reaching out for something to grip on to . . .'

Please don't say 'grip on to' again, either.

The purple lights start to pulse gently. I now notice that the shagging-fairy light has turned red.

The lighting now speaks to a combination of the fifth circle of hell and a knocking shop. I'm not sure which is worse.

If this was a gender-reveal party, the baby's pronouns would be de/mon.

From somewhere equally as hidden as the purple lighting comes the sound of monastic chanting. It is low, melodic and immensely disconcerting, in combination with the heaving Zitana bosom and the ambient lighting.

There's a part of me that's actually extremely impressed by the performance. Zitana has moved on from the time I worked with her, when she just used some soft spotlights during her stage show. I mostly made sure her promo materials were of a high enough standard, and that she got plenty of exposure in the national press. The actual stage show was easy to manage.

This is on a whole other level now, and I'm starting to understand why her house is so big.

None of this is really helping glean what afflicts me, though, so I'm not sure any of this was all that worth it. Annie is going to have a field day when we leave.

'Think back!' Zitana suddenly exclaims. 'Think back to that day, Charlie!'

'That day?'

'Yes! Think back to it! Hear the song in your mind! Feel the things you felt! Open yourself to me and let me know your essence!'

I'll be keeping my essence to myself, thank you very much.

And then, 'My Humps' by the Black Eyed Peas starts to play.

Aaargh.

Only this isn't the usual version of the song. It's an incredibly slowed-down rendition, echoing around the room from seemingly everywhere. Instead of sounding like an oversexed teenager, lead singer Fergie now sounds like a demon from the pits of hell itself. A monstrous thing of unknown dimensions, coming for me – and wanting to know what I'm going to do with all that junk in her trunk.

How the hell is Zitana doing this? I hadn't mentioned anything about the song until we got here today!

I know there's a logical explanation, but I am creeped the hell out anyway.

'*Think*, Charlie! Remember! Feel!' Zitana exclaims loudly, gripping the arms of her chair as she does so.

This is getting absolutely ridiculous. What exactly does she want me to remember? I was quite happy at Teddy's party. And then I had a panic attack when that bloody song came on. There's nothing more I can think of to explain any of it than—

Instantly, horribly, the sound of breaking glass and screeching tyres fills my head.

63

Only this isn't coming from Zitana's hidden sound system. This is coming from nowhere except my own mind. But I can *hear the noises*. As if they were here in the room with me.

And I can hear 'My Humps'. But it isn't slowed down anymore. It's at normal speed, but it sounds tinny. Small. On a low volume. As if it's coming from much smaller speakers than either the ones here today or at the bowling alley.

Small speakers.

Car speakers.

It's on the radio.

'My Humps' is on the radio, and I'm . . . I'm . . . I'm . . .

Crashing.

'Oh, bloody hell!' I moan, and clutch at the sudden headache over my right eye.

It's happening again!

I can feel my heart rate skyrocket, and the world start to go black. I'm going to have another bloody panic attack, right here in front of Prince.

Thank God the New Power Generation aren't here as well!

'Charlie?!' Annie cries, in exactly the same tone of voice as she used at the bowling alley, the last time she saw me in this state. Her hands fly out to grip my arm as I start to slump over.

Like a flash, Zitana is on her feet and around the table. She grasps me by both upper arms, and with a strength that's frankly terrifying, she sits me up straight and looks deep into my eyes.

'Say kumquat!' she commands.

'What?'

'Say kumquat, Charlie! Now!'

This woman is comprehensively insane. Here I am in the midst of a terrifying panic attack, and she wants me to start naming exotic fruit? If I have a coronary, will she require legumes?

'Say it!' This time her voice feels like it's taken on some sort of psychic quality, as if Zitana is tapping into some eldritch horror conjured up by the purple lights and shagging fairies.

I'd better do as I'm told, or there will be hell to pay.

'Kumquat,' I say in a shaky voice.

'Again, please!'

'Kumquat?' This time my voice is a little stronger.

And what's this? My heart is slowing.

'Once more!'

'Kumquat.' My vision has returned to normal. I feel a little tired, but the panic has passed.

What witchcraft is this?

'A simple psychological trick,' Zitana says, as if she's read my mind.

. . . having said that, we might be way past 'as if' at this stage. There's every chance Zitana is the real deal. She certainly looks and acts it. And she's triggered something in my psyche that I didn't even know was there.

Crashing.

'It's designed to bring a person out of a panic episode,' she continues. 'By engaging the speech centres of the brain and introducing an incongruity, it short-circuits the panic response.' She regards me for a second. 'You should be fine. Just take a few deep breaths.'

And with that, Zitana sweeps back around into her chair in one swift, fluid moment.

I take those deep breaths and start to feel remarkably calm, given what's just happened.

Annie's hand rests gently against the back of my head and I feel her fingers in my hair. It's super comforting. 'What's happening to him?' she asks Zitana, all trace of sarcasm or cynicism gone from her voice.

Zitana takes a breath herself. 'I think Charlie's many soul is repressing something that has impacted him greatly. Is that not so, Charlie?'

I swallow and nod my head.

Yes. That's definitely what's going on here.

But I don't understand it in the slightest.

I look at Annie, swallow hard and then tell her what I think is going on.

'I had a car accident,' I say, in as level a voice as I can.

Annie's eyes go wide. 'Oh, my God! When?'

'About five months ago.'

She looks shocked – and not a little hurt, if I'm honest. 'Why didn't you tell me?' she says.

'I didn't want you to worry . . . and we'd only been seeing each other for such a short time. I didn't think it mattered.'

'You didn't think it *mattered*?' she repeats, looking stunned.

'No. Because it was . . . nothing. I wasn't hurt. Everything was fine in the end. And it was that day you were doing your first gig at The Lexington Arms. I didn't want to put you off your stride.'

'Oh bloody hell, Charlie,' Annie says with a loud exhalation of breath.

'Honestly, please don't worry about it. I was fine. I *am* fine,' I tell her, squeezing her knee in as comforting manner as I am able. 'I wasn't hurt, apart from a bit of a stiff neck. Nobody else was really hurt, either – and I hated that car anyway. It was almost a relief to get it written off.'

It really was. I'd been wanting to get rid of that silly bloody MG for a couple of years, and getting it written off in that accident felt like a bonus, not a catastrophe.

'I was very lucky,' I tell Zitana, who arches an eyebrow. 'No. Truly. I hadn't really thought about it much at all. After a couple of days, it felt like a distant memory.'

She can't arch her eyebrow any higher.

'I was totally fine!' I insist.

'Well, you obviously *weren't*, Charlie,' Annie points out, trying to sound as gentle as possible. 'You've been suffering for weeks now.'

My face crumples in confusion. 'Yes, but . . . it was all *fine*. They checked me out in the ambulance, and then I got a taxi home. The insurance firm were very helpful – I knew I was right to get platinum cover – and they towed what was left of the MG for me. I had a hire car the next day, and the money in the bank within two weeks.' I look at Zitana. 'I don't understand why that would cause a panic attack five months later!'

'It's because your many soul is traumatised, Charlie.'

This is when I have to force my eyes not to roll. Zitana clearly has a talent for putting on a good show and coming across as the genuine article, but the many soul thing is still as silly as it sounded when we first got here.

She did stop me having to have another ambulance called over, though, so I resist the urge.

'Well, possibly . . . but I don't have a clue *why*,' I tell her. 'I wasn't thinking about the crash when I had the attack. Hadn't done for weeks. But that silly bloody song was playing on the radio when it happened, so I guess that explains it?'

'Oh, my God,' Annie says in a hushed voice. 'Is that why you've been walking around humming it, with a look on your face like someone just shot your favourite dog?'

'Is that what I've been doing?'

'Absolutely.'

'Blimey.'

'The crash obviously impacted you more deeply than you were aware, Charlie,' Zitana points out. 'The souls on the other side of existence have successfully communicated with your troubled many soul, and have gleaned what afflicts you.'

There's a somewhat smug, self-satisfied tone to her voice that I could do without.

Mind you, it's stuff like this that means she can afford a massive wigwam in her back garden, so who am I to judge?

'Okay, but what am I supposed to do about it?' I ask her.

She does not immediately answer, but the lights around us change once again. The purple hue disappears to be replaced by a rather pleasant blue tone, and the chandelier brightens considerably into a soft white light. The overall impression is like being in a Lenor commercial. One where sheets get wafted about a lot, with constant blue skies in the background.

We're going for super serene here, now that my trauma has risen to the surface. I'm quite grateful to whoever is watching all of this and fiddling with the light settings – probably Zitana's husband. It's very calming.

'Now that you have uncovered what your many soul has been trying to tell you, you must seek to quell its roiling humours,' Zitana says.

Okay, we're straying into near-incomprehensibility now. I wouldn't know what a roiling humour was if it bit me on the ankle.

Zitana senses this. 'You must find a way to achieve a sense of equilibrium again with your many soul, Charlie. You must seek both its forgiveness and its love.'

'And how do I do that?'

'See a doctor,' Annie mumbles.

'I don't need a doctor,' I argue. 'What say you, Zitana? How canst my humours be unroiled?' If she's going to lean on the flowery language, I figure I can give it a pop too.

'You must seek thine advice of those who ken the physical and emotional ailments,' she tells me.

'You what?'

For a moment, the rather haughty, composed expression drops off Zitana's face, to be replaced by a much more natural, exasperated one. 'Your girlfriend's right, Charlie, go and see a bloody doctor,' she says, in a completely different voice – one that sounds more like she comes from the other side of a council estate, rather than the other side of existence.

'Oh,' is about all I can say in response. I feel like I've witnessed a drawing back of the curtain here, and it feels a little weird.

Zitana straightens in her chair again, and the all-knowing expression returns. 'This must, I forswear, conclude our session. It has tired me beyond measure.' She passes a hand across her brow as she does this.

I think the freebie is over.

'Sorry,' I say, in a very British tone of voice.

Zitana smiles. 'Do not apologise, Charlie, the work can be tiring, even in very small doses.'

I hope she strings things out a bit more for the people who actually pay to come here and experience her light show. Not sure I'd be too chuffed about forking over seventy quid for fifteen minutes and a small cup of camomile tea.

Having said that, in my specific case, I think Zitana has done what I needed her to do – unbelievably.

I now have a much better idea why I've been so tense and disturbed recently.

The very fact I never even thought the crash had anything to do with my woes speaks volumes about how little I thought it had affected me – on the surface at least. I never made the connection.

But maybe I should have? A car crash – no matter the outcome – is a fairly traumatic thing to go through. I clearly didn't appreciate that at the time, nor subsequently. Not until today.

'Thank you for your time, Zitana, you've been very helpful,' I say, and actually mean it.

'Yes, thanks for that,' Annie echoes, in a very troubled tone. She's not happy I never told her about the crash. I can tell from the expression on her face.

But there was no need to! Not after we'd only been together for such a short time. I didn't want her to

think I was weak and stupid

worry about anything to do with me. That wouldn't have been fair on her.

It was something that happened, no real harm was done, and I moved on. Even the stiff neck wasn't that much of an issue.

From seemingly nowhere Zitana produces a leaflet. I immediately recognise the design, because it's an update of the one I commissioned for her. 'Please do tell your friends and associates about my services.' She smiles. '10 per cent discount if they say they know you.'

'No problem,' I tell her, taking the leaflet. I'm surprised to see that my hand is shaking slightly.

Annie and I rise to leave. As we do so, the lighting returns to the state it was in when we entered. I want to compliment Zitana on her stage production, but am worried I might offend her.

'I'm very impressed by . . . the way you conduct your sessions,' I say instead.

Zitana arches her eyebrow again briefly, before a knowing smile spreads across her lips. 'Thank you, Charlie. I still use a lot of what you did for me.'

Zitana then ushers us out of the wigwam and indicates with her hand down the driveway back to the car. She remains at the door, a wistful expression now on her face. 'Farewell, my friends. Take your many souls with you into brighter days.'

'We . . . er . . . will,' I reply, and turn to leave.

'And see that bloody doctor,' Zitana says, back in what I can only assume is her real accent, before stepping inside, and shutting the door on the wigwam with one swift movement.

Annie looks from the wigwam to me. 'Are you going to listen to her more than you've listened to me?' she asks, attempting to do the arched eyebrow thing, but not selling it quite as well. Zitana's had years of practice to perfect it.

I shrug my shoulders. 'I don't know. I'm going to have to think about it. She's helped a lot just by showing me what the hell has been going on in my head.'

'And what has been going on in your head?'

I shrug my shoulders again. 'I'm still not 100 per cent sure, but it clearly has something to do with that silly bloody crash.'

Annie reaches out and takes my hand in hers. 'Are you sure you're telling me everything about what happened now? It's okay if you're not. Talking about it could help.'

I give her a look of mild disbelief. 'No. Honestly, it hasn't bothered me. It could have been far worse, and it ended up being something of an inconvenience, but I promise you I haven't been walking around all traumatised by it. I'm as surprised as you are.'

Annie nods in acceptance . . . but there's doubt there. I can see it.

Maybe I'm a little more perceptive at reading her emotions than I give myself credit for. Is it doubt over whether I'm telling her the truth? Or doubt about me, because I kept something like a car crash from her? I don't know. Maybe I should ask?

Unfortunately, I don't get the chance right at this moment, as she starts to walk towards the car, leaving me to either follow or stay here with the shagging fairies. I heave a small sigh, and catch up with Annie as she opens the car door and climbs in.

There's a strange silence that descends between us as we drive back to her place. It's not an angry silence. Those are sharp things, where you fear that moving a muscle might cut you. Instead, this is a quietness born of – at least on my part – exhaustion and confusion.

It's only the fourth yawn emanating from my mouth that brings Annie out of her partial reverie. 'Straight to bed for you.'

I rub my hand over my face. 'I hope so.'

'Maybe what's happened here tonight will make you feel a little more relaxed?'

I nod in hopeful agreement. 'To be fair, that stupid song has stopped going round in my head for once, which can only be a good thing.'

Annie chuckles at this – but it's a very small, malnourished thing to hear.

As to the reasons why it's been going around in my head all this time, I guess I have more of an inkling now – but that's all I have.

I haven't thought about the accident in weeks, but I suppose this is probably the time to start. Anything that causes you that kind of panic attack and insomnia must have something more to it than I can currently fathom.

But what?

What am I missing about that day?

As far as I'm aware I came out of it totally

fine. I have plenty of time to get to everyone. No problem at all.

And Foo Fighters have come on the radio now. Who doesn't love a bit of Foo Fighters, eh?

I flick the volume up, and sing along to 'Learn To Fly' as the hedgerows pass by on either side of the car.

Everything really is okay.

Unfortunately, I can't help but let the mild feeling of panic creep back into my head by the time Dave Grohl gets to the second verse of the song. I've stopped singing, and am once more clenching my teeth hard as I look repeatedly at my satnav screen telling me how much time I have to get to Zenith Games.

Foo Fighters come to the end of their song, to be immediately replaced by the Black Eyed Peas.

Okay, so this is a very silly song indeed, but I force myself to sing along with it, in an attempt to ignore the voice of panic, and to stop my teeth clenching quite so hard.

My phone then starts to ring again . . . and it's Maurice once more.

Blimey, he's being very insistent.

But I'm not going to answer it. I'm just going to sing along to this very silly song, and—

Everything explodes.

I am thrust violently forward in my seat as the car's momentum is arrested by something very hard and very solid.

There's not much of the next few seconds I can truly grasp, but it involves a cacophony of breaking glass and crumpling metal, the hideous sensation of skidding, uncontrolled movement and the world outside rushing by me in a blur of blue and green.

I think I scream. I can't be 100 per cent sure, but my throat will be hoarse later that evening, so I think I do.

As fast as the whirlwind begins, it is over again.

The car comes to a rest askew on the road, and with my heart pounding out of my chest, I look out of the driver's side window to see that almost perfectly opposite me is another car. It's a black hatchback with red trim along its now crumpled side panels. Inside the car is the very shocked face of a teenage boy. I can see blood starting to well up from a small cut on his forehead.

Christ. He hit me.

Not that fast, otherwise we'd both be in a lot more trouble than we are. But the little sod definitely hit me.

There's no way I'm making the bloody meeting with Zenith Games now!

. . . calm down. You've been in a car accident. I doubt anyone's going to be angry at you.

Why, thank you for turning up, voice of reason. Nice to have you along.

My hand shakes violently as I press the window button, fully expecting it not to work.

But it does. Whatever damage has been done to my stupid MG does not extend to the driver's side door.

'Are you okay?' I shout to the teenager as the window fully winds itself down.

His window is smashed, so he hears me just fine. 'Yeah, I think so,' he says, blinking a few times.

'Alright . . . just don't get out of the car,' I tell him. 'It might not be safe.'

And indeed, when I look out of my cracked windscreen, I can see several vehicles coming to a swift halt ahead on the road. Best to just stay inside our cars until things calm down a bit. 'I'm calling the police,' I tell the kid – who looks horrified by this for a moment, but then nods. There are tears in his eyes. If he's anything more than eighteen I'd be amazed.

His insurance premium is going to rocket into the stratosphere after this.

Hell, mine will too, if there's no way to prove whose fault it was.

But whose fault was it?

I don't think I was distracted. I think I was concentrating on the road okay. But this road is pretty damned narrow . . .

Who knows?

That's for another time. Right now, though, my call has connected, so I flick the bloody Black Eyed Peas off the radio, and give the emergency operator the details of the crash, including our exact location, thanks to Google Maps.

By the time this call is over, I can feel that my heart rate has returned to more or less baseline. I'm quite impressed by this. I've never been caught in an emergency like this before, and I have to say I'm pleased with the way I've reacted to it.

I even manage to fire the MG back into life, and steer it slowly and very awkwardly into the conveniently placed lay-by at the side of the road, in order to try and free the road up for other users.

But even though I create a big enough gap between me and the teenager, nobody decides to try to squeeze through.

Odd.

But then people can be funny when these kinds of accidents happen. Best not judge them too harshly for not wanting to try and pick their way through it. Punctures from all the broken glass are a distinct possibility.

Unbelievably, an ambulance arrives a mere couple of minutes later!

I'm amazed.

They must have been in the area anyway, to get here so fast. I don't think they're going to be needed much beyond dressing the kid's cut, and checking us both over, but it's gratifying to see them arrive so quickly.

But do I even need checking over?

Probably time to get out of the car and find out . . .

. . .

Nope. I'm fine. Totally fine.

My neck feels a tiny bit stiff, but other than that, I have come through this accident unscathed. Thank God for that.

My car is another story. That's a definite write-off. As is the teenager's. He's out of his car too now and surveying the wreckage. He looks a lot more distraught than I do, poor kid.

The paramedics are now trotting over to us both, right at the moment I also hear a police car pull up behind me.

Well, that really is a level of service I never would have expected to get in these difficult, underfunded times for our emergency services.

Not going to complain, though. Hopefully someone can give me a lift home.

Thinking about what I'm going to do next reminds me of how many appointments I'm now going to miss today.

Best get on the phone as soon as I am able, to let everyone know what's happened, and that I'll have to reschedule with them.

Should I call Annie as well? Would she want to know?

No. I don't want to worry her. This whole damned thing could have been a lot worse, and I don't want to spoil her day, especially as it's an important one for her. The last thing I'd want to do is make her anxious right before she goes on stage.

And after all, the accident could have been a lot worse.

But it wasn't.

And what would Annie think of me if I interrupted her big day, whining about a teeny car crash?

I bet she'd be doubting her choice to start dating me.

No. No need to call her. It was nothing.

It's not fair on her, just before the show.

It was absolutely nothing.

And I've come out of it totally

Chapter Four

THE BOYS

'. . . fine,' I say out loud, to the completely empty room.

I then rub my fingers into my eyes, trying and failing to shift the memory of the crash.

I've been thinking about it a lot recently, you see. And I'd rather not think about it anymore, if I'm being honest.

But I will, because my brain currently has nothing else to do. Or nothing else it *wants* to do, anyway. It is bored.

I am bored.

Because even though I arranged that lovely holiday for Conrad and Eloise to make up for my hideous error at their party, the damage was well and truly done once it got out onto the socials. Work has dried up faster than a slug in a heatwave.

I can't say I'm surprised.

If someone can't get the gender of a baby right, what chance do they have with other details? Who are you going to employ to design and run your event for you? Someone who can tell the difference between a boy and a girl, or someone who can't? I guess I'm fine if the Royal Society for the Protection of the Androgynous comes calling at my door, but other than that, I'm in more than a little trouble with my career, it seems.

I have no work. I have no purpose. I have no idea what to do about it.

This all means that I am feeling thoroughly depressed, and sat on my couch at 11.34 on a Wednesday morning. I'm also still in my pyjamas – and constantly thinking about the car crash that caused all of these problems in the first place.

I'd like to just keel over to one side and get a nice relaxing mid-morning sleep, but given that my insomnia only appears to have increased with the added stress of no work coming in, the chances of that are none to even noner.

Bloody hell.

Maybe I should start day drinking?

. . . or at least do something more practical than just sit here, staring at the wall. The dishes could do with loading into the dishwasher, for starters. The garden outside the front of my flat could do with a cut as well.

I slowly turn my head in the direction of the bay window to look out at it, in order to make a full assessment of the situation, and nearly have a full-blown heart attack.

'Morning, Charlie,' Jack mouths silently from beyond the bay-window glass. He then grins and points down at my crotch. 'I can nearly see your cock,' he mouths – which, believe me, looks about as disconcerting as it sounds.

The sleep shorts are quite loose, though, I have to admit. I should have got dressed by now.

But then I wasn't really expecting my best friend to appear at my lounge window, having trampled his way across my decidedly uncut grass.

Slowly, Leo's head then appears beside Jack, from below the window frame, homing into view like a rising sun. He is trying very hard not to giggle.

Jack put him up to this. I have no doubt about that. Leo is not the type to stomp across someone else's garden for the sake of a terrible sight gag. Jack very much *is*, though.

As if to highlight this, Jack then starts to slowly drop below the window frame as Leo achieves his full height. Both of them continue to have enormous grins on their faces as this goes on, because of course they do. I stare at them with a look of the utmost derision on my face as they continue to perform this strange up-and-down motion for another two full cycles.

I know what they're doing. And it's not going to work.

Both of them then disappear below the window and a few more moments pass, before they reappear at the same time, having swapped sides. Leo has also put on Jack's battered old leather jacket, and Jack is wearing Leo's vastly expensive padded Barbour coat.

Leo is attempting to recreate Jack's near permanent look of good-natured scorn, while Jack is making a pretty good job of aping Leo's consistent gentle expression. He only looks ever so slightly like he needs professional help.

A traitorous burst of laughter erupts from deep in my chest.

Damn it.

They got me.

Jack laughs in triumph and points at me. 'Now let us in!' he roars, before dragging Leo away from the window and towards the front door.

I could just leave them out there. It looks like it could rain at any moment.

They'll piss off eventually.

I heave a sigh.

No, they bloody won't . . .

I get up from my sofa, and slouch my way out of the lounge and towards the front door. The Nirvana t-shirt I'm wearing only has three stains down the front of it, so that should be fine for my mates.

'Morning, dickheads,' I say as I open the door and allow them ingress.

Jack flicks a finger towards my genitals as he passes by me, making me recoil. Leo merely looks a little sheepish.

Both of them disappear into the kitchen to make coffee.

I stare down the hallway for a moment, watching them go immediately to work, bustling around the kitchen as if they own the place, and making the mess in there even messier.

I then return to the lounge and flop back onto the sofa, awaiting a cup of Jack's hideously strong coffee.

You never know, though, I guess it might perk me up a bit.

Eventually, both join me in the lounge, Leo perching on the arm of a chair, while Jack crashes down onto the sofa next to me. I have to stick my hand on top of the hideously strong coffee he's just handed me to stop it spilling everywhere.

'So, what's up, misery guts?' Jack asks, taking a sip of his own disgusting brown concoction.

'What do you mean?' I sniff, and then try my hardest not to let my face turn itself inside out as I sip my coffee.

'We haven't seen you for weeks, Charlie,' Leo points out.

'Been sat here wanking all that time, have you?' Jack adds, grinning from ear to ear. 'I thought with Annie being around, your horrifying addiction to horse porn would have calmed itself down a bit, but what do I know, eh?'

I choose to ignore this. It's always best.

'I'm . . . fine,' I say, sounding about as lame as I feel.

'You're clearly not,' Leo argues, drinking from what I have no doubt is a perfectly acceptable cup of coffee that he made himself.

'Things will pick up,' Jack says. 'I told you that. You just need to give all of those idiots a chance to forget about *you* being an idiot.' He pats me on the shoulder. 'It'll happen, though, I have no doubt.'

'Maybe,' I mumble.

Leo gives me a look. 'This isn't like you, Charlie. You don't sit around and *wallow*.'

'I do now,' I say, lip curling.

'No, you bloody don't,' Jack says. 'That's not the Charlie King I know and despise.' He fixes me with a distressing look of purest suspicion. 'What's really going on with you?'

'Nothing,' I say. Probably a little too quickly.

'Bollocks,' Jack rightly counters. 'There's been something up with you ever since that weird thing you had at the bowling alley. And young Leo the Lion and I have come here today to find out what it is. Can't have you sat around here, wanking to horse porn all day. Not healthy for you.'

'There's nothing up with me,' I protest, cheeks flaming.

I have not told my reprobate best friends about the crash. I do not want to discuss why such a simple thing could be causing me such extreme issues.

It's *humiliating*.

And Jack Bailey is the type of man to never let me live something like this down.

'Yes, there is,' Leo says. 'Something's happened to you that's . . . thrown you off-kilter. Changed you. I can tell.'

My eyes narrow.

Because you've had something similar happen, Leo? Is that why you're so astute about me?

I stare at Jack, who is also looking at Leo with slight suspicion.

I have to lean away a bit when he returns his gaze to me, though. 'Come on. Out with it.'

'There's nothing to say,' I mutter in a small voice, examining the depths of my coffee cup as I do so.

'We're not leaving until you fess up, boyo,' he tells me. 'From the looks of things, you don't have much else to do today. I'm still off thanks to the laboratory refit, and writer boy here can work whenever he wants to, so we literally have nowhere else to be, either.'

As if to underline this, he folds his arms dramatically, and stares at me.

Leo gently moves himself from the arm of the chair, to sit in it properly.

Oh God.

I'm not getting rid of them, am I?

'I was in a car crash,' I say in a dull voice, and take another sip of my disgusting coffee.

'Jesus,' Jack intones, once I've finished my tale of woe.

It actually feels good to have got it off my chest. Which surprises me. I'm still braced for all of Jack's jokes, and the look of intolerable sympathy on Leo's face, but I do think opening up to my friends has helped a little.

'That sounds pretty horrible, Charlie,' Leo says. 'I can't imagine not being able to sleep, and having that kind of thing going around and around in my head all the time. You must be exhausted.'

Yep. There's the look of sympathy I really didn't want to see. It makes my toes curl.

'You really don't have anything to worry about,' I tell them. 'I'm just going through a bit of a rough patch . . .'

Was the panic attack at 4 a.m. you covered up two nights ago so Annie didn't know about it part of that rough patch? It felt pretty rough at the time. And very lonely.

'. . . but I'm sure I'll get over it soon,' I finish, feeling almost out of breath, for some reason.

'Hmmm.' Jack isn't convinced. Mind you, Jack isn't convinced about *anything*, until he's seen a PowerPoint presentation, and had it independently verified by unbiased experts.

'Don't look at me like that,' I tell him. I almost wish he would start telling some awful jokes. The careful examination is much more unpleasant.

'I'm not looking at you like anything,' Jack retorts as he idly sips his coffee.

'Oh yes, you are. You both are,' I tell him.

Leo winces. 'Well, you do have to admit, you've not been acting yourself recently.'

'It's not that bad.'

Jack laughs in a humourless fashion. 'You cocked up a gender-reveal party, mate. *You.* Charlie King. The man who once planned out every essay he was going to write at university a year in advance. And mine. And Leo's. You live to make sure things go *smoothly*.'

'Alright, alright,' I concede. The gender reveal was, without a doubt, the worst mistake I have ever made. And boy, am I paying for it.

What about the car crash?

That wasn't my fault, though?

'We knew there was definitely something going on with you, and it's clearly all because of that accident,' Jack continues. 'It obviously hit you hard.'

'But it shouldn't have!' I burst out. 'It was *nothing*!'

'Car crashes are not *nothing*, Charlie,' Leo remarks, a slight look of disbelief on his face.

'This one was! I shouldn't be feeling like this!'

I don't know why I'm so adamant, but I am. All of this just makes me feel so damned . . . *weak*. People go through much worse than a little prang, and don't have these problems. Why is this happening to me?!

'We don't get to dictate how we react when something bad happens to us, mate,' Jack says, a hangdog expression on his face all of a sudden. I've never seen Jack look so uncomfortable before. It's extremely disconcerting. Like a deep-sea fisherman confronted with the prospect of a trek across the desert.

Leo also looks uncomfortable, but it's a more natural state for him, so I'm not nearly as perturbed by it.

'Maybe it would be good for you to . . . talk about it more?' Leo suggests.

This is officially the first time in human history that, in a conversation between three men, one has suggested talking more about a difficult subject. I feel like there should be a large brass gong going off somewhere close by.

'Maybe to someone like a doctor?' Leo adds.

That's more like it. Men are very good at advising their friends to talk about their problems. Just not to each other.

I shrug my shoulders anyway. 'I just don't think there's anything to talk *about*. There's nothing really wrong with me. I don't need to see a doctor.' I feel like I'm now repeating a phrase that I don't necessarily believe anymore. The same way if you say a word over and over again, it loses all meaning.

Jack's eyes meet with Leo's.

'There is something wrong, mate,' Jack says. 'And it's nothing to be ashamed of.'

My eyes flash as I look back up at him. 'Isn't it? I have a panic attack in front of dozens of people at a bowling alley. I screw up one of the biggest jobs I've ever had. I walk around looking like a zombie, and I can't get the lyrics to one of the dumbest songs in the universe out of my head!' I throw up my hands. 'It's all so . . .

bloody *embarrassing*! Can you imagine going to a doctor and telling them all that?'

I get up from the couch, affect a stiff pose and take on an officious look. 'What seems to be the trouble, Mr King?' I say in a posh accent.

I then turn my head and contrive to look miserable. '"My Humps", doctor! It's all about "My Humps"!' I snort with derision and throw my hands in the air. 'I'd sound like a talking camel.'

They both look at me doubtfully. I don't like it when people do that. It makes me want to curl up in a ball and die.

'Does Annie know about all of this?' Leo asks.

I make a face. 'More or less. I didn't really want her to. Thought it might ruin things between us.'

Leo throws his hands up. 'Don't be ridiculous! That's not going to happen.'

'You sure about that?' I argue. 'We haven't been together all that long. Things could go wrong fast if she thinks I'm messed up by something that's so trivial. Plenty more blokes out there that can cope with stuff like that much better.'

'Good grief, Charlie,' Leo sighs.

'And what did she reckon you should do?' Jack asks in a blunt tone.

The look on my face gets worse. 'Go see a doctor.'

'Well, there you bloody go, then!'

'No!' I exclaim. 'I don't need that. I don't *want* that.'

Leo grunts in frustration.

'But you've got to do *something*,' Jack points out. 'Can't carry on like this. There isn't enough horse porn in the world.'

'Give me a break, will you?' I snap, ignoring his attempt at humour.

I'm not being fair to my friend, but he doesn't understand what I'm going through. Neither of them does.

'It's okay, Charlie. We know what you're going through,' Leo says – and I think I should start promoting him as a mind-reading act, in support of Zitana.

'No, you don't,' I say in a sullen voice, sitting back down again on the couch. I pick up what's left of my coffee and drain it in one swallow. I'll get Jack to make me another one in a minute. The taste just about suits my mood.

'Yes, we do,' Jack says, with a sigh. He leans back a bit, and runs a hand through his straggly black hair. 'You don't think we know what it's like to have something terrible happen to us that has a knock-on effect? We're as human as you are, Charlie. It happens to all of us.'

My brow creases. 'No, it doesn't. Not like this.'

Jack looks exasperated. 'The Grampians, Charlie.'

I look at him, understandably confused. 'What about them?'

He rolls his eyes. 'I got lost there four years ago. Don't you remember?'

'Of course I remember. But you've never seemed that bothered by it. Not once it had been a few weeks, anyway. You made up that joke, didn't you? About getting grabbed in the Grampians? Didn't your brother get that t-shirt made for you?'

'Yes. He did. It's one of the reasons we don't speak much these days,' Jack says in a dark voice, and rubs his eyes with both hands. 'Look, I know I made a joke out of it at the time, but consider this . . . have I been climbing or trekking since? Have I taken Gormley anywhere for bloody ages?'

I think for a moment. Gormley is Jack's decrepit beige and brown mobile home from the 1990s he has parked on his driveway – and it's not moved in years. I'm not quite sure it could, judging by the rust on the wheel arches. And he certainly hasn't been anywhere on a hike. His Facebook used to be full of pictures of all sorts of wild and wonderful scenery, but not anymore. 'No. I guess not. I never really put two and two together until now.'

Jack was, for many years, a prolific climber. Not a weekend would go by without him taking himself off, usually alone, to go somewhere tall and pointy. It was never something I was into, but we did all go to Scafell Pike together one year in Gormley for our annual Shenanigans, I remember that.

And then there was the time I got him into that mankini . . .

I look at the pained expression on his face. 'So, did it affect you more than you let on, then?'

'Of course it did!' he says. 'I was up there for nearly *three days*.'

'But you found your way out eventually,' I counter. I find it deeply uncomfortable to think of Jack not being able to handle himself. If anyone is a rock in my life, it's him. A leather-jacket-wearing rock, who is as dependable as he is sarcastic.

'I was very *lucky*, Charlie. I had run out of food and water, and I was exhausted. I don't think . . . I don't think I had more than a couple of hours left in me when I stumbled across that farm.'

'You're too hard on yourself.'

'No, I'm not!' He actually sounds angry now. Which I don't understand at all. Getting lost somewhere like that could happen to anyone. Even the most experienced of climbers. It happens all the time. I made sure to show him a lot of accounts of people more experienced than him getting lost, to make him feel better.

Jack takes a deep breath. 'Look, all I'm saying is that it's been four years since that happened . . . and it's still . . . *with me*. The idea of going any place where I can see the horizon still makes me feel *sick*. I had to look at it for days, thinking it might be the last thing I ever saw. For four years, I've avoided any situation where I am completely on my own, or can't back myself up against a nice, solid wall. You had a car crash just a few *months ago*. Perfectly reasonable that you'd still be in a bit of a state about it.'

'That's different.'

I don't know how or why it is right at this moment, but I know it's different. *I'm* different.

'It's really not,' Leo says. 'We know what you're going through.'

'Do you?' I ask him, incredulous. I knew all about Jack's adventure in the Grampians, but I have no idea why Leo thinks he can sympathise with me.

'Yes, I do.' Leo's face has taken on a much darker expression. That's more disconcerting than Jack looking doubtful.

'And I figure it's about time I told you both about it,' Leo replies with a wan smile. 'What's happening to you has brought home a few things about me that I've been trying to ignore . . . and failing.'

Okay. This is unexpected. Both Jack and I have known something has been going on with Leo for a while now, but neither of us has felt able to ask what.

Leo is by far and away the most private of the three of us. He always has been. He's also a person who can be quite happy just in their own company. But there's been something about him for quite a long time that goes beyond that. A . . . I don't know . . . *fear*? He's seemed like a bag of nerves for so long.

'We have wondered what's been going on with you,' I say. 'And we've been desperate to ask you about it . . . but it never felt like it was the right time.'

Curse me to hell, but I feel much better turning the attention onto Leo. It's a relief to move away from my silliness.

Another slightly exhausted smile. 'It's not been something I have wanted to get into. But seeing you have that panic attack shocked me, Charlie. You've always been so . . . *together* in the past.'

I can't say anything in response to that, but my cheeks begin to flush red in shame and embarrassment. He's right. I have always been *together* in the past. I hate that he – and everybody else – had to see me so . . . *apart*.

'What happened?' I ask him, desperate to turn things onto him again.

Leo looks down for a moment and then back up at us. 'You're going to laugh.'

Jack blusters. 'We are most certainly not!'

'Come on, Leo! We'd never laugh at you!' I add in agreement.

'But you will, though,' Leo counters. 'Please just remember that this was a lot more frightening than it sounds.'

Jack, sensing Leo's vulnerability, changes his tone. 'We will, mate. Just . . . take it slowly.'

Leo grimaces. 'It's best I just get it out in the open as fast as possible.'

'Go on, then,' I say, my heart beating a little faster. What's he about to impart? Something grave and horrible, probably. That's what his face is advertising, of that there is no doubt.

Leo sighs, closes his eyes for a moment and then looks towards the ceiling. 'Gandalf beat me up,' he says, in a rather exasperated tone.

Silence.

Dead silence.

A couple of ice ages pass while Jack and I both digest this information.

'Gandalf *beat you up*?' Jack says, in a voice more level than a spirit.

'Yes. Gandalf,' Leo confirms.

'From *Lord of the Rings*?' Jack asks.

'From *Lord of the Rings*,' Leo confirms.

'Did he do it with his staff?' I interject, causing a small whine to come from the back of Jack's throat. He is trying ever so hard not to laugh. As am I.

We really do have to pick our way very carefully through this. Leo is clearly in a vulnerable moment, and any poor reaction from us will set him back.

But by Christ, do you have any idea how hard it is not to laugh when one of your best friends looks at you with a forlorn expression on their face and tells you they've been beaten up by bloody *Gandalf*?

'Why don't you give us a bit more detail?' Jack asks, and I can see that his hand is digging into his right knee. It's a commendable effort.

Leo nods. 'It was the last time I came out of The Channel. You remember? That nightclub I used to go to on Spring Street?'

'Yep, we remember, don't we?' I say, earning a nod from Jack.

Leo gives us a slightly shy half-smile. 'I know it was never somewhere you guys wanted to go, but it was an important place for me.'

'You met Travis there, didn't you?' Jack says, receiving a dark look from Leo for his troubles.

'Yes, I did . . . the little *shit*,' he replies.

'Let's not get bogged down in all that again,' I say hastily. Leo can get sidetracked very easily whenever someone brings up his ex. And we have bigger fish to fry here – instead of going over old ground for the millionth time.

'Agreed,' Leo says. 'Less said about him these days, the better.' He takes a deep breath. 'Anyway . . . I came out of the club that night, and figured I'd walk back to the flat.'

'That's over seven miles,' I admonish.

He rolls his eyes. 'It was summer. I was drunk. What can I say?' He shrugs his shoulders. 'It was dumb, I know that now. Largely because about ten minutes into my drunken walk home I was set upon by the entire Fellowship of the Ring.'

Jack leans forward. 'Leo . . . mate. Have you actually gone stark staring bonkers on us?'

Leo gives him a derisory look. 'No. I haven't. I was out the same night Fantasticon was in town.'

'Ah . . .' Light has begun to dawn on Jack's face. Puzzle pieces are falling into place.

It's not the biggest nerd convention in the country. Hell, I doubt it'd even make the top ten. But the civic centre has been home to Fantasticon for six or seven years now, and I've always taken something of a semi-professional interest in it, given what I do for a living.

Did *for a living, if we're not very lucky . . .*

'They were part of the cosplay competition,' I say to Leo, doing my best to ignore my unhelpful internal monologue.

Leo nods. 'And they were drunk too,' Leo continues, 'And I have to admit I was a bit rude to Frodo when he bashed into me as we both tried to negotiate the bus stop on Crammond Drive.'

I wince. 'Blimey.'

'We started throwing insults at one another.' Leo looks horrified. 'If it had been a group of big, burly lads, I would have just hurried away . . . but I was stupid . . . and very drunk.' He has a slightly haunted look on his face. 'Of course, his mates all defended him.'

'Well, they would,' I say. 'He's the ringbearer.'

Jack whines again.

Leo rolls his eyes. 'I know it sounds silly. But there were nine of them. Most dressed in armour of some description. A couple even had swords. And they were all absolutely *wasted.* They ganged up on me. Pinned me against a wall. It was bloody scary.'

'Blimey,' I say again.

I don't think I'd have felt any different, to be honest. A large group of threatening people surrounding you on a street at 2 a.m.

isn't something I'd ever want to happen to me, regardless of what silly costumes they may have been dressed in.

'I tried to tough it out like a twat,' Leo adds. 'And that's when Gandalf punched me on the nose.'

'Bloody hell!' Jack growls, in a complete change of mood, his fists clenching. 'If I'd have been there, Gandalf would have been wearing that staff up his magical arse.'

Leo gives Jack a thankful look. 'It bloody hurt,' he continues. 'May have even broken it. I don't know. I was too embarrassed about the whole thing to go to a doctor.'

Ignore that. It's nothing like your situation.

'The bruise ended up being *enormous*,' Leo confides, one hand absently poking at his nose as he recalls the damage done. Leo then rolls his eyes again and looks a bit dejected. 'If you both want to laugh now, you can do.'

Jack shakes his head. 'Nah . . . It all sounds very nasty, truth be told. The bastards!'

I nod my head vigorously in agreement. 'Yeah. No laughing matter, even if it was Gandalf.'

'It was horrible,' Leo says. 'And I was *terrified*. They were loud, obnoxious, incredibly drunk and didn't give a shit. Samwise was screaming right in my face, and Legolas even started nocking an arrow.'

'Christ on a bike,' I say, in shocked response.

The Fellowship are supposed to be the good guys.

'They were *feral*,' Leo says. 'Super loud, and super nasty. Called me all the names under the sun. I only managed to get away because there was a wall at the edge of the pavement I managed to clamber over. Twisted my bloody ankle coming down on the other side, but they didn't follow.' He thinks for a moment. 'Probably the costumes. Too heavy.'

'Did you call the police?'

'I did. They did pretty much nothing other than take a statement from me. The copper managed not to laugh when I told him what had happened.'

'Typical,' Jack snorts.

'Obviously nothing came from that,' Leo says. 'Not that I was expecting anything different.' He shifts uncomfortably. 'It stayed with me, though. Haven't been able to watch that bloody movie since . . .'

He trails off for a moment, lost in deep thought.

'Bloody hell,' Jack says. He then looks up at Leo with a somewhat uncertain smile on his face. 'I guess it could have been worse, though, yeah? At least it wasn't anyone dressed as characters from Warhammer. That lot are all absolute nutcases.'

Leo actually nods at this. Sometimes when Jack tries to make you feel better, it's best to just nod along, and hope he doesn't try again any time soon.

'I haven't . . . haven't wanted much to do with people since it happened – and that was eighteen months ago,' Leo continues. 'People . . . I don't know . . . *scare me* more than they used to, I guess?' He looks up at me. 'You remember when I told you I had the flu, and couldn't come to the beerfest? Yeah, well . . . that was a lie. I just didn't want you to see me banged up. You'd have asked questions about my nose. Questions I didn't want to answer.'

'You should have said something!' I counter. 'There was no need for you to be embarrassed!'

He gives me a pointed look. 'What? Like you shouldn't be embarrassed about what happened to you at the bowling alley?'

I make a face. 'That's different.'

'No, it isn't,' Leo says firmly, and deep down I know he's right. On the surface, though, I want to keep protesting.

'You see?' Jack says, getting up from the couch. 'The both of us know what you're going through. You're not alone, and you're not helping yourself by pretending that you are, or that there's nothing much wrong with you.'

I stare at him for a moment, trying desperately to think of something that separates my experience from what's happened to the both of them. I'm self-aware enough to acknowledge that there very probably isn't, though.

I can't sleep, Jack doesn't want to go anywhere in the big wide open, and Leo is now terrified of people. Especially wizards.

'So, what do we do?' I ask them both.

In response I get a couple of extremely blank expressions.

'Do?' Jack says.

'What do you mean . . . *do*?' Leo adds.

I hold up my hands. 'About what's going on? About how we all feel about these things?'

Jack shrugs. 'There's nothing to *do*,' he says. 'You just . . . just have to get on with stuff, and hope you feel better as time goes by.'

I give him a flat look. 'The Grampians were four years ago, Jack. You said it yourself.'

'Yes . . . But I put up with it. It doesn't ruin my life or anything. And I don't feel quite as bad these days. I'm . . . you know . . . *fine*.'

Leo nods in agreement. 'I didn't tell you what happened to me because there's anything that can be *done*, Charlie. I told you the police weren't interested. I just wanted you to know you're not the only one going through some stuff. I wanted to make you feel better about it. A trouble shared is a trouble halved, and all that.'

Jack slaps him on the back. 'Exactly!' He looks at me. 'Doesn't it make you feel better to know you're not the only one with a few issues? That you're not the only one with a problem? If we can cope okay, then you can too.'

I stare at them both for a second.

'No!' I eventually say. 'If anything, it makes me feel even *worse*.'

'What?'

'I had no idea my two best friends were messed up by things that happened to them ages ago!' I snap. 'Now I have you both to worry about!'

Jack's brow creases. 'No . . . that wasn't . . . We didn't . . .'

I chew on a fingernail. 'Bloody hell.'

This is no good at all. I thought I was the only one with problems, but now I have to deal with the realisation that my two best friends are as desperate as I am – if not more so.

What the hell am I supposed to do now?

'We have to find some way to fix things!' I then exclaim, with a wholly inappropriate level of sudden enthusiasm.

'*Fix things?*' Leo repeats, incredulous.

'Yes! Fix things!' I insist.

Oh, thank God for that.

I have *purpose*.

There is *something I can do*.

If there's one thing I hate more than anything else in this world, it's swinging in the wind, without a direction. I should not be sat in my pyjamas at 11.34 in the morning!

But here is *opportunity*.

Here is a chance to be proactive!

Ha!

'There's nothing to *fix*,' Jack protests. 'We've all got to . . . put up with these things, just like everybody else does. You just have to realise you're no different to anyone else. That we're all the same, and that it's fine to not be . . . you know . . . 100 per cent, all of the time.'

'No,' I say firmly.

'No?'

'No.'

'What do you mean, *no?*' Leo says, now with a rather anxious twang to his voice.

'I mean . . . we can't just *put up with things*,' I argue.

'We can't?' Jack looks mildly horrified now.

'No, we can't,' I insist. 'You two have been through some truly dreadful experiences that I had no idea about . . . but now I *do* know about them, there's something that I can do.'

'Is there?' Leo's expression is one of a man who's just given someone a ten-pound note, and received a warm hand grenade in exchange.

'Yes!' I jump up off the couch and start to pace up and down. 'There's got to be something that can be done to get the both of you through the trauma you've suffered.'

'That *we've* suffered . . . You mean all three of us?' Jack interjects.

'Whatever,' I reply, flapping my hand at him. 'I wish I'd known about it all sooner, but it doesn't matter. Now that I do, I can put my mind to work thinking about some ways we can overcome your problems.'

'We don't need help overcoming them!' Jack insists.

'Yes, you do!' I argue.

'No, we don't!' he insists back, just as hard. 'We're totally fine! Aren't we, Leo?'

'Er . . . yes?'

'You see!'

'But you're clearly not totally fine,' I tell him. 'Otherwise, you wouldn't have talked to me about how it's okay for *me* to not be *totally fine*, because neither are you.'

Aha!

My logic is absolutely unassailable!

Jack makes goldfish faces at me for a moment. Leo just looks like he wishes he was anywhere else. Possibly Mordor.

I have to convince them this is the right course of action. I can't stand to see them both feeling as bad as they obviously do. I must help them with their trauma!

And who knows? Maybe helping them will help me to feel better as well.

Yes, yes! That's it!

I will sleep better, and feel much more myself, if I can just get my two best friends through whatever it is they have that's hanging over them, because of their horrible experiences.

Thank God they came round today!

'I think we've made a terrible mistake,' Jack says to Leo, with a distraught look on his face. 'He's going to have me back in that bloody mankini again, isn't he?'

Leo shakes his head quickly. 'I don't want to wear a mankini, Jack,' he says, his voice laced with terror.

'Boys! It's not going to be that bad!' I assure them both. 'You know how I work . . . Just leave things with me, and I promise I'll come up with some ideas that will help.'

'Including for you?' Jack says, deeply suspicious of my intentions.

'Yes! Absolutely including me! Of course!'

His eyes narrow . . . but I am being incredibly sincere here, aren't I? Helping Jack and Leo will absolutely be of benefit to me. In the manner, and on the terms, that I have previously outlined.

Yes, indeed.

Leo points a shaky finger at me. 'Just . . . Just promise me you're not going to get us involved in anything too hare-brained, dangerous or bizarre. I know what you're capable of.'

'I promise,' I assure him. 'All I'm going to do is look into some methods of . . . I don't know . . . *therapy* that can help people who have suffered some sort of trauma. Whether it's Jack's agoraphobia, your fear of people, or my . . . whatever it is that's doing my head in about that car crash.'

The very fact that I cannot define what it is that troubles me is surely indicative of the fact it's not really all that bad . . . isn't it?

Jack's problem is obvious, as is Leo's. They're both having understandable reactions to what happened to them. One of them got lost and nearly died, and the other one got assaulted on a dark street. There's nothing like that for me. Nothing anywhere near that terrible.

And that means I can't be anywhere near as badly off as they are. I'm not like them.

'It's called PTSD,' Jack responds in a flat voice. 'You have PTSD.'

'Whatever, whatever,' I reply in a slightly irritated tone. 'The key thing is, we can do something positive here! All three of us! Together!' To underline this, I actively punch the air with a closed fist.

See?

Look how *healthy* I'm being! Look how proactive I am!

Surely that must be the right course of action?

'It would be nice to stop . . . stop being quite so scared,' Leo admits.

Jack stares at him for a second, before rolling his eyes. 'Oh, good grief. It's happening again.' The finger he points at me is ramrod straight. 'No bloody mankinis!'

'I promise.'

'. . . or other forms of ridiculous clothing.'

'Duly noted.'

'Or farmyard animals.'

'Absolutely not.'

'Or extreme sports.'

'Nope.'

If Jack's eyes narrow any further he'll lose his vision completely.

They stay like that for a second, before relaxing somewhat. 'Okay . . . I must admit, it would be nice to . . . you know . . . go

99

trekking again.' His eyes go a bit misty. 'Maybe even get Gormley out on the road again. Petra and Tyler would like that.'

I punch the air again. It's become a thing, and I'm too caught up in the moment to realise it's very probably not a *good* thing. 'That's the spirit!' I say, with deeply troubling amounts of excitement.

This is truly excellent.

I *will* help my friends.

I *will* make them feel better. And that means *I* will feel better.

It really is the perfect plan.

Everything will be alright. Everything will be totally

Chapter Five

NOT MUSHROOM IN HERE

'You want us to sit in Gormley, and drop magic mushrooms?'

'I do!'

Jack goes momentarily slack of jaw, before eventually gathering himself up enough to respond. 'Have you gone stark staring mad?'

'No, I have not.'

'Yes, you have,' Annie says, getting up from the kitchen table in a swift movement. 'It's a crazy idea, Charlie. You know it is.'

I shake my head in defiance.

I knew I'd get this kind of pushback.

But I am thoroughly prepared for it.

Hence the stack of papers in front of me.

Which I now begin to sift through. 'I've done extensive research,' I point out. 'This isn't some half-arsed experiment I'm proposing, Annie. I am taking solid, proactive steps to solve my problems with a holistic approach.' I don't want this to sound like something I've just read off ChatGPT, but it does, because it is. 'Nautilus assures me that there is a great deal of medical evidence to support the concept of psilocybin mushrooms having great therapeutic effect on trauma-related conditions.'

'Nautilus's real name is *Barry*,' Annie states in a tone that barely manages to contain her obvious frustration. 'And you only met him last week, because Zitana put you on to him.'

'So?'

'So, you're going to take the advice of a bloke called Barry – who's renamed himself after a submarine, and someone that you've known for less time than you've had a bottle of milk in the fridge?'

My attempts at reassuring her I know what I'm doing obviously aren't working.

I hold up some of the papers. 'But I have done extensive research as well,' I protest.

Annie lets out an exasperated grunt. 'I give up. You try, Jack. Maybe he'll listen to you? He's known you for much longer than me.'

'Annie's probably right, Charlie. This does all sound a bit dodgy,' Jack says, shaking his head.

Ha!

You see that 'probably' sat right there?

A man can work with a 'probably' . . .

'Look, I'm not saying it's guaranteed to have any effect, but I still think the evidence shows that it's worth a try. And I'm talking about a very, very low dose. Nautilus was very insistent on that.'

'*Barry*. His name is *Barry*,' Annie reminds us both. 'And Barry is not a trained healthcare professional. You need to go to see a doctor.' She looks at Jack. 'And it sounds like you do too, Jack, from everything Charlie has told me.'

Jack holds up his hands. 'Hey, hey. Let's not get crazy here. I don't think me not being keen on wide-open spaces is a good enough reason to go see an actual *doctor*.'

'Exactly what I've been trying to say!' I agree wholeheartedly.

Annie's eyes bulge for a moment in disbelief. Possibly at the entire male species. 'I . . . I can't . . . I . . .' she stammers, before letting out another loud gasp of exasperation, and exiting the kitchen, her feet stomping down the hallway.

Jack watches her go, before turning back to me with a slightly shocked expression on his face. 'Bit much, eh?'

'I know,' I agree. 'She's being a bit weird about this whole thing, to be quite honest with you.'

'Well, women are a strange and exotic species,' Jack replies in a knowing tone of voice.

'She does mean well, though,' I tell him – and somewhere, far off in the depths of deep space, a creature of bizarre shape and incredible dimension looks up from the purple leaf it's munching its way through, and shudders at the sheer enormity of how patronising I've just been.

'I'm still not sure about this whole magic mushroom thing,' Jack says, allowing the creature to go back to its lunch.

'Not the first time we've taken hallucinogens,' I say.

'We were a lot younger and a lot dumber back then,' he argues.

'They didn't do us any harm at Glastonbury . . .' I cajole. 'Made it even better, as I recall.'

Jack folds his arms and thinks for a moment. 'I'm not saying an outright no, but I'm not saying yes, either. And I'm not going anywhere near it unless Leo agrees.'

'Oh, I'm sure I'll be able to persuade him.'

Jack makes a doubtful face. 'I'm not so sure, Charlie. Leo was never one for hallucinogenic drugs, you know that. He always stuck to the mild stuff. He'll take some persuading. I bet you'll have a harder time than you think.'

'We'll see,' I say with a smile.

◆　◆　◆

'Stop looking at me like that,' Leo says uncomfortably as we all stand in front of Gormley on the driveway of Jack's semi-detached, on what is turning out to be a typically grey UK evening.

'No, Leo,' Jack replies. 'I am not going to stop *looking at you like this.*' His arms fold. 'I was counting on you to say no to this frankly idiotic scheme of his. I was relying on you to be the voice of reason.'

'He sounds pretty convinced about the whole thing.'

'Of course he does!' Jack leans forward slightly, his eyes widening. 'That's *Charlie*. Sounding convincing about the whole thing is his *raison d'être*.'

'You could have said no,' Leo quite rightly points out.

Jack shakes his head. 'No, no. We've long established that he can talk me into doing stupid shit, Leo. You're supposed to be the sensible one among us. The smart one. It wasn't you he had in the mankini, was it?'

'I guess not.'

'So, why in the name of ever-loving Christ did you let him convince you this was a good idea? You're my backstop, Leo. You're my last line of defence. My bulwark against the insanity!'

'He showed me a lot of paperwork.'

'*Hitler* had lots of paperwork too, Leo!' Jack remonstrates. 'Piles of the stuff, I'm sure! You don't invade Poland without a lot of admin behind you!'

'You're getting a bit carried away, Jack,' I say to him, shivering a little. 'Can we get inside Gormley? I'm cold.'

'Quiet, you,' he says, with a stern expression on his face. 'You are responsible for my current predicament, and therefore your mild discomfort is none of my concern.'

'I'm cold too,' Leo says.

This earns him a dark look.

But then Jack fishes into his pocket and pulls out the keys to the ancient mobile home. Continuing to look at us both very sternly, he moves towards Gormley's door and then turns to open it.

It's been years since I sat in Jack's pride and joy.

I wonder if the strange smell has gone away?

No. Probably not. It's probably got even worse.

There were no doubt other, better places I could have suggested for our therapeutic mushroom session, but Gormley still has a warm place in my heart – despite the smell. It was the scene of many a fun and exciting trip with me and my two best mates, and it feels appropriate to use him once again for this purpose. A bit of comfortable familiarity might help things go a little smoother.

I'm confident that this will go well . . . but taking magic mushrooms is still somewhat anxiety inducing, even at such small doses. Gormley's familiar rustic and rusting interior should keep that anxiety to a hopeful minimum.

. . . no.

I have no actual idea why it's called Gormley. Jack just started calling it that about a week after he bought it, and that was that.

It is the most incongruous, but at the same time, the most utterly *perfect* nickname for the rusting mobile home. If it could speak, it would speak in the voice of something you would absolutely call Gormley.

'Right, in you come, then,' Jack tells us both. 'Apologies for the smell. I've not had time to air him recently.'

It's not actually that bad, to be honest. It's a musty, old smell, rather than anything too obnoxious and . . . *recent*. If anything, the smell is sparking off some very happy memories for me, which is exactly what I was hoping for.

Even Jack and Leo have somewhat wistful expressions on their faces as we all pile into Gormley. The fear of what I have planned for tonight is temporarily overpowered by extreme nostalgia.

The three of us sit on the thin brown sofa cushions that surround Gormley's little Formica table at the rear of the mobile home. Given the vehicle's rather diminutive size, the space around that table is cramped, to say the least. Getting into a sitting position is not the work of a moment. There's a lot of sliding about and knee bashing going on. God help us if there was an emergency, because getting back up and out again takes even longer.

This won't be the first time we've sat like this and filled ourselves with intoxicating substances. We did Glastonbury three times in Gormley, and I think half the smell that still lingers in here is due to the amount of 'herbal remedies' we consumed between bands. Leo probably remembers more of those heady days than Jack or I do, thanks to his moratorium on anything stronger than a joint.

Ah, to be young again . . .

Young people don't suffer with chronic insomnia and unexplained panic attacks due to car crashes. They laugh such incidents off on their way to the next festival. I seem to remember Jack losing control of Gormley on a wet road one year, and nearly ploughing us into an oak tree, back when we were in our early twenties. He ran the side of Gormley down the bark of the tree, leaving a long dent that remains there to this day.

I think we actually *laughed* about the near-catastrophic accident after it had happened.

People in their early twenties are immortal.

And extremely stupid.

The look on Leo's face tonight assures me that at our advanced age, nobody thinks they're immortal anymore. Not when it comes to magic mushrooms, anyway.

'I'm really, really not sure about this,' Leo tells me, rubbing his face anxiously.

'Honestly, mate, it's going to be fine,' I try to assure him.

Jack harrumphs in a way his twenty-two-year-old self would have been thoroughly ashamed of. He certainly wouldn't have sat with his arms crossed and a suspicious look on his face as I produced a small bag of illicit drugs from my pocket, either.

But this is Jack the father, husband and chemical engineer we're talking about. Someone vastly divorced from the young idiot who cackled gleefully as he sped away from the oak tree that nearly killed all three of us.

'They look like something that's been at the back of my fridge for six months,' Jack points out as I wave the baggie of magic mushrooms in the air, peering at them somewhat doubtfully. 'No wonder we never buggered about with the things years ago. Expensive . . . and resembling a wart.'

I have to admit his comparison is pretty accurate. The magic mushrooms are little black and grey bullets of squishy nastiness that look like something you'd produce from the nose of a coal miner, rather than something you'd stick in your gob.

Nautilus assured me they were the good stuff, though. Just enough of a single dose to be able to evenly split between three, for a mild hallucinogenic experience all round. One that is meant to both connect you with, and release the pent-up dismay about, your own brand of personal trauma.

In California, there is a whole medical practice dedicated to this kind of therapy . . . and it's proved to be extremely popular. People swear by it.

I feel like Jack is much more likely to swear *at it* – and me – as I open the plastic baggie, and tip the mushrooms out onto what I hope is Gormley's clean Formica table.

'I'm not fucking eating that,' Jack announces.

'I agree,' Leo says, with a look of disgust on his face.

I have to confess I feel much the same way. There is a total of nine of the weird little black and grey mushrooms. We are meant to consume three each. That should be just the right dose, according to Nautilus.

My gorge rises if I have to eat boiled vegetables, so I'm not sure how my stomach is going to react to those horrible little things.

'Oh dear,' I say in a disconsolate voice. This plan of mine looks to be falling at the first hurdle.

I look up, expecting to see a triumphant look on Jack's face. But instead, he continues to look quite dismayed. He regards the disappointed expression on my face for a moment.

'Hang on,' he says, raising one finger, and gets up from the sofa. He walks towards the kitchenette that runs down Gormley's right-hand side, and opens the small cupboard above the little gas stove. From it, he produces a half-full bottle of Jamaican spiced rum – his favourite tipple.

Both Leo and I can't keep the surprise off our faces.

'This has been here . . . *a while*,' Jack says, examining the bottle closely. 'Forgot all about it until we came in just a minute ago. I think it's probably a good five or six years old, but alcohol never goes off, does it? It's alcohol. How can it?' He sits back down and plonks the bottle on the table next to the coal miner's bogies. 'Eating those things with a swallow of this should make it a bit easier.'

'Not sure we should be mixing alcohol with magic mushrooms,' Leo says, ever the cautious one.

I wave a hand. 'It'll be fine,' I promise, grabbing the bottle and unscrewing the cap. 'Who wants to go first?' I say hopefully, knowing full well what the reaction will be.

'You,' Jack demands.

'Absolutely *you*,' Leo agrees.

Both of them sit back, regarding me with expressions that scientists who study mice would recognise.

I sigh.

I guess I shouldn't have expected anything else.

With the bottle of rum in my left hand, I gather up three mushrooms in my right. My heart is beating fast as I do this.

Is this a good idea? I mean, really?

What other choice do you have?

We could just go to the doctor, like Annie suggested?

What? And have the embarrassment and indignity of trying to explain why we're so weak and out of control? Be quiet and eat your black bogies.

With a grimace, I open my mouth and deposit the mushrooms on my tongue. Leo lets out a snort of disgust, while Jack looks on with fascinated horror. I very quickly take a large slug of the rum, and swallow hard. There's a moment when one of the mushrooms slimily slimes against the side of my gullet, but the otherwise inevitable dry heave is suppressed by the extremely strong taste and heat of the rum.

'There,' I say, trying not to gasp. 'That wasn't so bad!'

Only because my throat is on fire, instead of slimy.

'Hmmm,' Jack intones . . . but also takes the rum from my hand and picks up his own three mushrooms. 'I swear to God, King . . . if this ends in my untimely death, I will haunt you for the rest of your natural lifespan.' He throws the mushrooms into his mouth and takes a much, much larger glug of rum to accompany them down. Once he's done, he slams the bottle back on Gormley's table and looks daggers at me. 'And I will be *naked*, King. You will wake up to my ghostly penis swinging in your face every single morning.'

'It's not big enough to swing,' I retort, quite comfortable that Jack will not have to carry his threat out. I doubt this experiment will end in any of our deaths.

I *think*.

Jack slides the bottle over to Leo. 'Your turn, champ.'

Our friend regards the bottle with mounting horror – and then summits the mount when he looks back at the three remaining mushrooms. 'I can't.'

'Yes, you can,' Jack says.

'I don't like rum,' Leo argues.

'Yes, you do,' Jack insists.

'No, I don't.'

Jack – possibly buoyed by the rather large amount of Jamaica's finest he's just consumed – laughs and pushes the bottle even further in Leo's direction. 'There's no way you're getting out of this now, boyo,' he remarks. 'I can lock Gormley's door from the inside and keep you trapped in here if I have to.' He leers at Leo. 'And rum gives me the worst farts imaginable, Leo. Do you remember?'

Leo's face goes the kind of ghostly white Jack was threatening me with just a second ago. 'Yes. I remember,' he says.

As do I.

Nothing was guaranteed to clear Gormley of two-thirds of its occupants than a long, sonorous, drawn-out Jack Bailey fart. The idea of being trapped in here with one is enough to make me regret my life decisions.

Leo feels much the same way, as he picks up the mushrooms in one shaky hand, pops them onto his tongue in much the same hesitant manner as me, and takes a pull of the rum, forcing himself to swallow both.

I've never seen a bulldog chewing a bleach-soaked wasp before, but I bet it would look quite like whatever it is that Leo's face is doing at the moment.

He gasps for air like a man drowning in his own regrets, spluttering rum over Gormley's table, and sits back with a look of exhausted terror on his face. 'I hate the both of you,' he says, having carefully thought about it for a few moments.

'No, you don't,' Jack says, taking another swig of rum, before popping the cap back on.

'How long . . . How long do we have to wait?' Leo asks, still gasping for breath a bit.

'Nautilus says the psilocybin requires thirty minutes to one hour to affect the brain's chemical composition,' I report with confidence. Trying to maintain an air of clinical detachment in the way I speak about this whole thing makes me feel better, for some reason. Like it genuinely is a therapeutic medical session, rather than three idiots sat in a rusting mobile home, dropping 'shrooms.

'Once that happens, we should be able to engage in clear and insightful memories of our trauma, which we can analyse dispassionately in conversation with one another, thanks to the calming effect of the chemical.'

'Riiight . . .' Jack says, seeing through my little charade incredibly easily.

'Okay,' Leo nods in shaky understanding. 'What shall we do in the meantime?'

Jack reaches under his seat and into a cupboard, producing a pack of playing cards. 'How about a bit of gin rummy?' he suggests.

It does not take thirty minutes to an hour for the psilocybin to affect the chemical composition of my brain.

It takes barely ten.

I've only just got myself a good hand for the first time in the game, when I start to feel . . . *quite odd*.

'Are you playing?' Jack asks, staring at me.

'Give me a chance,' I reply. 'I haven't had time to look at my hand properly yet.'

'You've been staring at it for nearly five minutes,' Leo remarks.

I blink. 'Have I?'

'Yes,' Jack says, his face like thunder. I wonder if he's going to fart?

This makes me giggle briefly.

'Stop it, Charlie!' Leo says.

'Stop what?' I ask.

'Laughing like that! You've been doing it for thirty seconds and you've gone very red.'

'Have I?'

Jack eyes me. 'The 'shrooms are kicking in, aren't they?'

'No, they aren't,' I tell him, shaking my head quickly.

'Charlie!' Leo cries. 'Stop shaking your head like that! You're going to do yourself an injury!'

I look at him. 'What on earth are you on about, Leo?'

'You've been sat there wobbling your bloody head about like a bowl of jelly for a minute,' Jack tells me.

Impossible! What's he on about?

But then . . . I do seem to have developed something of a sudden ache in my neck. Great. That's the one thing that I thought I'd managed to get rid of in all of this mess, and I think I've just brought it back.

'Oh my,' I say, touching the end of my nose with one hand. I think this takes me no more than a second, but it could be three hours in reality. 'My nose has gone very numb,' I tell my friends.

'Oh, good grief,' Jack says. 'You're high as shit. Already.'

I slam my cards down hard on the table. Never have I been so insulted in my entire life!!

'I AM NOT HIGHHHHHHHHH!' I tell him, in what I think is an angry tone of voice.

'No?' Jack's face is a heady combination of disdain and amusement. 'Then why do you sound like a moped going eighty in a thirty?'

'My insides!' Leo suddenly barks, making us both jump.

'What?' Jack snaps, clearly quite perturbed by the sudden outburst.

'My insides have coagulated!' Leo says, the horror on his face now taking on proportions so epic in nature that it's a wonder his eyeballs haven't rolled out of his head. Leo then grabs his stomach and starts to massage it. 'They've become incoherent! Can you see their incoherence? Why must they disentangle in this manner??'

I can't help but let a loud bray of laughter escape from my mouth. It probably goes on for a day or two.

Jack realises what's happening and buries his head in his hands. 'You're both gone now, aren't you?'

'Oh! Oh!' Leo exclaims. 'They've reintegrated!' The look of relief on his face is palpable. 'They've reasserted their coherence, and have become infallible!' He rubs his stomach again, this time in apparent glee. 'My tummy-ness is restored! I can feel the sedentary connections obliviating!'

So, magic mushrooms apparently turn Leo into a walking, talking dictionary of gibberish, while they slow me down to one-tenth speed, like a sloth with arthritis.

Jack appears to be completely untouched by their influence. Thus far anyway.

'I knew this was a bad idea,' he says, his hands still firmly clasped around his head.

This makes me giggle.

For about thirty minutes.

As I do this, Leo starts a stock check of the rest of his body parts. His biology degree is working overtime. 'Ah! My cranial sacks remain oscilliant!' He seems delighted by this turn of events. As am I. I giggle for a further seven hours. 'And my limbic stanchions can be pulpated quite freely!'

I have no idea what a limbic stanchion is, but it brings me no end of joy that Leo's can be pulpated quite freely. I'm so happy when my friends are happy. It's all that matters to me in the world.

Jack sits back up again, and takes another shot of rum. 'This is going to be an extremely long evening,' he intones.

Leo points a shaking, excited finger at him. 'Yes! Long! My longs are fine too! Especially the exterior ones!' Leo then stands up and unbuttons his jeans. 'Would you like to see my main exterior long?'

'Sit down!' Jack barks and pushes Leo back into his seat, before he has a chance to whip his exterior long out for us both to get a good look at.

'Ow!' Leo protests as his arse slams back onto the incredibly thin cushioning. 'Be careful, Jack! You'll hemorate my googlins!'

Oh no!

The last thing I want is for Leo to have his googlins hemorated! I peer at Jack with disgust. 'Why would you do that, Jack?' I ask him. 'Why would you want to hemorate Leo's googlins?'

'I'll hemorate your bloody googlins in a minute, you imbecile,' he growls.

'Pfft,' I snort, 'don't be so angry all the time, Jack.'

Hmmm. That's an interesting sensation, isn't it? The way the air flows between my lips when I purse them like that. I think I'll continue to do it for the next three weeks at increasing speed and pressure.

All Jack can now do is sit back in disbelief as one of his best friends makes stupid noises, while the other continues to check his body for non-existent organs.

'Yes, indeed, Charlie,' Jack says. 'This really is turning out to be a great therapy session. Can't wait to analyse our traumas in dispassionate conversation, and implement the valuable findings in my day-to-day life.'

I'd like to respond to this, but I'm far too busy flapping my lips together and making a terrifically satisfying *brrrrr* noise.

I don't know why he has to complain so much. This is a thoroughly enjoyable way to spend your time. Right up there with the heady, hectic nights we've had in Gormley in the past. I tell Jack as much.

He looks at me in extremely certain terms. 'This is nothing like those times, Charlie. Isn't that right, Gormley?' Jack then cocks his head, as if listening to something. 'Yes, I agree completely. He is an idiot,' he then says.

'Who are you talking to, Jack?' I ask him.

The look I get in response is withering. 'Who the hell do you think I'm talking to? It's Gormley.'

I blink in surprise. 'You're talking to *Gormley*?'

He rolls his eyes. 'Well, of course I am, you cretin. He's the only one here I can have a decent conversation with, given how high you two are.'

I giggle again, understanding coming to me in an instant.

Thirteen months later I reply. 'I think you're high too, Jack,' I tell him.

'Don't be so bloody ridiculous,' he says, and again listens to something that quite clearly isn't there. 'Yeah, you're right, Gorms. This was a bad idea. These two obviously can't handle the 'shrooms.' He pauses again for a moment, before laughing and slapping his knee. 'Yes! You're so right, Gormley! You always know the right thing to say!' Jack then stands up and starts to tickle the roof. 'Who's a good boy, then?' he says, in the kind of voice it's impossible not to use when stroking a dog.

This is clearly too much for me, and I spend the next eleven decades laughing out loud.

I'd like to be able to fill you in on what goes on for the next hour or so, but it's all rather a blur. I'm pretty sure all I do is sit there continuing to giggle like I'm – well . . . as high as a bloody kite. Leo continues to feel himself up in a manner that becomes more and more disturbing (and therefore hilarious) as the minutes pass, while Jack goes around stroking every one of Gormley's surfaces – apparently to the absolute delight of the mobile home. If it could, it would kick one leg out and make happy little yipping noises.

At no stage are any of us able to talk about our traumas, or converse calmly about the things that are troubling us. If this is a mild dose, then I'd hate to see what a large one would do. I'd probably be unscrewing the top of my head off right now, if I'd taken four mushrooms, instead of three.

Things only take a turn for the dramatic when Leo reaches across the table and grabs my arm. 'I'm okay, aren't I?' he asks me in a somewhat desperate tone. 'My thuribles are fine, right, Charlie?'

I pat his hand. 'Your thuribles are perfectly okay, Leo,' I promise him.

'And what about my hipolicals? They don't feel in line with my chakramis *at all*.'

I really don't know what to say, other than to reassure him that both hipolicals and chakramis are operating at peak maximum efficiency, as far as I can tell.

'My nose hurts, though,' he says, this time in a much more scared voice. 'I can still feel where he hit me. The evil wizard.' He takes on a distraught look. 'They were *all around me*, Charlie. In the dark. I had nowhere to go! I was trapped!'

Even in my current state of heightened psilocybin-powered hilarity I can pick up the sudden change in Leo's temperament. I try to control the giggling, and squeeze his hand a little tighter. 'It's okay, mate. Nothing is wrong. You're okay.'

He whips his hand back. 'No. You're wrong, Charlie! I'm not safe! There are too many people!' His head whips back and forth. 'I should never have come here tonight! Why did you make me?'

'I . . . I wanted to help . . .' I say, rather pathetically.

He shakes his head. 'You can't help, Charlie. No one can. I'm trapped. My nose hurts and I'm trapped.' He then violently rubs his face. 'I have to get out of here!' he tells me, and tries to get up from the table, awkwardly banging his head on Gormley's roof as he does so.

'Hey! Be careful, Leo!' Jack warns him. 'Poor old Gorms needs to be treated kindly, don't you, Gorms?' Jack pats Gormley's roof again and smiles broadly at the reaction only he can hear.

'I have to get out! Before they come . . . Before they come and surround me again,' Leo states, and spends what feels like the next twenty-five minutes extricating himself from the confines of Gormley's little Formica table trap.

Once he's done this, he makes for the door.

'No!' Jack screams in terror, and wraps his arms in what he must think is a protective manner around Leo. 'Don't go out there! Stay in Gormley, where it's safe! It's too big out there, Leo! Far too BIG!'

Leo struggles. 'Let me go, Jack!' he wails.

'No! I can't. I don't want you to get hurt out there! I don't want you to get lost!' Jack wails, and I can see tears in his eyes.

'But I'm not safe in here!' Leo protests. 'I'm not safe anywhere!'

'You are safe! You are!' Jack insists. 'In here! In Gormley, you are safe! I promise. That's why I come in here. And Gormley loves me being inside him, don't you, Gorms?'

Again, Jack listens for a response, but his face falls in an instant. 'Gorms? Gorms?! Speak to me, Gorms!' he almost screams.

'Let me go, Jack!' Leo cries, and attempts to get free of Jack's clutches. All this succeeds in doing is making the both of them bash against Gormley's little Formica table, sending the bottle of rum falling to the floor. It smashes as it hits the faded linoleum.

The sound of breaking glass immediately catapults me *somewhere else.*

I am still sat in the mobile home, but at the same time I'm sat in the driver's seat of my old MG.

And I'm *crashing*.

Once again on that country road, and once again being flung around in my seat as my car connects with the one being driven by that teenage boy.

Only, when I look out of the window as the MG is hurled sideways, the teenage boy and his car are nowhere to be seen. Instead, the crash is happening with a giant black and grey mushroom. I bounce off the hideously slimy thing and come to rest once again, the same way I did in real life.

The teenage boy and his car are back again . . . sat across the road from me just like they were, but now we are joined by the mushroom, which lies a little beyond both cars, up the road to my right.

And it is *pulsating*.

Hideously, terrifyingly, pulsating – in a slow, awful rhythm that reminds me of a heartbeat.

My heartbeat, to be precise. Because like everything else on this strange hallucinogenic trip, my heartbeat has been slowed to a crawl. As have my movements.

For some reason I feel like I should be jumping out of the car and running towards that giant pulsating mushroom, despite how noxious and evil it looks.

I must get to it.

I must touch it.

I must lick it.

I must know it . . .

Every fibre of my being wants me to go over to that mushroom, because something is very, very wrong with it, and I must do something to help.

It should be a bright, shining mushroom. Full of life and vigour. Not the pulsating, cancerous thing it has become. It is sick. It is going to die, if I don't so something.

I open the car door, which takes four weeks, three days and seventy-eight minutes.

I climb out of the car, which takes six centuries.

I start to walk down the street, and time stretches out in front of me like a path I can never reach the end of. *Ice ages* are in front of me. *Epochs* of time I can scarcely comprehend. The formation of the universe lies between me and the mushroom.

But I must help it! I must save it!

I must!

'Charlie!' I hear a voice scream.

And suddenly I am returned to what passes for the real world.

But I am still on a road.

The one outside Jack's house.

With a set of headlights coming right at me.

A car horn blares, and I feel hands roughly pulling me backwards. I stumble, my heels catching on the kerb behind me, and can do nothing to stop myself from falling.

Jack, Leo and I all come crashing down onto the grass verge in front of Jack's house. The feel of cold, wet grass up my back and legs goes a long way to pulling me out of my drug-induced state. Enough to bring me back to the present, anyway. The memory of that pulsating mushroom is still crystal clear, though. No matter how hard I shake my head.

'I . . . I . . . I couldn't do anything to save it!' I wail at both of my friends, the tears now coursing down my cheeks.

'Save what?' Jack asks as he rises from the grass, spitting some out of his mouth as he does so.

I lie there looking at him for a moment in an agony of ignorance. 'I don't know!' I eventually screech. 'A big mushroom, I think? I don't know!'

'Let's maybe get you inside,' Jack says, his face a picture of genuine concern. 'And we'll lock the door, so you can't go off on any more almost fatal adventures.'

I rise to my feet, and suddenly feel a bone-cold chill. 'How long have I been out here?'

Leo glances at his watch. 'We lost track of you about forty-five minutes ago,' he says. 'We were . . . somewhat distracted.'

Jack barks a laugh. 'That's putting it mildly. You were trying to bury yourself under the driver's seat, and I was caressing Gormley's hot plate.'

'Are you . . . Are you both feeling better?' I ask them, very much hoping they are.

Jack nods. 'I feel a lot straighter than I did an hour ago,' he tells me, before holding a hand up in front of his face. 'Everything is a bit blurry, and I feel like I'm walking about on a cloud, but other than that, things have calmed down a lot, yes.'

Leo nods. 'All I can see now is the streetlights above us leaving tracers across the sky, whenever I look away from them. I also have a very dry mouth.'

I look up, and sort of see what he means. Each street lamp looks like the burning eye of Sauron to me, but other than that, and the cold I feel down my back, the world seems to have returned to something akin to normality. 'I guess Nautilus was right. The dose was a small one.'

Jack groans. 'Yes . . . but I was expecting to feel a bit happy and light-headed for a few hours. That's the kind of small dose I thought it would be. Not one that makes you think your caravan is a dog for twenty minutes before bringing you crashing back to earth.'

'Let's get inside, eh?' I say, shivering. 'My excursion into the unknown has left me very cold and wet.'

Jack nods, and walks us back up to the house, where he invites us into the lounge, and pumps the central heating up a bit.

He then makes us all a coffee, and when I've had a few sips of that, I start to feel a little warmer, and a little more myself. The effects of the mushrooms really are wearing off now – although the memory of what happened to me on them most certainly is not.

'You want to talk about it?' Leo asks me.

I look at him blankly. 'I don't know. It was horrible. And I don't understand it.' I roll my eyes. 'I thought doing this might help us all understand things a little better, but it's only made it *worse.*'

'That's just you, I think, champ,' Jack says. 'Leo and me know what's going on with us. We told you that.'

I nod in a resigned fashion. He's right. I'm the only one who still can't quite fathom why he's having such a hard time of it.

When I tell them both about the flashback to the crash and pulsating mushroom, the pair of them think for a second about what the hell they should respond.

'It meant nothing,' Jack says, with no small degree of surety. 'You were high as shit on mushrooms, so no wonder one popped up in your hallucination.'

'He's probably right,' agrees Leo. 'Don't spend too much time over-analysing it. You'll drive yourself mad.'

I heave a sigh. 'I wanted this to work, damn it.' I look from one to the other. 'Did either of you get anything from the experience?'

'A headache,' Jack says in a deadpan voice.

'Not really, Charlie. Sorry,' Leo adds. 'If the mushrooms were supposed to relieve some of our anxieties, I think they just managed to do the exact opposite.' He looks uncomfortable. 'I never want to feel that kind of dread again.'

I'm not all that sure whether he's referring to what he felt while tripping, or what he felt when he was whacked by Gandalf.

I am disconsolate at this news.

I did so want this to work.

Jack gets up and comes to sit next to me on the couch. He pops an arm around my shoulder. 'Look, try not to let it get you down too much,' he says. 'We had a go at something that was a long shot anyway, and nobody got hurt.'

'I was nearly run over.'

'. . . apart from you nearly getting run over, yes. But let's gloss over that and just be grateful that none of us suffered some sort of permanent mental breakdown, and are now squatting on my roof naked, throwing their own shit at passers-by.'

I guess this is a good point. If you look at it from a certain angle, and have at least four shots of rum in you.

'It accomplished nothing, though,' I argue.

I *hate* that. I can't tell you how much I *hate* that.

'Hey,' Jack says, squeezing my shoulder. 'It's given you a new, lifelong fear of mushrooms, hasn't it?'

I give him a look built on foundations of the purest disdain. 'Thanks for that.'

I'm trying to sound dry and humorous, but there's a catch to my voice that betrays something far more honest.

I think I *am* afraid of mushrooms, now. Or at least what mushrooms may represent. That pulsating, nasty thing sat there on the road terrifies me, and I have no idea why.

Aaaargh!

It's all so *frustrating*.

'I think it's time for me to go home,' Leo says, rising from the chair he's sat in. He looks about as exhausted as I feel. Whatever stimulant effect the mushrooms were having has clearly worn off for all three of us.

'Taxis,' Jack demands, also rising. 'There's no way either of you are driving.'

'Had no intention to,' Leo says. 'Everything is still quite fuzzy, and I keep jumping at shadows. I'll pick the car up tomorrow.'

'Me too,' I agree. 'Let's face it, my track record with driving hasn't been great recently, so best I don't get behind the wheel right now, eh?'

My poor attempt at humour falls completely flat. Neither of them laughs. In fact, they both look at me with something more akin to pity.

On my way out of the door some ten minutes later, when my taxi arrives to pick me up and after Leo's has already left, Jack holds me back for a second and says, 'Please don't let this get you down, mate. Just pass it off as another one of our famous group cock-ups and move on. Just more Shenanigans. You know, like Satan's Arse?'

I shudder at the memory.

Around Leo's birthday every year – which falls a week and a half after mine, and two weeks before Jack's – the three of us take ourselves off somewhere for a boys' weekend away. We've done it for the past fifteen years without fail, other than during the pandemic. We rotate who gets to choose what we do, and one year it was Jack's turn to arrange the trip.

He found Satan's Arse, and took us into it.

Satan's Arse was an Airbnb we rented in France for our weekend away, back when the service was first getting up and running – and the place was so named because everything in it was cursed by the lord of hell himself. We spent a day and a half there before vacating. It was a waking nightmare of dirt, broken equipment, trespassers, farmyard animals and at least one World War II-era land mine.

But I would frankly stay there for a whole month, rather than go through what I'm going through at the moment. I might not sleep any better thanks to the chickens, but at least I wouldn't have the nightmares, and a permanent cloying sense of abstract anxiety.

I also wouldn't eat the bloody mushrooms.

I'm too tired to point all this out to Jack, who I know is just trying to help. 'I won't,' I tell him. 'On to the next thing.'

Jack's expression goes flat. 'Next thing?'

'Taxi's here!' I tell him, pointing down the driveway – and making off in the direction of it, before he has chance to further question me on what I meant by that.

I'm not giving up.

Not at all.

Okay, psilocybin clearly wasn't the answer, but there is one out there *somewhere*. I just have to find the right thing for us to try that will unlock it.

Because I can't stand to see Leo looking as scared as he does, and Jack's bravado doesn't fool me for one moment. Even in my drug-addled state, I could see the fear on his face when he was holding Leo back from running out of the door.

Maybe the mushrooms were more useful than I first thought. They've certainly highlighted just how much their experiences have impacted my best friends.

What about you? What did it highlight for you?

I don't have an answer for that. I'm as in the dark as I ever was. I still don't understand why the silly bloody car crash is doing what it's doing to me.

So frustrating!

The conversation I have with Annie when I arrive at her place is not what you'd call a constructive one. She was disappointed with me, as you'd expect. This made me feel like I weighed about a hundred tonnes.

There's part of me that wishes I'd just gone back to mine, on my own – which is something I hate to admit.

But I went to her flat, and I let her tear a few strips off me, because the whole thing with the mushrooms did end up being a very stupid idea – no matter how much research I'd done about it beforehand. And I didn't want to have an argument with her. Not at all. Keeping things happy between me and Annie is my paramount concern.

But I should have gone home alone. That would have been better . . .

Needless to say, I hardly get any sleep that night, and when I eventually do, I'm woken from it by a very concerned-looking Annie.

'Wass'up?' I say, rubbing my eyes.

'You were moaning about a giant mushroom, Charlie,' she says. 'No. More than moaning. Whining. Like a scared dog.'

'It's nothing. Honestly,' I tell her. 'Just the after-effects of what we did earlier. I'm fine. Everything's fine.'

Annie closes her eyes briefly and tries very hard not to look annoyed. This just makes her look upset, though, which is worse. 'Charlie, why are you trying to shut me out?'

I stare at her for a moment. 'I'm not.'

'Yes, you are,' she sighs. 'And I don't really know why. We've been together over six months now. We should be . . . closer.'

My panic levels rise. 'We *are* close,' I try to reassure her. 'I've never felt closer to anyone, to be honest with you.'

'It doesn't feel like it.' She runs a hand that's shaking slightly through her hair. 'You keep telling me everything is fine, but whining about a giant evil mushroom in the middle of the night is *not fine.* You do need to see a doctor. But you won't listen. I wish I knew why you were being like this with me.'

I'm suddenly aware of the large space that exists between us in the bed. This should be impossible, as it's only a small double. I reach out across the strange gap and take Annie's hand. 'I'm sorry you feel like I'm shutting you out, but I'm honestly not. I'm just going through a few things at the moment. Temporary things, that I'm sure I'll come out of . . . that I'm sure I can fix.'

'How can you be sure?'

I shrug. 'Because I always have in the past. There's not been any problem I couldn't solve. And I don't see this being any different. I just need a little more time, that's all.'

Annie looks into my eyes for a moment. 'Mr Fixit. That's you.'

I laugh. 'Probably.'

'But what if this is something you can't fix, Charlie?'

I shake my head. 'No, I don't believe that. You have to trust me. Just give me time. Please?'

She continues to study me for a few moments. I find it both a wonderful and an uncomfortable feeling in equal measure.

'You just need time,' she says.

I nod hard. 'Yes! That's right.'

'I can give you that,' she eventually says with something of a sigh.

But what she doesn't say is *how much* time she's going to give me.

. . . that's okay, though. I can work with what I've got. I *always* work with what I've got. I will get this problem sorted out. I *will*. Annie won't have to worry anymore. She won't feel like I'm shutting her out, because there will be nothing to shut out. I'll be *fine*.

And hey, look at it this way: I know not to try something as stupid as magic mushrooms again, don't I? That's useful information to have. That's *progress*. I am learning valuable lessons. And that's a *good* thing.

'If it's okay with you, I'm going to try to go back to sleep now,' I say to her in a lighter tone of voice. The space between us in the bed feels like it's a bit smaller now.

'Alright, but if you start screaming about toadstools, I'm waking you up again.'

I chuckle. 'Fair enough.'

We're both trying to sound light and breezy, but I doubt anyone looking in from the outside would believe it for a second.

Annie must have been very tired, because she goes back off to sleep in seconds, but I don't drift off for another hour or so. I keep thinking about the strange and worrying sense of space I felt between Annie and me just now.

A space that's probably just about big enough to fit a giant, pulsating mushroom . . .

Chapter Six

LOSING HER

Things . . . settle.

They always do. That's just the way life is. Bad or good, time tends to flatten out the peaks and troughs, the mountains and the valleys – even if the valleys you do have to wade through are still full of liquid poop.

. . . I never claimed to be good with words. I'm an events co-ordinator, not a writer.

A good six or seven weeks go by, and my life enters a rhythm that I can just about cope with.

I continue to sleep very badly, and the nightmares don't go away, but it reaches the stage where I just become used to it . . . and carry on regardless. 'My Humps' still lingers, but there are entire days when I don't find myself humming it. The earworm has become slightly less active.

Thanks to the social media fallout from the disastrous gender-reveal party, I still have had no more new clients come in for my work. And I don't feel like anything I'm doing for my few existing clients is particularly *good*. Zenith Games are pleased with the events programme I present to them . . . but they are not delighted with it. I'm giving them their money's worth, but that's about all. Nothing else. There's none of my usual extra flourishes that keep the client coming back time and time again.

They'll pay me what I'm owed for this project – but do I think they'll be employing me again in the future? I very much doubt it.

Everyone can tell I'm flat. And flat doesn't promote business well. Unless you're a company that makes irons.

So, my work very definitely continues to suffer, in one way or another.

And Mr Fixit hasn't been able to fix anything when it comes to Annie, either. The space in the bed has only got wider. We haven't had sex in over a month. I just don't feel like it. I cite tiredness and stress from work as the causes – and that is more or less the truth. My job has always fired me up in more ways than one, but the lacklustre way I'm going at it these days has robbed me of my drive in the bedroom as much as in the boardroom. I'm staying over at hers less, just to avoid putting myself in the situation where sex might be on the cards. It also means she doesn't have to cope with me starting awake at 3 a.m. quite so much.

I'm deathly afraid that all of this is going to drive her away from me. Our relationship is just not long term enough to survive my continued lack of oomph. Sooner or later, Annie is going to want to get away from me. I know that for a fact.

But I keep telling her things will get better, as much to convince myself as her.

Eventually, it will.

It *has to*.

That's how things work, isn't it?

The troughs flatten out. They always do. And the trough I'm in at the moment will go away sooner or later. I just have to ride it out. And keep wading through the poop, in the meantime. I will get my mojo back sooner or later.

Meanwhile, life goes on . . .

And on this particular night, that means attending Annie's latest stand-up gig.

I have to confess, I'm more than a bit nervous as I take my seat for the show. Not least because she's trying out new material tonight, and I'm a little apprehensive about what it might contain.

After all, comedians do draw from real life, don't they?

Oh dear . . .

She really did want me to come along tonight, though. Was quite insistent about it, actually. So here I am.

This is only the third time I've been to see one of her gigs, and I want it to go well for her. It usually does (there was that one incident with Captain Vomit she told me about, but that's not the kind of thing that happens on the regular, thankfully). She's a professional, after all. She knows what's she's doing. Even if someone is upchucking their dinner in the third row.

I can't imagine having to deal with something like that. I'm not good with surprises. Or vomit. There is nothing I can do to prevent somebody like Captain Vomit turning up again. Nothing I can do if some other unknown quantity comes along to screw with her routine.

I don't know how I'd cope.

I probably wouldn't . . .

And I'm also nervous tonight because I'll be hanging out with Annie after the show, and I'm not sure how that's going to go. It might depend on what I'm about to hear in this new routine, I guess.

Annie has been more than a little . . . *distant*, of late. I can't say I blame her.

It's not bad enough that I think she's about to end the relationship just yet, but it certainly is enough for me to absolutely understand that things are not 100 per cent fine between me and her.

Largely this is, of course, my fault. I say Annie is the one who's been distant, but it's really me who's doing all the drifting away.

I'm tired. I'm anxious. I'm twitchy. I'm sad.

And I don't want her to see any of that. That's not the way Charlie King is meant to be, especially with his girlfriend.

Hence why I'm now sleeping at her place less. Hence why I'm making excuses not to see her.

And she knows this. She knows what's going on. That's probably why she was pretty adamant I come to the gig tonight.

She is most definitely not happy with the way things are between us at the moment.

I know this. I'm not stupid.

And I *have* to do something about it. I have to prove to her that things will be okay. That everything will be as totally fine as I keep promising her it will be.

Even if I have no answers to what's troubling me, I have to make sure the questions don't end my relationship with a person I am most definitely head over heels in love with. And have been for quite a while now.

I *have* to do something. I have to make an *effort*.

. . . after I've sat here and listened to her latest routine, that is.

The lights go down on the stage here at The Palisade as Annie walks out to the applause of the audience. She's the second to last performer this evening, so she'll get a good half an hour of time to show everyone just how funny she can be.

I settle back into my seat, hoping Captain Vomit isn't sat two rows behind me.

131

'Good evening, everyone. Welcome to the show,' she says with a smile. 'My name is Annie, and I'm absolutely *knackered* . . . I've been fighting off a bad case of hay fever all week, you see, so if I sound a bit bunged up, that's just some extra realism I'm adding to tonight's entertainment.'

No word of a lie. I keep having to duck when it looks like she's going to sneeze.

'I thought it'd bring some authenticity to the routine,' she continues. 'You're absolutely welcome. Though, for those of you in the front row, I'd think about putting your coats on. When I sneeze it's like the big bang, only without so much majesty of a newborn universe, and a lot more snot.'

First big laugh of the evening. That's lovely to hear.

'Do you ever find that there's something about being sick that brings out the absolute worst in people?' she says to the audience, obeying the first rule of stand-up: connect with the crowd as fast as possible.

'I mean, the minute I feel even slightly ill, I turn into the biggest diva imaginable. I lie there like Elizabeth I on her deathbed, with my hand to my forehead.' Annie affects the ridiculous pose she was working on three weeks ago, while *Location, Location, Location* was on its advert break.

'*Fetch me the physician! I am not long for this world without his dreadful ministrations!* And meanwhile, my boyfriend will be standing there, completely unfazed, just watching me with a dumbfounded expression on his face. *It's a slight head cold, baby*, he says. *You'll survive.*'

That's not really true, unfortunately. Stand-ups may base their material on real life some of the time . . . but it's less than people think.

'Sadly, unlike Elizabeth I, I am not in a position of power to have his head chopped off,' Annie tells her new friends, who are enjoying the routine as much as she'd hoped. 'Which is probably just as well. He'd just shrug it off and tell me he's *totally fine*. Because he's a man, and that's what men do.'

Aaah . . . well, that's interesting, isn't it?

Gulp.

'And I don't know what's worse, to be honest – actually being ill, or how fast everyone around you loses patience with you for it. If I'm sick for more than forty-eight hours, my friends are like . . . *Really, you're STILL sick? Have you tried . . . just . . . not being sick? You know . . . for our sakes? Please?*

That is very true. Her friends seem to be an eclectic bunch, and some of them have – shall we say – a healthy amount of *self-interest.*

'They start suggesting that I should manifest my way back to good health – as if it's my fault I've somehow invited a virus to squat in my immune system without paying rent. *Maybe if you just visualised yourself being healthier?* they say, with a well-meaning expression on their face that would certainly result in some head chopping if I was Elizabeth I.'

Heh. That'll be a reference to Mitzy. Mitzy thinks she can visualise anything in this world, and have it come to her. This is possibly true, given that her husband is the CEO of a bank.

'Okay, then!' says Annie, affecting that look of barely contained comedy anger she does so well. 'Just let me visualise a world where my nose has stopped running like Usain Bolt on amphetamines, and where you've been turned into some sort of chocolate pudding. Because right now, chocolate pudding is of far more use to me!'

The audience agree. Of course they do. Chocolate pudding is always better.

'But I think the worst part of being ill is all the advice people give you. Oh, my God, the endless, unsolicited advice! Especially from people who suddenly turn into herbal medicine experts, the moment they see you start to sniffle. *Oh, have you tried ginger root with turmeric, echinacea and haloumi?* they say. *Have you heard of the healing power of crystals? If you insert a lapis lazuli up your bum, you'll be right as rain in no time!*

She wasn't sure about the lapis lazuli gag. I don't know why, it's a killer. The laughter around me confirms that.

'They're only saying this stuff because they want to sound smart. Knowledgeable. Because they spent twenty minutes on Facebook the other day researching what things you can stick up your bum – and accidentally found out that lapis lazuli instantly cures the flu when inserted lengthways.'

Big laugh. Not surprising. Bum gags always get a big laugh. We're a simple bunch, when you get right down to it.

Annie is really hitting her stride now. She once told me that the exact same joke can be met with a few titters or a massive wave of laughter, depending on when you deliver it. It's all about the timing. We're now far enough into the routine that even the jokes she's not sure about still land.

Annie then takes on a thoughtful expression. 'Although, thinking about it for a moment, one perk of getting sick is the excuse to cancel absolutely everything. You know, to *legitimately* cancel plans. It's a guilty pleasure of mine. I'll ring whoever I'm meant to be seeing, coughing my lungs up.' Annie actually pulls out her iPhone at this point. '*Oh, no, I'm so sorry, I can't make it tonight. I feel rotten, I couldn't possibly come out*, I say. And then the second they hang up, I'm back in bed, in my pyjamas, the TV remote in hand and a cup of tea in hand, watching true crime stories on Netflix. Do you know how soothing an unsolved multiple mass murder in Alabama can be when you have bronchitis?'

Lots of Netflix watchers in the audience tonight, judging from the reaction to this.

'I do text my mates for sympathy when I'm sick – despite everything I've said about how they react. I'm a glutton for punishment. You get the absolute worst responses back when you're trying to get sympathy. I'll send a message that says I'm really unwell and feel awful – and without fail, my friend Olivia just responds with a thumbs-up emoji. A bloody thumbs-up emoji. I'm on death's doorstep, and all she's got is the pictorial equivalent of *Good for you, babe! So proud of you!*

It's the mindless look of encouragement Annie plasters across her face at this moment that makes this gag so funny.

'It's like no one knows how to be properly sympathetic anymore. I blame social media. Mind you, I blame social media for most of the world's problems these days. It's a knee-jerk reaction. We've all got the combined empathy of a potato. It's a little hard to be empathetic with other people, when you're mainly worried about how your arse looks on Instagram.'

She lets this joke sink in for a moment, revelling in the laughter. I can tell she's enjoying herself.

'Your brain turns into the worst possible roommate the second you're stuck in bed,' she says, having allowed the cadence of the audience's laughter to subside a little.

'*Oh, are you planning on lying down for a nice rest?* it'll say. *In that case, I'd like to remind you of every single embarrassing thing you did while you were at university. Or how about that time you called your new boyfriend, Charlie, "Dad"? That was great, wasn't it?*

She did do that. She was absolutely horrified.

'Speaking of my boyfriend – and I probably shouldn't, to be honest, because he's here in the audience tonight. But he knew what he was getting into when he met me. And frankly, he should have walked away when I called him "Dad" that time, so he's only got himself to blame.'

I laugh at this – but a little uncomfortably. The idea of the routine being turned onto me is not something I relish.

'My boyfriend, Charlie, bless his little cotton socks, refuses to believe he can ever get sick. Like, genuinely. The man could be coughing up an entire lung, and sounding like a deflating accordion, and he'll still tell me he's fine, and that it's just a tickle in his throat.'

Okay. This stuff is all made up. I don't think I've been sick around Annie once so far in our relationship. Certainly nothing that's needed any medical—

Oh.

Oh, I see . . .

'And I get it,' Annie continues. 'No one likes being ill, but he takes the whole "mind over matter" thing to near Olympic levels of insanity. He's convinced that if he just denies he's got anything wrong with him, his immune system will eventually comply with his wishes and go: *Oh, sorry, mate! Didn't mean to inconvenience you. I'll just fight off this virus without you even noticing! You get back to whatever it is you're trying to do . . . probably wanking.*'

I sink in my seat a little bit. Nobody here knows me, but I sink anyway.

'Honestly, his confidence would be admirable if it wasn't so bloody delusional. I remember once when he had a fever. He wasn't sweating buckets. They were bloody barrels. I'm pretty sure I could have fried an entire full English on his forehead, that's how hot he was.

'I tell him that I think he might have a bit of a fever. He just scoffs – and gives me a look like I've accused him of some grave and hideous offence. He says he's fine, and that he's just running a bit hot today . . . as if he's some sort of racing car on the forty-third lap of the Monaco Grand Prix – instead of what he actually is, which is a soaking-wet idiot with glowing red eyeballs.'

This must all come from a previous relationship, because none of this is about me.

While, of course, at the exact same time, it is *absolutely* all about me.

'So, naturally, I go to check his temperature with one of those fancy forehead thermometers. I press it to his head, wait for the little beep, and it comes back at thirty-nine degrees. That's Celsius, by the way – for any Americans in the audience – which is roughly one degree away from spontaneous human combustion. But he just brushes it off like it's nothing! *Oh, come on, those things are never accurate. You should do it the old-fashioned way.*'

The impression of me is eerily spot on, even if those words have never come out of my mouth.

'Old-fashioned way? What do you want me to do? Break out a bloody cauldron? Find some eye of newt? Maybe sacrifice a goat to the great lord of darkness and glean what afflicts you from its entrails? What is it with men and acting like modern medicine is too New Age for them?'

This is all very funny – for the audience, that is. But I can detect a distinct amount of frustration in Annie's voice that's seeping over into the performance.

'He'll just power through the problem. Or try to, anyway. He'll insist on carrying on regardless by going to work – like he's some sort of martyr. I'll tell him he's practically delirious, but he'll insist on going out, as if he's desperately needed by someone, somewhere . . .

'Oh, are you? Are you needed by people to breathe pathogens all over them? Are there people in this world that require being covered in a warm, fresh layer of spittle? . . . Actually, I don't think I want to know the answer to that question. There are some weird buggers floating about, so I wouldn't it past someone to get their rocks off at being sneezed over.' Annie makes a hideous face. 'Ugh. Can you imagine sneeze porn? It'd be the first time in porn history that Kleenex would be used for its primary intended purpose.'

137

This gets a massive laugh. One that I don't join in with, because I'm too busy reading in between all the lines Annie is throwing at me.

And, just in case it wasn't clear what's really going on here, the next thing she says is a lot more blatant.

'Of course, my boyfriend absolutely refuses to go and see a doctor. For *anything*. No matter how serious it is. It's like he thinks the GP will tell him off for wasting their time.'

She doesn't look at me once while she's saying this.

'This is hilarious to me, because when I'm sick, he's the first one to ask if I want to see a doctor. When it's me who's hacking up the lung, it's a totally different story from when it's *him*. I'll sneeze once – and he's already googling my symptoms, got multiple windows open to medical websites and is convinced I've got dengue fever.'

I wish this part wasn't true, but God help me, it is. I was literally on Google yesterday trying to find things to help her with her hay fever.

'But he's not this bad when he's just got something like a cold. Oh no. It can be anything wrong with him. Physical or mental. He could be walking around with his arm hanging off, and several voices talking to him from beyond the ether, telling him he needs to start the killing again – and he'd still just take a couple of ibuprofen and tell me not to worry about it so much.'

Now her gaze does rest on me. And I really wish it hadn't.

'I'm looking at him right now,' she says, with an expression I find to be quite unreadable. 'I can see him squirming around in his seat like a landed trout. Stand-up comedy is fine when it's all made up, but when it skirts a bit too close to home, he gets uncomfortable, bless him. I called you "Dad" on our third date, Charlie. This is all entirely a hell of your own making.'

Her eyes linger on me for just a split second, before moving to somewhere else in the crowd.

I thought I'd come here to see a stand-up routine, but I think I might be having an argument. A very one-sided argument, but an argument nonetheless. Annie is *not* happy.

'I'm being a bit unfair to him, but he can be an absolute nightmare about this kind of thing. But he is a man – and they've raised avoiding health problems to some sort of art form.'

Ouch.

'I actually think most of us spend way too much time avoiding things, don't we?'

Oh, thank God, she's changing the subject.

'Honestly, if we put as much energy into actually doing things as we do avoiding them, we'd probably be a generation of Olympic athletes and brain surgeons. But no, we are the kings and queens of procrastination! Largely because of social media. You see? I said I could blame pretty much anything on it, and I meant it. We love to put things off . . . ignore the issue . . . pretend it doesn't exist . . . deal with it *later*.'

. . . or maybe she's not.

'But let's be real: we never actually get around to the "later" bit, do we? We just kind of slowly let things rot away in the background – like that pot plant your aunt bought you. The one you know you should have watered a lot more than you did. And now it's a brown twig on the kitchen windowsill, and she's coming over in half an hour, and what the hell are you going to do now, Annie?! B&Q is a twenty-minute drive away! Do they even have begonias at this time of year? Oh God! Oh God! Nooooooo!'

The audience are in stitches. I'm chewing a fingernail.

'. . . sorry. Having a flashback there. I still have PTSD about that incident. Or should that be PPTSD. Pot plant traumatic stress disorder.'

Is she still referencing me here? Is the pot plant meant to represent my car crash? I just can't tell anymore.

'It's not just pot plants. It's *everything*. The little things, the big things, the mildly irritating things that make you shudder if you even think about them.

'You know when you get that slightly unsettling noise in your car? The one that sounds a bit like a tiny poltergeist having a tantrum under the bonnet? Do you deal with it? Do you go to a mechanic, like a sensible adult that doesn't spend all their time on TikTok? No, of course you don't. You just crank up the car radio and decide that it's a problem for Future Me!

'But of course Future Me is just Past Me, with another six weeks of denial and TikTok videos piled on top of her. I could've fixed this problem when it was a tiny rattle, but now the car sounds like it's auditioning for the part of the trash compactor in the next *Star Wars* movie.'

Is she saying she thinks I'm in some sort of denial? About what, though? I'm telling her the truth about what I remember of the car crash. I'm not hiding anything. And I'm not in denial about seeing a doctor. I'm just not.

Absolutely bloody *not*.

'Honestly, it's everywhere,' Annie says, her arms open wide. 'Every single part of our lives is just one giant case of the *I'll do it tomorrow*s. And even when we do finally face the difficult stuff, we tend to be pretty inept at handling it, because we're so out of practice.

'I tried "facing things head on" once . . . And it was bloody awful. I only ended up making things worse. I tried to end things with this guy I'd been seeing. This was years ago, way before the current boyfriend who I once called "Dad". The one who's sat in the audience, praying he doesn't get another mention in this routine.'

So very, very true.

'I tried to end things directly with this other bloke – who I'd only really been seeing on a casual basis up to that point. I told him

140

it wasn't working and that we should go our separate ways. You know what he did? He started bloody *crying*. And the next thing I know, he's talking about how he's never felt this way before about anyone. That's when my guilt reflex kicked in – and somehow, I end up in a full-blown relationship with someone I was trying to dump. I ended up dating him for another four bloody months, just because I was too polite to say: *Actually, could you . . . could you possibly leave now?*

To underline the joke, Annie picks up the microphone stand and starts making brushing motions. This has them rolling in the aisles.

Is this about me? Does she want to brush me away? Is she just being too polite with me?

'You know what? I think we all just need to get over this fear of dealing with stuff, don't you? We need to learn to just rip off the plaster. Get things done. Be a bit braver about it. Sort it out properly! And quickly!'

I blink a couple of times. I feel like my girlfriend is reading my mind, live here on stage tonight. And it's far more disconcerting when she does it than when it's Zitana in her purple suit.

'No more procrastination! No more TikTok! Just ball up all of those problems in one glorious bigger ball, and throw it in the rubbish bin!'

Some of the crowd clap at this.

'I've decided my new mantra is: *Just get it done.* The moment I hear myself say that I'll deal with a problem later, I force myself to do it right there and then. Got a difficult email to write? Just send it. Need to go to the doctor about something? Book the appointment. Got a stubborn boyfriend who won't do what you ask? Invite him along to your latest gig and embarrass him in front of a bunch of complete strangers . . .'

Oh boy. Mission accomplished, sweetheart.

'Just do it now, and then it's out of your head. Face your fears all at once! Deal with your issues with no delay!'

Annie's clenched fist rises high into the air, much to the delight of the audience, who clap and cheer.

The triumphant expression disappears from her face and she looks back down at the audience with a lopsided grin.

'. . . and, you know . . . if that doesn't work, you can always just shove a lapis lazuli up your arse. That should take care of everything.'

Bringing a joke back when the audience least suspect it is a guaranteed way to get a huge laugh. Which gives me ample opportunity to slide out of my seat, and get the hell out of here. Clearly my girlfriend and I need to have a conversation after her show. I just hope it's not one that ends with her pushing me away with a microphone stand.

'Well, that went well,' I say, with a slightly sick expression on my face, as Annie enters the dressing room that the kindly staff of The Palisade have provided for her.

'You think so?' she says, picking up a bottle of water from a side table and taking a long swig.

'Yes. Lots of interesting material, I thought.'

Annie's eyebrow arches as she methodically screws the top back on the water bottle, looking at me quite intently as she does so. 'Yes, there was, wasn't there?'

'Went down very well with the crowd.'

'Yes, I'd say so.'

My mouth has suddenly gone quite dry. 'Felt like some of it wasn't really aimed at them, though.'

'No?'

'No. Felt like it was more . . . aimed at someone more specific.'

Annie places the bottle of water down on the table very carefully. 'Well, Charlie, they do say that the best comedy feels like it's been written especially for you.'

I nod, equally carefully. 'Makes sense.'

Annie folds her arms and simply chooses to look at me. It's clearly up to me to fill the silence.

Which is quite problematic, to say the least.

'I guess . . . I guess maybe the stuff about sickness and facing up to your fears was probably aimed at me?'

Annie's face crumples a little. 'Not *aimed* at you, Charlie. I'm not trying to be horrible to you. But is it partially about you? Yes. I base my stuff on real life, and what's going on with you is the main thing in my life right now.'

'It is?'

She looks a little horrified. 'Of course it is, Charlie.' Her brow furrows. 'I'm really worried about you.'

Why do I feel so embarrassed and ashamed when she says this?

Annie catches the look on my face. 'There's no need for you to feel so bad about feeling so bad, Charlie. And please stop pushing me away.'

I shake my head. 'I'm honestly not trying to do that.'

'You're not? The way you've been acting these past few weeks makes me feel like you are. Like you STILL don't want to talk to me. I put all that stuff in my routine because I had to say it all to *someone*. Might as well be paying customers.'

My shame grows. I can't stop it.

'The bit about getting rid of the guy you couldn't stop dating . . .' I say, my entire body feeling like it wants to convulse. 'Is that . . . Is that how you've been feeling about me? Would you rather I wasn't around anymore?'

Annie looks aghast. 'Of course not! That wasn't about you. I don't want to split up with you! I want to be with you!'

'I want that too!' I say, and make a move towards her. She holds up a hand.

'That's lovely to hear, Charlie. But I'm not sure I quite believe it. I'm not sure we have a future together at all.'

'Why not?'

'Because I don't think you trust me. I don't think you trust yourself. And you're avoiding me. You're avoiding the problems that you're having . . . for some reason.'

'I don't mean to,' I mumble, falling back against the dressing room wall.

'Nevertheless . . .' She leaves this hanging in the air, looking at me with eyes that are slightly glossy. She's probably said all she's wanted to say tonight. Both on stage and in here.

I'm losing her.

She says she still wants to be with me . . .

But I'm losing her.

Because there's something wrong with me, and she deserves better than that.

Annie yawns and rocks her head back and forth. 'I'm tired, Charlie. I think I'd like to go home now, take a long bath and get some sleep.'

I give her a dull nod. 'I'll go get the car . . . and I'll . . . I'll drop you off.'

Her eyes grow a little more glossy. 'Okay, Charlie. That's fine.'

I can't bear to look at her anymore. I can't bear to be in the room with her.

No. You can't bear to be in the room with yourself. *Big difference.*

I leave quickly, letting Annie collect her things, and make my way out of the rear exit of The Palisade. As I reach my car, I try to take a deep breath, which for some reason I find very hard to do.

You know what? I think we all just need to get over this fear of dealing with stuff, don't you? We need to learn to just rip off the plaster. Get things done. Be a bit braver about it. Sort it out properly!

Oh God, I wish I could just *sort it out.*

Nothing would make me happier! Then I'd be the man Annie fell for in the first place.

Then I'd be a man that she does want to stay with, and not one she wants to push away with a microphone stand.

But that's not who I am right now, is it?

Not at all.

I'm something else. *Somebody* else.

I just wish I could bloody understand WHY.

Chapter Seven

POLE POSITION

. . . but Bryan and Delta should be able to help me with that, though, shouldn't they?

Yes, yes.

They can help me understand WHY.

They can help me sort myself out – so that I don't lose my lovely, patient girlfriend.

They've got to.

Otherwise, my already difficult life is going to get a hell of a lot *worse*.

Bryan and Delta should be able to help me out *a treat* – along with helping my two best friends, into the bargain.

I know Jack and Leo very well, and I know that if I'd come up with another therapeutic session idea too soon after the mushrooms they would have had none of it.

Timing is everything in life, and while I feel like I've lost my mojo in a lot of ways, I don't think my ability to time things right is one of them.

Two months is more than long enough for my best friends to reflect on their experiences while on the magic mushrooms, and reach some conclusions.

Mainly that they are both carrying some deeply rooted anxieties around with them – probably even more than they realised before that night in Gormley.

On the four occasions I see them in that eight-week period, the conversation often returns to what the mushrooms highlighted for each of us. It's playing on their minds as much as it is on mine.

And at no point in these conversations do I mention anything about Bryan and Delta.

Not until I know Jack and Leo are ready to hear it.

Bryan and Delta O'Dowd are a couple whose business I helped get off the ground a while back. I didn't end up doing a whole lot of work with them, as they only needed some guidance about what kinds of events they should hold to drum up business, and who to target for attendance – but I enjoyed my short time with them, nonetheless.

I never actually thought I'd be in a situation where I'd want to take them up on their services – but the same could be said for Zitana, and look what happened there.

Bryan and Delta are the owners and runners of Motive888, a company dedicated to giving clients a good kick up the arse.

Proverbially speaking, of course.

Both ex-soldiers, they are the kinds of healthy, attractive, forthright people that are built to motivate others – usually through the mediums of shouting, activewear and a complete intolerance of negativity.

They run one-, three- and seven-day boot camps out of their rather lovely farm, buried deep in the countryside – where they can scream positivity at their clients as loudly as they like without upsetting anyone.

I know for a fact (because I used it in the promotional material I designed for them) that these boot camps have helped people motivate themselves out of the kinds of rut I currently find myself in. Unlike Nautilus and his bloody mushrooms, Bryan and Delta have multiple testimonials from customers that prove they know what they're doing. And they're genuine reviews as well. I know, because I've done my due diligence on this one to an almost paranoid degree. Not making the same mistake twice.

And I'm not making the mistake of suggesting a day-long boot camp at the Motive888 farm to Jack and Leo until I'm fairly sure they'll agree to it.

Which they do, after a trip down the pub, where I get them both good and drunk before suggesting it.

'Oh, screw it, why not,' Jack says, rocking back and forth on his bar stool a little. 'I could do with a bit of motivation in my life.' He slaps his stomach. 'And losing a few pounds. They do that, don't they? These people you're on about?'

I nod enthusiastically. 'Yes. They have a long record of helping people lose weight and rediscover their sense of self-worth.'

'The stuff it says here about how they help people with their phobias *is* interesting,' Leo pipes up, looking up from his phone. He's less drunk than Jack, but still susceptible to a bit of light cajoling. Especially when Bryan and Delta's website is so well put together and informative. I like to think I had a hand in that when I helped them get the business kickstarted.

'It certainly is!' I agree.

Jack nods approvingly. As well he might. Agoraphobia is specifically mentioned as a phobia that Bryan and Delta have tackled in the past, with a great deal of success for those suffering from it.

'I can't do it for another couple of weeks,' Leo says. 'The paper is way too busy for me to have a day off. It's the council elections next week as well, which will mean things will get even busier.'

'No problem,' I assure him. 'I can book us in for next month.' And then I drop the bombshell that should head off any last objections. 'My treat,' I tell them with a smile.

'Are you sure?' Leo asks, a bit doubtful.

'Of course. It's my idea.'

'Alright, I'm in,' Jack announces confidently. 'Should be a nice day out in the country, if nothing else.' He smiles broadly, but I know that underneath that smile is a broad vein of anxiety that has come to the surface more and more since the night of the mushrooms. This will do him a power of good, I just know it.

'Okay, let's do it,' Leo agrees. He isn't trying to hide his anxiety at all. It's writ large across his face – and has been for a long time.

I'm afraid to say I see much the same expression when I look in the mirror these days.

But Bryan and Delta O'Dowd should have some help for all of that!

With my friends convinced into joining me, all I have to do now is book us on the course, and buy myself some new activewear that won't make me look too fat.

Or too skinny.

I have one of those physiques that can go either way.

Ring ring.

Ring ring.

'Are you going to answer that?' Jack asks, glancing over at me with a look of annoyance on his face. 'Could be Annie? Or some work for you?'

No. I'm not going to answer it. Not even if it is work. Or Annie.

I'm not going to answer my phone because right now I'm having too much of a hard time processing what's in this bloody waiver I'm being asked to sign.

It's making me sweat.

And it's not even hot in here.

Even my heart is racing a little, reading all about what may or may not be likely to happen to me in the next eight hours of my life.

I send the call to my answering service, allowing me to fully concentrate on what I'm about to let myself in for.

When you hear 'boot camp', you think of people dressed in army fatigues making you do jumping jacks and press-ups, don't you?

And I'm sure those will be part of today's fun and games, but I'm not sure they would, and I quote: *cause strain to the human body that only those with a decent level of physical fitness should take part in.*

What else have these people got in store for us?

Enough to require an entire A4 sheet's worth of tiny writing, that's what.

'You going to sign that, or what?' Jack asks, impatient. 'My biro's out of ink.'

'Have you read this?' I reply, pointing at the offending page.

He shrugs. 'Eh. All these are the same when you do one of these outdoor physical-activity-type things. They have to cover themselves legally, don't they?'

'It is pretty thorough, though,' Leo remarks. 'I'm not sure I like the sound of *group activities that could cause injury if instructions are not listened to, and may still result in injury, however unlikely.*'

Nor do I. I don't like the sound of it at all.

'And what does *participants may be exposed to emotional and mental thought processes that could affect them in a profound manner* mean exactly?' Leo continues.

Jack snatches the pen out of his hand. 'Stop worrying so much. It's just all legal stuff.' He signs his sheet with a flourish, and hands Leo back the pen, before exiting the small cabin we're stood in to go and join the small crowd of other boot campers.

Leo signs his sheet as well, with a lot more reluctance, and makes the same move outside, offering me a tight grin as he does so.

I stand there hovering over the damned thing, in an agony of indecision.

Why am I so reluctant? This was my idea, after all.

But I never expected this kind of warning prior to doing it. It's . . . rather confronting.

I never felt like I've had a problem with confronting things before the accident. I've always taken Jack's path, rather than Leo's. But these days, that's changed. For reasons I still can't fathom.

My heart is racing as I look down at the sheet of paper, the pen a mere inch from it.

And then, my poor old heart nearly jumps out of my chest when my phone starts ringing again.

'No!' I wail, and thrust a hand into my pocket. I pull the stupid phone out, and hit the red button again without even looking at who's calling.

I can feel the beginnings of a panic attack.

The hot flush. The throbbing face. The hitching breath.

It's a feeling I've become all too familiar with.

I think I'm up to at least nine or ten of them since the bowling alley.

No. No. This is not going to happen, I order myself, taking a long series of slow, deep breaths. That's what Google told me to do.

I'd be up to well over a dozen panic attacks without this helpful breathing method – and sure enough, it does the job now as well, calming me down again.

Sign the stupid sheet, and let's get outside into some fresh air.

I scrawl my signature at the bottom, and go to join my friends. By the time I'm standing by their side, the panic attack signals have completely disappeared, thank God. Maybe just getting past the hurdle of signing the waiver was all I really needed to do.

'Good morning, everybody!' Bryan O'Dowd says in a voice that entertains not a jot of doubt. It *is* a good morning as far as Bryan O'Dowd is concerned. And therefore, it must objectively be a good morning to everybody, because his tone of voice demands it.

As does his clipped and extremely neat ginger beard. Bryan O'Dowd is a man very concerned with his own appearance. The clipped beard and all-over suntan convince me of that.

'We're so pleased to see you all here today!' Delta O'Dowd adds, also in the tones of someone who is 100 per cent sure of everything that has happened to her, or will ever happen to her. Her golden hair shimmers in the sunlight. She is equally tanned.

Both of them are dressed in activewear. Purple, grey and black activewear that echoes the colours of the Motive888 logo. That was my suggestion when I put together their launch event. Continuity is incredibly important in marketing. One of the first lessons I ever learned, and still one of the best.

I am *also* dressed in activewear.

Or more accurately, I am dressed in a pair of new black Primark jogging bottoms that will be saggy at the knees in about five minutes, and a blue Primark t-shirt. That's about as close to activewear as I get.

Leo is dressed in an expensive olive-green tracksuit combo from Lululemon, a brand I had never heard of until he told me about them. This happens quite often with Leo's fashion choices.

Jack is in a Metallica t-shirt and a pair of jeans. In deference to today's activities, the jeans are somewhat looser than normal.

We're all wearing Adidas trainers, because we are men of a certain demographic and generation.

Joining us is a selection of other people who need a good kick up the arse. Not least for their fashion sense, in some cases. Activewear can – and does – really bring out the worst in people. Never have so many human beings dressed so inappropriately for their shape and size.

Everyone has an expression of combined hope and doubt on their face. As if they are all seeing this as something of a last resort for whatever ails them.

I wonder if they have partners who are drifting away? I wonder if there's a space in the bed between them as well? Do they have problems at work? Do they feel like they've lost something of themselves?

Probably.

Or at least something very similar, I'd wager. Otherwise they wouldn't be here.

Standing in a field on a farm in the middle of nowhere with two suntanned ex-soldiers feels like the kind of thing that could be considered a last resort.

I can understand that. Bryan and Delta O'Dowd seem to understand it too, given what they say next.

'We know all of you are here because you need a little pick-me-up for your lives,' Delta says, a look of what I assume is genuine empathy on her face. 'You've no doubt tried plenty of other avenues with no success. We believe our programme will be the thing you need to finally progress.'

'What we hope to accomplish with you today,' continues her husband, 'is the first step on a better, brighter path for you all. We're not here to fix all of your problems, but we do believe that we can give you a foundation on which to build.'

'A strong foundation is needed to tackle any issue,' Delta says. 'You'll leave here today feeling that you have one you can stand on, finally.'

That all sounds . . . lovely? But I'm not quite sure how it helps *me*.

Jack is nodding along, though, and even Leo looks relatively impressed. I guess I'd better just give Bryan and Delta the benefit of the doubt at this stage.

'Around the farm, we will be engaging in several activities that will both challenge you and challenge your perceptions of yourself,' Delta continues.

'We've specially designed these activities to focus on one aspect or another of how we learn to deal with, and effect change upon, our problems,' Bryan assures us.

Which again sounds lovely.

But a bit . . . *woolly*.

I know woolly when I hear it. I've been in the promotions business for a long time, and can spot woolly from a mile off. Especially when it's multi-coloured and at a gender-reveal party.

I'm starting to wish I'd done a little more work with the O'Dowds than just a single launch event. My due diligence might not be what it could have been, even though I read all of those glowing reviews.

You spent hours on the mushrooms and look what happened there.

Which is a fair enough point. Thank you, brain.

Bryan and Delta then split us up into four groups of three. Bryan takes on two of those groups, while Delta handles the three of us and the remaining people also in need of a strong foundation.

We are then told that we will move around the expansive grounds of the farm, engaging in different activities as we go. I look over at Jack's face as Bryan tells us all this, wondering how he's feeling about the word 'expansive'. His expression is unreadable, but his body language is stiff. The farm is surrounded by trees and hills, though, so I don't think the horizon is going to pop up and give him a heart attack any time soon.

From what Bryan tells us, it feels like the day is extremely well run, and very well organised. Which goes some way to quelling my doubts over the aforementioned woolliness.

What brings them back again is when we descend a slope, following Delta to the end of a nearby fallow field, and discover what lies in wait for us, as the first of today's activities.

It's a tug of war.

I've paid a grotesque amount of money three times over to come and have a game of tug of war with my mates.

Good grief.

'This is what we call "The Balance",' Delta tells us as we congregate around the large circular, white rubber mat. 'Here we will start to interrogate how being off balance physically and mentally can increase your dissatisfaction with your life.'

Ah, so it's a *pretentious* tug of war. Got it.

And for the next half an hour, the full pretentiousness of the tug of war becomes very apparent. Delta, marching back and forth between the three of us and the other group, says a lot of stuff about the push and pull of modern life. She expounds on the need to know when to pull at a problem, and when to let it go. The idea that we're only really pulling against ourselves comes up quite a bit, as does the notion that we need others to work with, in order to improve our lot in life.

You see?

Woolly.

I certainly feel like I'm wearing a large woolly vest, given how much I'm sweating by the end of the forty-five minutes we spend playing at tug of war.

All six of us are very hot and bothered. Delta is all about the inner reflection, but she's also all about making you work your bloody arse off.

The fact she does it in a very reasonable tone of voice, with plenty of encouragement, is almost a disappointment. This is meant to be a boot camp. Why am I not being shouted at? Why am I not being called a worm? Why is my parentage not being called into question? That's what happens at boot camps. I've seen the movies.

'That certainly got the muscles going,' Leo remarks as we start walking back up the slope, in the direction of whatever Delta has in store for us next.

'Glad we won, though,' Jack says with a grin.

'The only thing that won was *our ability to understand the balance we need to maintain within ourselves*,' I remind him, in a haughty voice.

'Nah, we pulled them over. We won,' he says, adamant. 'And they had two fatties on their team. We did good.'

Not quite sure Jack is taking away from the experience what Delta wanted him to, but that's Jack for you. Never one to conform, if he can help it.

The next activity is an obstacle course. Delta calls it 'The Path'.

Oh *joy*.

I'm starting to get the feeling that what Bryan and Delta have very cleverly done here is take a bunch of basic military exercises and dress them up with some pat psychology.

'Obstacles meet us every day on our paths in life,' Delta says, walking back and forth in front of us as we survey the thing we're about to clamber over. 'Here, we will learn that those obstacles can always be overcome with help and guidance from those around us.'

I'm going to be pulling a fat lad up a cargo net, aren't I?

In fact, there's a little more to it than that. Rather than just throwing us at the whole obstacle course at once, Delta leads us through it in four sections, each with differing obstacles that are meant to highlight one aspect of our internal struggles.

I'm not sure how running through old tyres is meant to represent my doubts and fears, but the crawling under fake barbed wire does remind me of how slowly I feel I've been moving in general recently.

Delta makes us attempt these sections first on our own and then with the help and encouragement of the others.

And damn me, if it doesn't start to have the desired effect. Climbing up a cargo net is easier when you know you have other people there to help you, if you need it.

Delta is good at this.

By the time we get to run the whole obstacle course an hour later, it does feel like I'm achieving something. And when I successfully cross the finish line, I feel a small measure of triumph, which is an emotion quite unfamiliar to me.

I actually feel the most positive I have in weeks.

Bloody hell.

'That was pretty cool,' Jack says as we walk towards a small patch of woodland at the edge of the farm.

'Agreed,' Leo adds, and pats me on the back. 'You did good suggesting this,' he tells me. 'Feels great to be out and about, doing a bit of exercise.'

'Surrounded by thick woodland and lots of nice people,' Jack throws in, making Leo's smile falter a little.

Still quite a way to go with these two, clearly . . .

And I'm not sure how the next exercise will help either of them, to be honest.

There are poles, you see.

Long wooden poles that rise a good fifteen feet off the ground, and have small, round platforms nailed to the end of them.

I spy a couple of long, very sturdy-looking ladders leant against a nearby tree – and some conclusions start to be drawn in my head that I don't like the look of one little bit.

'Now this is an exercise that will challenge you a little more!' Delta tells us enthusiastically. 'But you should be feeling more confident after the "The Balance" and "The Path". Do you?'

She receives a chorus of nodding heads, some more certain than others.

We may be feeling more confident, but those are some bloody high poles.

'That's great!' she says, punching the air. 'You should all be ready to take on the last challenge before lunch . . . "The Truth".'

Everybody is looking up at the height of those poles with no small degree of trepidation. Delta acknowledges those looks by holding out her hands in a mollifying gesture. 'Don't worry! The poles are perfectly safe. You honestly have nothing to worry about.'

You might say that, Delta, but I'm pretty sure you're about to make me stand on the top of a big wooden pole, so I'll do a little bit of worrying, if it's all the same to you.

'The truth can be a complicated thing,' Delta informs us. 'And the way we can best understand that complication is through the simplicity of externalised experience. By placing ourselves in a challenging environment designed to focus the mind, our internal thoughts can become more focused – thus allowing ourselves a better understanding of our own personal truths. It is up these poles that this may be accomplished. In our isolation, we may achieve objectivity.'

She gestures up to the top of the poles.

I'm starting to think this is why the waiver sheet was so long.

I don't see any patches of blood on the ground around us, but they could have been washed away by the rain.

But then Delta goes over to a large wooden bin that I had previously not noticed, and produces a safety harness.

My heart slows a little.

She then goes on to explain that each of us will put on one of the harnesses around our waist, which clip onto a metal ring in the centre of the wooden platforms.

'This is about sitting with ourselves, so that we might interrogate our internal biases and confirmations,' she tells us. 'As I say . . . it is safe, but challenging.'

I am challenged by how unconvinced I am by the whole thing at this point, and I'm afraid my internalised personalised truth may be that I think this is a load of old dangerous bullshit.

However, Delta is at great pains to assure us that we're not in that much actual danger of falling off the poles. She doesn't say we're in *no* danger, though, but I guess that's the point.

The next ten minutes are all about putting on the harnesses and climbing up to our respective platforms. I am the fifth one to go up, leaving only Leo on the ground.

I'm very sweaty and nervous by the time Delta locks me in place, despite the safety harness and assurances.

This is dreadfully high up. *Bone-breakingly* high up, in fact.

I look over at Jack, who's sat cross-legged and grinning. Mostly because we're surrounded by trees, and can't see more than a few metres in any direction.

Leo isn't grinning as he's clipped into place. Not one bit.

'It's not that bad once you've been up here a few minutes,' Jack tells him.

And he's kind of right. My legs still feel very wobbly, and my palms are still slick, but I do feel a little calmer after a couple of minutes. It probably helps that the sun is poking through the treetops above us, and a warm, pleasant breeze is blowing.

It also helps to not look down too much.

Unfortunately, this is quite hard when Delta starts talking again, requiring our attention. She stands in the centre of the six poles, and it feels like we're some kind of ethereal host of gods, passing judgement on a mortal below us.

The Gods of Sweat and Anxiety, perhaps.

Delta then gives a short spiel about how we will spend an indeterminate period of time at the top of the poles, during which we should fully embrace the isolation of our situation, and think about what truths we think we know.

. . . yeah, this is a lot woollier than the obstacle course.

But the course of my life for the next several minutes is set. I am to sit here at the top of this pole, on what feels like a platform just a little bit too small to feel comfortable . . . and reflect on my internal truths.

But what are those, exactly?

Well, there's certainly the fact that my job is in the shitter. That's both an internal and external truth. I know that every time I look at my bank account.

And it's definitely the truth that there's a space between my girlfriend and me that's widening every single day. It's the reason I'm up this pole . . . and possibly up a creek without a paddle.

Oh, and it's the truth I can't get a good night's sleep. Which is another reason I'm in pole position right now.

Along with the fact I can't understand why I'm suffering so much grief from that stupid car crash.

That's about it, though.

What about the fact you're terrified of going to see a doctor? That's the truth, isn't it? If you're being honest with yourself, while you're up here on the pole.

I'm not terrified of going to the bloody doctor. It's just a massive waste of time.

You sure?

Yes. It's embarrassing. That's all.

160

But maybe a doctor would get to the bottom of things quicker than doing all this malarky?

No, they wouldn't.

They could, though?

No!

Maybe that's what you're actually scared of. Getting to the bottom of things. Nobody likes being at the bottom, do they?

'Bugger off,' I say out loud, drawing Jack's attention.

'You alright?' he asks.

'Yep, totally fine,' I say, trying to ignore my mental dialogue for all I'm worth. If this is what Delta meant by understanding our internal personal truths, then I don't want a bit of it.

'Where's she gone?' the fat lad says, looking down at the ground.

We all slightly lean over our platforms to discover that Delta has disappeared.

When did that bloody happen?

'I'm sure she'll be back in a minute,' Leo says, sounding as confident as it's possible to be, when you're hooked to the top of a long pole by a small carabiner. Which is to say, not very much.

'Yeah,' I agree. 'I'm sure she will.'

Spoiler: she wasn't.

In fact, twenty minutes go by before I start to get what I would call 'proper' anxious.

'Has something happened?' I wonder to my fellow pole sitters.

Jack shrugs. Leo looks as anxious as I feel. The young woman whose name I think is Rachel looks at me blankly. Pete the plumber, whose bulk and muscle would have been instrumental in the other team's victory in the tug of war had he not gassed himself out in thirty seconds, shrugs his shoulders. 'I'm hungry,' says the fat lad.

'I reckon it's all part of it,' Jack says.

'You do?'

'Yep. I certainly hope so, anyway.' There's now a look of dismay on Jack's face that he's trying very hard to cover, but is obvious nonetheless. Does agoraphobia mix with acrophobia, by any chance? Is he sliding from one to the other the longer we stay up here?

'It's probably okay,' Leo agrees. 'She talked a lot about facing the truth while isolated, and I guess this is probably part of that. She did say it would be challenging.'

'Well, the truth is my arsehole is starting to pucker from being all the way bloody up here,' Jack intones, looking down at the ground.

'I don't like it,' says Possibly Rachel. 'Delta!' she calls out, which makes me jump. I'm more nervy than I thought I was.

The height isn't bothering me all that much anymore. Been up here long enough now for that to settle a bit. But the idea of being stuck up here with no way down is a whole other problem. There's no way I could unclip myself and get down around this platform without falling off.

Perhaps Leo is right. Perhaps this is deliberate.

Needless to say, Delta does not respond to Possibly Rachel. The little wooden copse we're in remains relatively silent, other than the buzzing of a few bees and the sound of the gentle breeze in the tree branches.

Funny how oppressive silence can become extremely quickly, isn't it?

A further ten minutes pass.

That's now a good half an hour stuck at the top of a pole.

Fat lad was only slightly ahead of the game, because I'm hungry too now. It's very definitely lunchtime – back down there in the world not at the top of the pole.

162

'Delta!' Possibly Rachel calls out again. For the fourth time.

This time Jack joins in. 'Delta!' he shouts in a louder, more strained tone. There is an edge of panic to him now. The space around us has probably widened in his mind quite considerably.

'I'm sure everything is okay,' I say, trying to believe it. 'Like Leo says, this is all part of the game.'

Another ten minutes pass.

And then I hear something in the distance that ratchets the fear up to proportions most epic.

'Christ, is that a police siren?' Pete the plumber asks.

'Yes,' I say, my mouth very dry. 'I think it is.'

'Delta! Bryan!' Jack shouts once more – and this time we all join in.

Still nothing.

No response.

Other than another siren joining the first.

In my head I try to triangulate the sound with where I remember the farmhouse being.

Gulp.

'I want to get down,' says the fat lad.

'Don't try it,' I warn. 'There's no way you can get underneath that platform and not fall off. The poles are all way too smooth as well. You'll plummet like Batman in the TV series – without the cool ending.'

'We're stuck,' Possibly Rachel says. 'Oh, my God, we're actually stuck!'

'It'll be okay,' I say, desperate for everyone not to start panicking. 'Someone will come and find us.'

'What if one of them was an axe murderer?' Possibly Rachel then says, eyes bulging.

'What?'

'One of the other clients. Maybe they were here because they wanted to stop killing, but the urge was too strong, knowing we were all isolated out here on this farm.'

'Unlikely,' I say in a dry tone.

'But it could happen!' she replies, adamant.

'Maybe give the Netflix true crime stuff a rest,' Jack tells her. 'This is a bad enough situation without getting into the realms of fantasy.'

'Then what are those sirens about?' Possibly Rachel asks him, pointing in their rough direction.

Jack doesn't have an answer for this. None of us does.

'I need a wee,' Leo then pipes up. Strangely, he now looks the calmest of the six of us. Even Pete the plumber is red-faced with what I hope is panic, and not an incipient heart attack.

If Jack's phobia is exacerbated by being in this predicament, then Leo's worries over having violence done to him again are probably lessened by it. Hard for anyone to give you a clout if you're up a fifteen-foot pole.

'Me too!' the fat lad says.

I look at my watch. We've been up here nearly an hour now. Not such a long time in the grand scheme of things. But when you're up a pole, it feels like a lifetime.

None of us have our phones to call for help.

I know this should send me into even more heights of panic, but weirdly it doesn't.

They were popped in lockers back in the hut, where I signed my life away to Bryan and Delta O'Dowd.

. . . who could be lying in a pool of their own blood right now, while Possibly Rachel's axe murderer tries to fend off the local constabulary.

We are, very much and completely, bloody *stuck*.

Which is more than a bit on the nose when it comes to parallels for my current problems, when you think about it.

My eyes go flat.

Of course it is.

'It's bullshit,' I tell my fellow pole sitters.

'What?' Jack snaps, now fully caught up in the throes of heightened panic.

'Everything's fine,' I tell him.

'How can you know that??' Possibly Rachel near shrieks.

I roll my eyes. 'Because today is all about giving us things to do that parallel what's going on in our heads. And right now, the six of us are stuck up a pole with no way off. We're stuck fast with a problem we can't do anything about.' I look around the peaceful wooden copse. 'It's about as good a metaphor for personal struggle as I can think of, to be honest with you. That's the bloody internalised personal *truth*. No doubt about it. That's what Delta wants us to realise.

'Aah,' Leo says, relaxing visibly.

Pete the plumber and the fat lad both take on expressions of deep thought. Jack still looks worried, but not quite as much.

Possibly Rachel is having none of it. 'No! No! Everybody up there is dead! And we're going to die here as well!'

I don't know what troubles her in life, but I'm willing to bet it's something exacerbated by watching too much true crime drama and TikTok videos.

'Please try to calm down,' Leo tells her. 'My friend is right, I think. He's very good at understanding what's going on around him.'

Blimey. *Am I?*

'Yeah, you are,' Jack remarks, reading the surprise on my face like an open book. 'If there's one thing about you that never changes it's that you know people. You know . . .' he waggles his hands around. 'You know . . . *stuff*.'

'Oh,' I reply, not really knowing what else to say.

The funny thing is, I'd have probably agreed with the two of them up until a few months ago. But if you can't understand yourself, how on earth are you meant to understand anyone else?

'No! I won't calm down!' Possibly About to Have a Panic Attack Rachel cries, and then does something that returns my heart to its previous high rate.

She unclips her harness.

'Wait! Don't do that!' Jack shouts, his arms out. We all make the same gesture towards her, our own harnesses pulling tight as we do so.

Instantly, we hear Delta O'Dowd's voice over a loud tannoy. 'Please remain calm, Rachel, everything is okay.'

I knew it.

I absolutely bloody *knew it.*

And then, from a specific patch of the forest floor that looks exactly like any other patch of the forest floor, Delta O'Dowd jumps into view like Rambo.

She rises quickly out of a trapdoor, beneath which I spy a little dugout room, with a couple of small TV screens, a camping chair and a bottle of water.

She's been down there this whole time.

I start to laugh. I don't know why, but I just can't help it.

Definitely Rachel looks down at Delta in horror, still locked in whatever nightmarish fantasy she's driven herself into. She probably thinks it's the axe murderer, come to finish her off.

This just makes me laugh even harder, which probably sounds cruel, but I can't help myself.

'Are you alright?' Jack asks, looking at me like I've gone crazy.

He might not be too far off the mark.

I point downwards. 'She jumped out of a little hole,' I remark, sending me off into another gale of laughter.

Jack smiles at this, and then starts laughing as well. As does Leo.

Pete and Fat Lad just look at the three of us like we've gone bonkers. There should be nothing about being up a pole for an hour that sends you into hysterics.

But there is.

Oh, my God, there truly, truly is.

Delta immediately goes over to Definitely Rachel's pole with a ladder and proceeds to help her down off it. By the time they get to the ground, Definitely Rachel has calmed down considerably.

Delta then moves the ladder to my tree, but I wave her off. 'Oh no. I'm fine. Get everybody else down first,' I tell her. 'Start with my friend Jack.' She gives me a speculative look, and moves over to Jack's pole instead.

I'm quite happy up here now, truth be told.

Because it's very *easy* up here, isn't it?

And the breeze is nice.

I'm not afraid anymore. Because somebody just jumped out of a hole with all the answers.

I chuckle at this, watching Delta get everybody else down before me.

A sudden urge to tell her to just leave me up here for a few more hours hits me. I don't care if it's lunchtime anymore. I don't care what the rest of our boot camp activities might be. I just want to stay up here, on my pole, where everything makes some sort of sense. Where I'm still the guy who understands people. Understands . . . *stuff*. Where I can get to the truth of the matter, with no real effort.

My humour dribbles out of me like sand from a tightly grasped hand.

Because *down there* is where I have to go, any minute now. And *down there* is where all the problems are. Where I have absolutely no idea what the truth is.

I know in that moment that whatever we get up to for the rest of today, it's not going to help me much. Any more than the bloody mushrooms.

Because metaphors aren't going to do me any good, any more than psilocybin did.

Let me stay up here, I plead to Delta O'Dowd silently.

Read what's going on behind my eyes, and let me stay up here on my pole.

It's lovely up here. Calm. Peaceful.

Up here I feel totally—

'Time to come down, Charlie,' Delta says, now at eye level with me. She holds my gaze as she says this.

How many like me have come through here? How many like me have wanted to stay up at the top of the pole? How many know this whole thing is a lost cause?

More than a few, I'd bet, judging from the way Delta is looking at me right now. 'If you come down, I can explain what we've just done,' she tells me.

'I think I already know,' I reply, in a low voice.

I then swallow hard, and unclip the harness.

Back on the ground, Delta spends a good ten minutes clarifying what the little experiment we've just been through is all about. She comes out with a lot of what you'd expect. Mainly that sometimes the truth eludes us, and that everything we see, hear and feel can persuade us that the truth is one thing, when in reality it is completely another. Not being able to get to the truth can make us feel stuck in place. Unable to move on. Unable to see that we actually have less to fear than we think we do, when a situation is looked at objectively.

I'm not sure Definitely Rachel agrees with her, judging from the fact she still looks pale and more than a little perturbed, but I certainly have a better idea now of why the waiver was so detailed. Scaring the crap out of people so they understand their own minds better is always going to be something you need a lot of legal protection to do.

'And well done to Charlie for understanding what The Truth was really all about,' Delta then says, inclining her head towards me. I think she's being genuine, but I'm not entirely sure. 'It's actually quite rare for someone to put two and two together so effectively.'

I'll take that as a compliment.

But you should see me trying to get to the truth when I'm not up your pole, Delta. I don't think you'd be quite as ready to pay me compliments then . . .

With her sum-up complete, Delta bids us walk back towards the farmhouse, where our much-needed late lunch awaits. The rest are eager to get to it, and take off at a fast clip. But I drag my heels, for some reason.

Delta sees this, hangs back a little and takes my arm gently.

'You worry me, Charlie,' she says in a hushed voice, so that nobody else hears.

My eyes go a little wide. 'Why's that?'

'These boot camps are meant to help people with the things that are troubling them.' She cocks her head. 'But you really don't know what's troubling you, do you? You have no idea what your truth is.'

I shake my head. 'Not really, no. I said in the email to you that I was having trouble sleeping, and kept getting . . . panicky because of that car accident I was in. How it was affecting everything important in my life – my work, my relationships. But I feel like there's more to it than I know . . .' I drift off, as unable to explain to Delta as I am to anybody else, including myself. 'I'm thrashing around, looking for answers, and none are coming.'

She pats my arm. 'Well, that's fine. Not everybody gets to know what walls they have to climb over. Not right away.'

That's a tremendously nice thing for her to say, and the absolute most useful thing I'll take away from this entire day.

'I guess not,' I respond. 'Thank you.'

'My pleasure.' She gives me an earnest look. 'Just try to engage with the rest of today as something fun to do. Don't overthink it. I fancy half your problem might be overthinking things.'

'You might be right,' I say, with a half-smile on my lips.

There's actually no *might be* about it. I *do* overthink things. Always have.

But doesn't Delta see that because I overthink things, I'm good at my job? Good at my life?

I understand *stuff*, Delta. Like Jack says. You don't get to understand *stuff* unless you do an awful lot of thinking about it.

But if you stopped thinking, maybe the answers would come? Maybe the truth would come?

That's not how answers work.

That's not how answers *ever* work.

I look up the gentle slope at my two friends, who are now in animated conversation with Pete, Fat Lad and Definitely Rachel. The five of them certainly look like they might have some answers.

I suddenly feel crushingly *alone*.

I think.

I believe.

There might be a chance . . .

Just a small one.

That I might not be, if I'm being completely honest about it . . . *totally fine*.

I should have stayed up on the pole.

Chapter Eight

SHENANIGANS

'AAARGH!' I scream. Because there really is nothing else you can do when Legolas has just bitten you on the ankle.

'Hah!' Leo exclaims with glee. 'Exactly what you deserve!'

Jack says nothing. He just gives me a look of absolute disgust.

The rest of the Fellowship of the Ring giggle. Frodo is actually laughing so hard that I think he may have peed himself. He clearly feels that poking Legolas up the bum was the best decision he's ever made, given what has happened as a result. But where's the professionalism? I was promised *professionalism*, damn it!

As I desperately try to pull Legolas's wriggling body away from my ankle before he can savage it any further, I am forced to reflect that I may have made something of a major error.

Allow me to explain:

Annie's stand-up routine told me I should stop procrastinating, and do something about my problems. Or should I say, *our* problems. Mine and my best friends'. She told me I should stop putting things off. Okay, then.

And then Bryan and Delta convinced me that getting to the truth of what those problems are is very important. Which also made a whole lot of sense.

I fear the way I have chosen to interpret those pieces of advice has not been *particularly* constructive . . .

It was such a *lovely* plan, though. The kind I am well known for.

But everything went wrong when Legolas started savaging my ankle.

That was never part of my *grand master plan*.

If, at any time in your professional or private life, you feel that having a poodle dressed as Legolas savage your ankle is part of your grand master plan, I suggest you seek medical advice at your nearest opportunity.

Mind you, if I'd done that, then I wouldn't be in this situation in the first place, would I?

There should be a much longer road between not wanting to go to a doctor because you're embarrassed and getting your ankle savaged by a cosplaying poodle, but that is clearly not the case.

The road is very short, and begins with Shenanigans.

Shenanigans (with the capital *S*, that's very important) has been an annual tradition for Jack, Leo and me for over ten years now. With our birthdays all happening in close proximity to one another, it's always made for a fabulous excuse to bugger off somewhere together for some fun. We rotate who gets to choose what we do, so that it never becomes boring.

Jack was the one to come up with the name and the concept, but of the three of us, I've always been the one to figure out the best ideas. Which is something you'd expect to be the case, given my job.

In fact, both Jack and Leo have tried harder and harder over the years to match my Shenanigans – with limited success. The crown has never been taken away from me. If anything, their efforts have backfired the more they have tried to equal me. There was the Airbnb from hell in France. And one year Leo arranged a three-day cruise to the Canaries and back, which was like spending seventy-two hours in a washing machine, thanks to the Bay of Biscay being rough as shit the entire time.

It's always better when they both keep things simple, and allow me to do the clever, complicated stuff.

When I'm in charge, Shenanigans has always been a roaring success – even if I do say so myself. The laser-tag weekend, for instance. That was amazing. As were the two nights in the Scottish castle, where we lived like lords of the manor for a weekend.

Whatever I've arranged for Shenanigans in years gone by, it's always gone down very well with my two best friends, and has thus become something both of them look forward to greatly, when it comes around to my turn.

I'm afraid that this year I have rather taken advantage of this trust to do something that I very probably shouldn't have.

'Get him off me!' I squeal. You'd think a small poodle would be easy to extract from your ankle, wouldn't you?

Not this one, though. Legolas has jaws like a bloody vice. The wriggling little sod must be part limpet.

Frodo is now doubled over with laughter. *Unbelievable.* He's the one responsible for my plight! He's the one who poked Legolas up the bum and sent him into this irrational rage. This is all Frodo's fault!

No, it bloody isn't. The only person responsible for this mess is you, Charlie King. This idiotic scheme was all your idea. Now shut up and pull harder before it breaks the skin!

This is unfortunately not something I can readily disagree with.

. . . but it seemed like a great idea at the time.

It honestly did.

I figured it would be a great way to confront trauma, in a strong and effective manner, and thereby get over it nice and quickly. No more procrastinating. No more putting things off. Understand the internal personal truths, deal with them – and move on!

You see? I'm only following the advice people have given me. I can't really be blamed for what has transpired.

Stop looking at me like that.

'Ow! Bloody hell! Get it off me!!' I screech again.

But nobody comes to my aid, because the Fellowship of the Ring are all too busy giggling their heads off, and my two best friends have no intention of helping me, because of what I've done to them here today, on the uplands of Dartmoor National Park.

Because that's where all this happening. Did I forget to mention that?

I've somehow manufactured a situation where a small poodle is savaging my ankle in front of a group of laughing children, all dressed as the Fellowship of the Ring.

On *Dartmoor*. Miles away from the nearest first aid kit.

I appear to have lost my bloody mind.

I found them on one of the online catalogue services I subscribe to for work.

Tall Poppies Talent Agency is one of the many child talent agencies that exist across the country. This one was close enough to Dartmoor to suit my purposes quite nicely.

I wanted to give Leo the chance to face his fears, you see. I wanted him to be able to face up to the Fellowship of the Ring again in a way that would allow him to move on from his trauma.

But because I am a very considerate friend, I didn't want it to be too much of a challenge for him. I didn't want him to be too scared, so . . .

You see? Makes perfect sense, doesn't it?

And agency owner Poppy Mulbray was more than happy to accommodate my wishes – no matter how ridiculous they sounded. As long as I passed a thorough security check, found and bought the costumes myself, arranged transport in the minibus there and back, and agreed to have her along as a chaperone, I could certainly employ nine members of her little troop of stars for my purposes. It would just cost me. An awful lot. Especially at such short notice.

But I was very pleased to pay Poppy a vast sum of money and put my scheme into motion. Because I am a man who can organise things at short notice. Because I am a man who can get things done, when I really want to.

And, more accurately, because I am an ocean-going, five-star, gold-plated *idiot*.

My poor savaged ankle is testament to that.

I shouldn't complain, really. Having Poodlelas savage my extremities is probably a very suitable punishment for tricking my best friends into coming out into the middle of nowhere for a spot of extreme confrontational therapy.

. . . which – as I have now repeatedly said in an attempt to make myself feel better – sounded like a great idea *at the time*.

That time being several gin and tonics deep on an otherwise dull and depressing Tuesday evening, all alone in my flat.

The whole extravagant notion sounded like an idea that absolutely played to my strengths. A big, bold, beautiful event – organised by someone who knows how to bring things together quickly, and *spectacularly*.

Visiting Zitana and the O'Dowds didn't accomplish anything really positive, because I was too *passive*. I just arranged a meeting with someone who I thought could help . . . and went along to it, allowing other people to take the initiative away. I just *sat back*.

But that's never been a successful way of doing things for me.

All my greatest triumphs in life have been when I've been the one to take the lead. When I've been the one to be in control. The one to plan things out properly, and create an unforgettable event for everyone concerned.

As soon as I realised this, I finally understood why neither of my previous attempts to help my friends had done any real good. I was too passive. Not proactive enough.

It has to come from *me*, doesn't it?

I have to be the one to put things together.

I am the event organiser. I am the co-ordinator.

Sorry, I am *The Co-Ordinator*.

It really does need capital letters to sell it properly – and possibly some black sunglasses and a leather jacket.

And who *hasn't* heard of desensitisation therapy?

I mean, really, when you get right down to it?

It's *famous*.

Everybody knows about it.

You take someone with a phobia or fear, and push them to their limits, by exposing them to it. That helps them conquer that fear, and get past it.

I've seen it work. Everybody has. Go on YouTube and have a look!

People who hate snakes get snakes thrust at them. And the snake-hating people get used to the snakes, and their fears *go away*. So much so that they end up hugging the snakes, and taking them home as pets.

Probably.

Heights!

People who suffer from a fear of heights always get better when they are exposed to being up really high. You just get used to it, don't you? It becomes *familiar*. You can't be scared of something that you're really familiar with, can you?

Why, I'd imagine there's nothing you can't get over a fear of, provided you're exposed to it for long enough.

Other than death, maybe.

Or thermo-global nuclear warfare.

Furthermore . . . how well would you get over a phobia if you were exposed to it in a really *big way*? Like, if they threw a really big snake at you, or made you stand at the top of the Burj Khalifa?

Surely that would do a great job of desensitising you to your fears, wouldn't it?

A good, sharp shock to the system!

That'd do it. That'd make *all* the difference.

A good, sharp shock, delivered – let's say – out in the wide expanses of Dartmoor for one friend's trauma, and involving a collection of child actors dressed as characters from *The Lord of the Rings* for the other's.

What a brilliant plan!

Because the mushrooms and the poles didn't really do any good, did they?

But this? Dartmoor and the Fellowship?

Yeah. That sounds like a very sensible and effective way to deal with serious mental health issues . . .

I am a very clever person, completely in control of my faculties – and not at all someone who is entering into the realms of total irrationality, based on their combined desperation and lack of sleep.

'AAAARGH!'

I just can't cope anymore. Poodlelas is destroying me. He is the flame of doggy punishment in which I must burn.

I should have stayed in bed this morning. I should never have gone through with any of this stupidity.

But it all seemed like such a good idea at the time . . .

'Come on, Jack! Look at the time!' I wave my hands in my friend's direction, trying to hurry him along. I am very excited about today, and really want to get the show on the road as soon as possible.

It will another three hours until Poodlelas launches his savage attack upon my person. I have no idea that such a horrible fate awaits me.

For now, I am excited. Because today I will properly help my two best friends come to terms with their traumas.

. . . if only I can get Jack into the bloody limousine I've paid a small fortune to hire.

'I've put a lot of effort into these Shenanigans, Bailey, the least you could do is be dressed when I come around to pick you up.'

Jack winces. 'Alright, alright. It's not my fault you plied me with enough rum to get a smuggling conviction last night.'

I contrive to look deeply offended by this. 'Me? I didn't do anything, except facilitate the orders you kept giving me. Leo told you to go a bit easier, because of what we're doing today. You knew we had an early start.'

Jack looks at me with disgust. 'Alright, Mum, keep your hair on.' He pulls on his leather jacket with another wince. 'This had better be good, Charlie. I do not get up at 7 a.m. This is not a thing that I do.'

'It is today!' I exclaim, making him wince a third time. 'Now come on, Leo is waiting in the limo, and I don't know if he'll be able to resist the Toblerones in the fridge for much longer.'

Do you have any idea how expensive a limousine with a fridge containing Toblerones is? Not to mention one that comes with pretty unique and special blacked-out rear windows that no one can see in or out of?

The first thing wasn't really necessary for today's entertainment, but the second most definitely was.

I don't want either of my two friends to see where we're going until we get there.

They're going to be so *surprised!*

Jack nods approvingly as he climbs into the limo, and sees Leo.

'Morning,' our friend says to him, from around a mouthful of Toblerone.

'Not so loud,' Jack replies, slumping into the incredibly comfortable seat. He then looks around the cabin. 'He's pulled out the stops for this one, and no mistake,' he remarks to Leo, who nods in agreement.

'There's champagne in the fridge,' Leo points out. 'And sushi – for some reason.'

I truly have spared no expense today. I want them both to feel as relaxed and happy as possible.

Jack nods approvingly once more. 'Right then. Best we get underway.'

I nod happily, and knock on the blacked-out partition between us and the driver. The limo pulls gently away from the kerb, and as it does, music starts to be piped into the cabin. It's the kind of chilled-out lo-fi stuff that always puts me in a relaxed state of mind.

. . . or at least, it *used to*, before . . . you know.

A glass of champagne will make me feel better.

'Relax, chaps,' I tell my friends. 'We have a couple of hours' drive before we get to where we're going.'

Leo frowns. 'You're being very cagey about this.'

I nod. 'Yes, I am. I want it to be a surprise.'

Jack also looks a little suspicious.

I pour him a glass of champagne. 'Here. Have this. Hair of the dog.'

He looks at the glass for moment before taking it. Once he's had a swig, he visibly relaxes into his seat a little. Leo continues to munch on his Toblerone.

Yes, yes. That's it. Get nice and comfy. Enjoy the ride, chaps . . . Desensitisation therapy always works better with a relaxed subject.

This is all going to go so well!

And for the next three hours, it most certainly does. By the time the limo pulls up at the destination I have arranged, the three of us have emptied at least one champagne bottle, and the sushi and Toblerone are no more. We're all full of booze, fish and chocolate.

'Oop . . . we've stopped!' Jack exclaims, and then giggles.

'We have!' I concur.

'So, what's next, then?' he says, leaning forward. 'Strip club? Backstage at a gig?' He looks at Leo. 'Must be something great. He wouldn't have brought us all the way out here otherwise!'

Leo nods enthusiastically. 'I'm sure you're right. This is Charlie we're talking about.'

Despite the champagne buzz, I am instantly suffused with a feeling of deepest guilt. Or maybe it's *because* of the champagne, I can't really tell. Either way, I have brought my two best friends out here on false pretences, and this is the moment my conscience has decided to berate me for it.

Turn us around. Tell the driver to take us back. It's not too late.

No! I want to go through with this. My friends need my help, and I'm going to give it to them. I *have* to give it to them.

I hold out my hands. 'Now, this is going to be a little different to the kinds of things we've done before,' I tell them. 'I wanted this trip out here to mean something, for both of you.'

'Out here?' Jack remarks, eyes narrowing.

At that moment, the door to the limousine opens gently, to reveal the wide-open expanse of the Dartmoor uplands. Jack's face bleaches white in an instant.

'What the hell . . .' he says, his voice suddenly all a tremble.

'Don't be angry at me,' I say, putting a hand on his shoulder and giving it a squeeze. 'I know how this kind of thing has made you feel, and I want to face it with you. With the both of you.'

He looks at me in horror. 'You bastard. This isn't Shenanigans.'

'Yes, it is, Jack. The most important Shenanigans there has ever been.' I point out of the limo. 'And it's easy. Honestly. It's a lovely sunny day out there. All we have to do is get out, and have a look around. That's all. Then we can get back in the limo. I have an afternoon arranged for us at a luxury spa down the road. Just do this little thing for me, and we can go.'

I'm not altogether being truthful here. The spa is definitely booked . . . but there are a couple of other things we have to do before getting there.

'Oh, for Christ's sakes, Charlie,' Leo says. 'You've lost your mind.'

I shake my head. 'No, I haven't. This is going to help Jack. It really is.' I turn back to him. 'Come on, mate. Just do this one little thing for me?'

He stays silent.

'You can't put things off forever,' I continue, my voice cajoling. 'Seize the moment . . . *get it done*. Know the *truth*.'

'You bastard,' Jack moans.

I squeeze his shoulder. 'You can do this. Trust me.'

And I really mean it. He can. This is Jack Bailey we're talking about.

We sit there in silence for another few moments, with Jack staring out of the door at the bright blue sky and scrubby bushes beyond. Then he wipes a hand over his mouth, clenches his fists briefly and then slowly starts to pull himself up and out of the limousine.

'That's it, Jack!' I say triumphantly. 'You're doing it!'

And he is. First at a snail's pace, then all at once.

Before I know it, Jack is completely out of the limo.

'Yes!' I crow with glee.

Leo passes me to also get out of the limo. 'You'd better know what you're bloody doing,' he tells me with a snarl.

This takes me aback a bit. Leo does not snarl. Especially at me. What's he going to think when—

No! This is working! Don't ruin it!

It's my turn to get out of the limo, and when I do, I see that Jack is plastered against the side of the vehicle, and Leo is stood next to him, one hand gripped on Jack's jacket sleeve.

I close the door, and tentatively get closer to them both. 'You see, Jack? That was easier than you thought it would be, wasn't it?'

'Go to hell,' he tells me in a low voice.

I nod. 'Okay, I will . . . But not before we've taken a little walk up the road a bit. How about it? You've come this far . . .' Cajoling again. Wheedling. Manipulating.

I will lie in bed later tonight hating that tone of voice more than I've hated anything about myself before. I will replay the words I use in my head. The inflections. The persuasions. And I will cry tears of frustrated rage that I could have been so stupid . . . and so unkind.

I pull at one of his jacket sleeves, while Leo's hand remains clasped to the other. 'Come on,' I repeat. 'You can do this.'

Jack licks his very dry lips, and takes a step forward. Leo's expression darkens considerably.

'Yes!' I exalt. 'Well done, Jack!'

He even looks up at me and nods. And then he takes another step. Into a wide-open space that must feel like it goes on forever.

Dartmoor is a beautiful place. But even I feel a little disoriented by how far you can see. That's not a common thing to be able to do in the UK at all. It's just too small to have wide-open vistas that go on for miles.

I should know. It took me ages to find somewhere big enough for my purposes.

But here, under the blue vaults of heaven, and surrounded by the flat, scrubby moorlands that stretch on for miles, I can understand why Jack would be afraid. You could wander alone out here for the rest of your life. Alone with nothing but your thoughts.

Jack takes another step. I don't cheer this time.

From off to our left a flock of crows takes flight, disturbed by our passage. Jack lets out an exclamation of terror.

'It's fine!' I cry, trying to reassure. '*You're* fine, Jack.' I point up the way a bit. 'Let's just get to that big clump of bushes, eh? Let's get there, and we'll call it a day. You're doing very well.'

'Am I?' he asks me, and I feel him tremble all over as he says this.

I nod hard. 'Yes! You're doing brilliantly. I'm very proud of you!'

He nods as well. 'I am doing it.'

'You are,' Leo agrees, giving him a smile of his own. This one is more gentle. More patient. More

honest

Leo-like.

The three of us continue towards the large crop of bushes, which are just the right size to hold several children dressed as characters from a well-known fantasy epic.

My heart rate rises as we draw closer.

But Jack's stage of this adventure has gone well, hasn't it? No reason to suggest Leo's won't too!

'That's fine,' I eventually say. 'That's far enough, Jack. Why don't you have a little look around? Take a few deep breaths as you do it.'

Jack nods again, and does exactly that.

As he does, the deep frown lines of terror start to evaporate, and his body begins to untense. So much so, that I am able to let him go, and stand back a bit. Leo does the same thing, but with a lot less surety about his movements.

'Are you okay?' he asks Jack.

'Yeah. I . . . I think so,' our friend responds. 'If I just stand here, and don't try to think about things too much, I think I can . . . I can . . .'

Oh God. There are tears in his eyes. This is so hard for him.

What the hell am I doing?

'If I just stay here,' he repeats, 'it's not too bad, as long as nothing—'

'I AM THE SERVANT OF THE SECRET FIRE!' shouts a high-pitched but surprisingly powerful voice. 'I AM THE FLAME OF ANOR!'

'Jesus Christ!' Jack screams as the sound cuts through the Dartmoorian silence.

From behind the large clump of bushes, and very much on cue, emerges a tall kid of about ten years old, dressed as Gandalf the Grey. He is holding his staff and plastic sword mightily aloft, and has a look of grim resolve on his face. Good, good. He's playing the part well. That's just what I wanted.

Behind him come several more children, dressed as Frodo, Sam, Merry, Pippin, Aragorn, Gimli, Boromir and—

That's a poodle. I did not request a poodle.

That was not part of my grand master plan.

From behind the bush, Poppy Mulbray pops her head out. 'Sorry, Charlie!' she stage-whispers. 'Noah got the runs and couldn't make it. I thought Coco might make a nice alternative? I had a Christmas elf-dog costume lying around, so . . .'

I stare at her in disbelief.

No, Poppy Mulbray.

A nice alternative would have been finding a different child to play Legolas . . . or just not bothering with a Legolas at all.

A poodle was *not* required. Not in any way was a poodle *necessary*.

Legolas wanders over to where Frodo is now stood, flops to the ground and starts scratching at his little green overcoat. The Hobbit gives him a pat on the head and looks up at me with a broad smile on his face.

I am aghast.

Not least because Frodo shouldn't be smiling. Those were not my instructions.

Happily for Jack, this decidedly unexpected turn of events has smothered his agoraphobia completely. 'What in the actual buggery is that?' he says, jaw dropping open.

'G-G-Gandalf?' stammers Leo, one hand instinctively going to his nose, until his brain catches up with events a little more, and realises how short the wizard actually is. The chances of this Gandalf being able to bonk him on the schnoz are slim to none – which was kind of the whole point, wasn't it?

Jack looks at me and blinks. 'What is going on, please?'

The Fellowship surround us as they have been instructed to do. They all contrive to look mean and moody, which is *also* what they have been instructed to do. Results are mixed.

Gandalf, Aragorn, Boromir and Gimli aren't doing too bad a job, waggling their plastic swords for all their worth, but the four kids playing the Hobbits are all entirely too bloody cute. Two of them are girls. They are all tiny. There's an unhealthy amount of pure sweetness and light pouring off all four of them that should come with a health warning for anyone with diabetes.

Legolas is licking his genitals.

Realisation is now dawning on Leo's face about what I've done here.

'You're bloody mad,' he says, utterly dumbfounded.

'Now hang on, Leo—'

'Stark-staring, off-your-chump, away-with-the-fairies *mad*.' He sweeps a hand around. 'Did you think this would do for me what the moors are doing for Jack?'

I nod my head slowly. 'Yes. Kinda.' I clear my throat awkwardly. 'I thought, you know, facing up to the same people that made you scared that night might snap you out of your trauma a bit. The same way being up here is helping Jack.'

'*Helping?*' Jack interjects, his face a picture of unmitigated misery.

Leo stares at me for a second before replying. 'You absolute *maniac*.' He looks around at the Fellowship again, who are continuing to point their plastic swords at us in a moderately effective manner. 'Can you just answer me one question, Charlie?' Leo's voice is being kept very level only by dint of heroic effort on his part, I am sure.

'Okay?'

'Why are they . . .' He looks understandably incredulous. 'Why are they *children?*'

I shrug. 'Well . . . you know . . . I didn't want to scare you too much, did I?'

Leo's eyes bulge. I can't tell if he's about to start laughing, crying or vomiting. Possibly all three are on the cards.

Oh dear. Things aren't going well, are they?

He looks fit to burst. 'And you thought that the best way to help me with my fear of being beaten up by fully grown adults was to bring a load of small children out into the middle of nowhere and . . . *present them to me?*'

My face collapses. 'Well, when you put it like that, it doesn't sound all that great.'

'No, Charlie!' Leo snaps. 'It bloody well doesn't, does it?'

I point at Gandalf. 'Would you like Gandalf to threaten you a bit with his staff?'

'No, I fu—' He stops himself just in time. 'No, I'm *bloomin'* well wouldn't!' He throws his hands up. 'Honestly, Charlie, I'm actually scared you might be losing your mind. You're doing all this weird stuff. You're not making much sense. You're all over the place!'

'No, I'm not,' I protest. 'I'm just trying to help you both.'

'We're not the ones who need help!' Jack snaps. '*You* are!'

It's at this point that Frodo – undoubtedly now bored to tears with all this adult nonsense – decides to poke Legolas up the bum.

The poodle jumps a bloody mile, howling at the top of his canine lungs as he does so.

'Theo! That's very naughty!' Poppy Mulbray exclaims from her semi-hiding place. 'We talked about this, remember?'

'Sorry, Mummy!' Theo replies, but I don't detect much actual regret in his voice.

Poodlelas, now in an extreme state of agitation, has to make a split-second decision between fight or flight.

Sadly for me, he chooses fight.

And what he chooses to do is enter into mortal combat with me.

'AAAARRGH!' I scream . . . because there really is nothing else you can do when Legolas has just bitten you on the ankle.

◆　◆　◆

'Coco! Leave him alone! Come here!' Poppy Mulbray demands, emerging fully from the bush. She could have done this a lot sooner, to be honest with you, but I did stipulate she stay out of sight in my instructions. It's only now that I'm being savaged that she quite rightly decides to disobey orders and step in.

It's the right decision, as Poodlelas finally lets go of my ankle, and bolts back to his owner.

I inspect the damaged area to find that my jeans have been shredded, but thankfully my skin has not. I'm likely to wind up with a nasty bruise, though.

'This farce is over,' Leo says in a tone that brooks no dissent.

'Agreed,' adds Jack, with equal veracity.

The two of them give me a look that Sauron would have quailed from, and walk back over to the limousine. They climb in, and immediately slam the door behind them – thus leaving me to my own devices.

'Are your friends mad at you because of us?' Frodo asks, a worried little look on his face.

'No,' I tell him. 'Absolutely not!' I look briefly back at the limo. 'They're mad at me because . . . because I made them come here today when they didn't want to. And because . . . they think I need to do something *I* don't want to.'

He considers this for a moment, his little face a picture of thought. 'Mummy says sometimes we have to do things we don't want to. Like brush our teeth . . . and not poke Coco up the bum. She says it makes us *better*.'

For some reason I find it difficult to look into his eyes. So instead I turn to his mother. 'Thank you for your time, Poppy. The minibus will be back very soon, won't it?'

'Yeah, it will,' she says with a smile 'I just have to call the driver.' She looks over at the limo. 'I hope you can sort things out with your friends.'

I sigh. 'So do I.'

'Mummy says saying sorry is important!' Frodo pipes up again.

I nod gravely. 'Mummy is right, Theo. Mummy is absolutely *right*.'

I give him, Poppy and the rest of the Fellowship a rather half-hearted wave, and walk slowly back over to the limousine.

Gingerly, I open the door and lower myself in.

I am greeted by a pair of faces more granite-like than the bedrock of these moors.

'Shall we . . . Shall we go and have a nice spa?' I say to them, pathetic hope etched across my face.

'Just tell the driver to get going,' Jack says, face like thunder. 'I'm going to have a drink, and decide what the hell I'm supposed to think about this idiotic adventure of yours. You will keep quiet while I do this. *Very* quiet.'

I go to say something.

'He said *quiet*,' Leo snaps.

I swallow hard.

Oh dear.

Jack opens a second bottle of champagne, pours himself a glass, and does the same for Leo. I get nothing. Which is to be expected.

I knock on the partition window, and the limo driver – who has sensibly kept himself out of all this stupidity – pulls away, and drives back in the direction of the nearest main road. He knows what his job is. He was given pretty specific instructions, just like the Fellowship, and he's following them to the letter. Good man.

A rather uncomfortable hush descends.

Jack and Leo are both taking sips of their champagne when, from the car's very competent audio system comes the ear-splitting sound of 'My Humps' by the Black Eyed Peas.

'Jesus Christ!' Jack exclaims for the second time today, spilling champagne down himself.

Leo squeals like someone's just inserted something.

Oh *God*.

I'd forgotten all about this bit.

In all the misery of being savaged by a poodle and having my best-laid plans go completely sideways, the last part of my desensitisation therapy had completely slipped my mind.

My part.

Because what better way to confront my personal trauma than to sit in a car and listen to the bloody song that sparked the whole thing off in the first place?

It seemed – as did everything I've done today – like a *good idea at the time*.

'My humps! My humps! My lovely lovely lumps!'

As the hideous, annoying, brain-melting song ramps up, the driver guns the limo's engine and we pick up speed as we hit the main road. Inside the cabin, I can't see anything of the world outside. And all I can hear is Fergie telling me about her bloody humps again for the millionth time.

'Shut that shit off!' Jack wails, banging on the glass partition, and spilling even more champagne.

Hearing the song again is definitely having the desired effect on me. I am now facing (and possibly even reliving) the crash that sent me down the path to eventual poodle savagery – to an extent that I wasn't really prepared for.

Of all the stupid decisions I have made today, this could possibly be the worst one of the lot. Which is saying something.

I should never have done this.

What the hell was I thinking??

My hands fly up to cover my ears. My eyes squeeze tightly closed.

I can't cope with this! I can't handle this!

'I can't . . . I can't . . .' I wheeze at my friends as the world starts to swim.

I can't even say what it is that I can't do now – which is breathe.

I'm having another panic attack. This one completely and utterly self-inflicted.

What the bloody hell *was I thinking*???

Gasping, I slam my hand on the button that unwinds the limo's window, and stick my entire head out of the side of the vehicle, once the glass is low enough for me to do so. This gives me an excellent and terrifying view of the passing scenery.

My hair is whipped away from my sweaty forehead, and the tears are stolen from my eyes by the roaring wind.

But the fast, fresh air is like a slap to the face. It's a little hard to continue a full-blown panic attack when your face is going at fifty miles an hour.

'Charlie! Get back in here!' Jack demands – but I don't capitulate. I'm still on the edge of panic, and I don't think that's going to be helped by confronting the two people I've just put through a load of unnecessary misery to prove a point I'm not so sure even exists.

No. I think I'll just stay out here, thanks. With my head in the slipstream, and pretty much all thought driven from my head by the roaring wind. It's nowhere near as calming as being at the top of the pole, but it might be even more effective.

However, I then see another car coming straight towards me, and the panic strikes me again like a hammer.

This is too damned much!

That car is going to hit the limo, and the world is going to turn into an explosion of sound and fury – before we come to a final rest, with a teenage driver looking out at us, a small cut on his head and a dazed expression on his face.

But the elderly man will be gasping for breath and clutching his chest in agony.

The two cars

three cars

will be in a mangled heap in the middle of the B road.

It'll take the recovery services quite some time to clear the two cars

three cars

so others can move on with their journeys.

But at least me and the teenager are okay, and will only need a cursory examination by the paramedics.

They work on the old man at the side of the road, but it's obvious it'll do no good. I even hear his sternum crack when they start CPR on him. They are desperate. I am desperate. Everyone is desperate.

And even though the crash was quite horrible, I will go home feeling pretty okay about the whole thing, other than the annoyance of having to find another car for work, of course.

But that's okay. I never did like that stupid MG.

It could have all been a lot worse.

I cannot bear it. I cannot think about it. He died right in front of me. He died because I crashed into him. I cannot bear it. I cannot deal with it. It cannot be part of me. It cannot. It cannot.

I can't.

I CAN'T.

I

The other car – a large white BMW – speeds past the limousine safely, but there is a car crash going on in my head, nevertheless.

I know I'm crying, and I know my friends are desperately trying to get my attention. I know I have also slumped back into the limo seat, and am shaking in a manner that's probably causing the both of them great concern.

But I can do nothing to alleviate this, because I am . . . *detached.*

The world as it exists has been driven away for the moment, because the world as it *actually was* the day of the crash is enveloping my entire conscious mind.

The horror of it.

The reason I haven't been sleeping. The reason I've been having panic attacks. The reason I haven't been able to let go of this obsession with fixing my friends' problems.

Now I understand – and oh, my God, I truly wish that *I did not*.

And with the horror of the truth comes the grotesque shock of how my own brain could have lied to me for so damned long.

How can that even happen?

How could I have lied to myself like that?

My memories are coming back thick and fast, but it feels like my mind is splintering. Because there are two Charlie Kings. The one who's been struggling with his life for months and months, and the one buried deep down. The one who *remembers*.

Remembers it all. Every brutal, hideous second of it.

And now he is in the ascendency, and I think I might need some sort of hospital treatment very soon, because I feel like my heart is about to explode.

'Charlie!' Jack screams, shaking me. 'Charlie!'

'What's wrong?!' Leo adds, his voice filled with terror.

Somewhere off across the depths of time and space, my body feels the limousine coming to a halt. Unlike what's happening in my tortured mind.

They won't stop.

The flood of memories.

They

'My humps, my humps, my humpy lady—'

Everything explodes.

I am thrust violently forward in my seat as my momentum is arrested by something very hard and very solid.

There's not much of the next few seconds I can truly grasp, but it involves the cacophony of breaking glass and crumpling metal, the hideous sensation of skidding, uncontrolled movement, and the world outside rushing by in a blur of blue and green.

I think I scream. I can't be 100 per cent sure, but my throat will be hoarse later that evening, so I think I do.

As fast as the whirlwind begins, it is over.

The car comes to a rest askew on the road, and with my heart thudding out of my chest, I look out of the driver's side window to see that there is one car right across the road from me . . . and another further down the road. The one closest to me is being driven by a young lad. He has a cut on his forehead and looks dazed, but is otherwise okay.

I look further around to my right and see

I DON'T WANT TO.

Look.

I SAID I DON'T WANT TO! DON'T MAKE ME!

LOOK, DAMN YOU.

I see the crumpled wreck of another car, a much older one. I think it's a Datsun Cherry, probably built before I was even born. The entire right-hand side at the front of the car is staved in, as is the entire rear of the vehicle. It's clear that the front damage was caused by my car, and the rear by the teenager's car slamming into it. That's what drove it so far forward and out of my immediate line of sight.

My hand shakes violently as I press the window button, fully expecting it not to work.

But it does. Whatever damage has been done to my poor car does not extend to the driver's side door.

'Are you okay?' I shout to the teenager as the window fully winds itself down.

His window is smashed, so he can hear me just fine. 'Yeah, I think so,' he says, blinking a few times.

'Alright . . . just don't get out of the car,' I tell him. 'It might not be safe.'

And I don't get out of the car, either, taking my own advice.

YES, YOU DO.

No. I stay safely in the car, call the police and await their arrival.

NO.

Yes, yes. That's what I do. I stay in the car and watch the other cars coming to a halt before they reach the scene of the accident.

NO. YOU GET OUT.

No, I don't. I call the police and

GET OUT.

No. Please. I don't want

GET OUT.

My car door opens, shrieking in metallic pain as it rubs against the crumpled front panel. My legs feel ten times shakier than my hands, but I have to go and see if the other driver is alright. I have to check.

I have to know.

It's very, very obvious almost immediately that he is not.

He's an old man. In his seventies at least. And he's gasping. His chest is hitching up and down at a rapid pace. His face has gone as white as a sheet, but there are huge dark rings around his eyes.

As I approach the car, he looks at me, agony etched across his face.

'Oh God! Are you okay?!' I exclaim, knowing full well that he most certainly is not. He tries to raise one hand, and small shards of shattered windscreen glass cascade off it as he does.

'Don't try to move!' I tell him, desperate not to see him do anything that would make the situation worse. 'I'll . . . I'll call the police,' I say, which earns me the slightest of nods.

That's all my cowardly little heart needs to turn away.

That tiny nod.

Permission from a dying old man to do something else – anything else – than actually try to help him. Actually try to prise his door open, and see if there's any lifesaving measures I could take to save him.

195

But I don't know any!

I never have!

*YOU SHOULD. YOU SHOULD BE ABLE TO HELP, YOU
USELESS BASTARD.*

I drop the phone twice trying to call 999.

*Later that night, I will look at the heavily cracked screen and think
it happened during the accident.*

No. That's not right.

I will know *it was caused during the accident, because my brain
will have already started the work of building a very secure, thick and
impenetrable wall around the truth of what happened here today.*

*It will concoct a much easier and less horrific story to tell myself,
and everybody I love. One where everything is cleared up quickly, and
nobody is hurt all that badly.*

A story where everybody is totally fine.

TOTALLY FINE.

'Hello, this is the 999 service, what's your emergency, please?'

'Please help!' I almost scream. 'There's been an accident! He's dying!'

'Please calm down, sir. Where are you?'

'He's dying!' I scream again. 'He's dying!'

It's all I can say. It's all my brain will allow me to say.

HELP HIM, YOU USELESS BASTARD.

*Then the teenager is standing right by me, and is taking the phone
out of my hand. His face is as white as the old man's, but he looks calm.
Far calmer than me, anyway.*

*The young kid talks to the operator on the other end of the call,
while I suffer some sort of breakdown. I slump back against the side
of my car, shaking all over, my breath becoming increasingly hard to
catch.*

*This will be the first panic attack I have. It will be followed by
many more, culminating in the largest one of all in the back of a hired
limousine.*

I don't know how much time passes, but there's a woman now at my side. I have no idea who she is, but she's nice. Her voice is kind, and she has blonde hair that reminds me of my new girlfriend, Annie.

The woman helps me to the side of the road – where I will sit in a daze for a good thirty minutes, watching other people move my shattered car to the side of the road, and also trying their level best to help the old man in the Datsun Cherry.

I am useless.

I am a lump.

A lovely lady lump.

I am unable to do anything except take short, unsatisfying breaths and let my brain do the work of constructing a fiction that will let me get through the rest of my life guilt free.

A fiction that will supplant the teenager's role in the aftermath with the version of me I wish actually existed. Someone calm and capable, who can easily arrange for the police to come. Someone who can make sure my car is parked off to the side of the road, in the lay-by.

Yes, yes. It's me that did those things. Not my teenage friend, who doesn't seem too bothered by that small cut on his forehead at all. It was me.

That's the Charlie King everybody knows. That's the Charlie King I know.

Not this useless little thing, sat at the side of the road and barely able to comprehend the scale of what's just happened.

It sits there and watches as the paramedics arrive. It stares on as they try their level best to save the old man's life.

It doesn't do much of anything as other paramedics check it over, and declare it uninjured, apart from the very obvious shock of being in a car accident.

But after this has happened, the useless lump starts to be taken over by Charlie King again. The man in control. The man who knows how to organise. How to problem solve. How to make things better.

Constructing events is my bread and butter, after all. So why can't I construct a version of this day's events in my head that is so much easier to deal with than the truth?

Of course I can.

As long as I don't look over at where the paramedics have given up trying to save the old man's life. As long as I don't engage with any of that again.

I'll just keep looking the other way.

Down the road I was driving along before all this happened.

Yes. That's the way to handle this. Look forward. Put all of this behind you.

Forget it.

When the police come to talk to me, I make sure to keep looking down the road, and never back. When I call my insurance firm to tell them about what's happened, I keep looking down the road, and never back.

When I am eventually told I am allowed to leave the scene, I make sure I head down the road a little before calling an Uber. I never look back.

It's much easier once I am away from the scene of the accident.

Much easier to lie to myself. Much easier to believe the story my brain is telling me.

So much so that by the time I get home, I am pretty much back to normal. On the surface at least.

And when I get calls from both the police and the insurance firm over the next couple of days, the fiction has set in so much that I can easily forget that those calls ever happened, mere minutes after they are complete.

The foundations of my lie are strong. They will not buckle.

The lie of being Totally Fine.

That will be my story moving forward.

The story of Totally Fine.

And it will be a good story, a convincing story — that absolutely feels like reality, right up until I hear that damned Black Eyed Peas song again.

Because all stories have holes. They have places where the truth of them falls apart, no matter how hard the writer tries to prevent that from happening.

My story falls apart slowly at first . . . but then the dissolution becomes more and more rapid, until one day the whole thing unravels completely in the back seat of a limousine, surrounded by panicked friends.

And now the story of Totally Fine has fallen to pieces, what on earth does it get replaced with?

THE TRUTH.

Please.
No.

Chapter Nine

USELESS LUMP

She looks at me in a way I've never seen before.

It's fast. The expression barely registers on her face for a second. Almost imperceptible, if you weren't looking for it very carefully. But I know Annie's face quite well now. I've even seen it blown up on theatre posters and under the harsh lights of a stage. I know it well, and can easily pick up on any expression, no matter how brief – including this one.

And this is a look of distrust.

It's a look that says *I'm not sure I know who you are. Not really.*

She does her best to hide it, because she thinks I've probably told her the truth. And she knows I'd never lie to her.

But still . . .

There's a crumb of doubt there, isn't there? There has to be.

Because the whole thing sounds so fantastically *unlikely*, doesn't it?

How can a human being completely rewrite an event in his life, without even realising he's done it?

I can scarcely believe it myself.

And so, I can't really blame Annie for that almost imperceptible look of distrust, because I'm not 100 per cent sure I can trust myself anymore, either.

'Do you want another cup of tea?' she says, getting up from her kitchen table. She doesn't look at me as she says this.

She hasn't looked at me much since I got here from the ridiculous theatrical event I staged yesterday, and confessed all to her about what was actually happening with me.

It was the most difficult conversation of my life – coming hot on the heels of the *second* most difficult conversation of my life.

Do you have any idea how humiliating it is to tell your two best friends and your girlfriend that you don't know your own mind? That you've unwittingly concocted a fiction in your head to help you deal with the fact that you totally fell apart at the moment when you needed to display a little backbone? That you are, in no uncertain terms, a useless lump?

That first conversation with Jack and Leo was made with my breath still hitching in my lungs, and my face flushed with sweat. Their anger at me for Dartmoor and the Fellowship was more or less immediately overridden by their concern for my welfare. I am extremely lucky to have people in my life like that. Stupendously lucky.

I really should try to remember that more.

Because here I am, letting them down at every juncture. Disappointing them at every turn. Making stupid decisions, and lying to them about fundamentally important things.

Jack and Leo were incredulous as I tried to explain what the hell was happening in my stupid brain. But I *think* they believed me. They certainly sounded like they did when they got me over to Annie's place, and told her what had happened across the day, and how the revelation had come to me in the back seat of the limo.

I, being the useless lump I am, just sat there while Jack did most of the talking. I was exhausted, and embarrassed, and didn't really know what the hell to say.

Let's just hope that my subconscious doesn't decide to memory hole the evening as well – and create some sort of alternate reality, where everything is fine, and me and Annie watch a nice movie together with a bottle of wine.

'Here,' Annie says, plonking a cup of tea down in front of me, and bringing me back to the present with a jolt. Annie is angry. Of course she is.

Because she remembers me telling her I was *totally fine*. She remembers how I said that nobody was really hurt. She remembers Charlie King resolutely telling her, with a smile on his face, that the accident wasn't that big a deal.

And then months later, she learns that somebody died that day. That Charlie King just *forgot* to mention that the car crash he was in led to the death of an elderly man.

Further, Charlie King also lied about the fact he sat there for what seemed like an eternity, and watched the paramedics trying to save that elderly man. And about how he was such a useless lump by the side of the road, while everybody else busied themselves with the clear-up.

Lies, lies, lies.

All from Charlie King's mouth.

And what's this? What's this crowning turd on top of the shit sandwich?

Why, it's Charlie King trying to claim *he had no idea he was lying*!

What kind of insane bullshit is that?!

Not only does Annie find out that I can easily manufacture a convincing lie to cover up a horrible truth, but she also discovers that I can sugar-coat that lie with an even bigger one, by claiming not to realise I'd done any of it!

'Thanks,' I say, in response to the cup of tea. I peer down at it. It looks weak. As if it was made in an absent-minded hurry, by someone who'd rather be doing anything else.

She flashes a brief, noncommittal smile at me, and sits back down, picking up her iPhone again and losing herself in TikTok — where the liars can't do her any real harm.

'Do you want to talk about it anymore?' I say in a small voice.

She looks up at me from a video about how to air-fry a bacon sandwich. 'Um. I'm not sure. We covered it all last night, didn't we?'

She's right there. We went on until well past midnight, in fact. And we only stopped then because I'd got into a circular pattern of repeating the same apologies and anxieties over and over again.

But I have a small piece of new information I thought I'd share with her this morning. Something I've found on Google.

Only, I'm terrified to actually tell her this, because Google is where I was inspired to plan all of the crazy stuff I've done recently. I very much doubt she's going to want to hear that I've been on there again — researching more lunacy.

This is different, though.

Because *dissociative amnesia* is a thing, apparently.

Annie's eyes go flat when I mention Google. I hoped they would widen again when I told her about the condition I think I'm suffering from, but they don't.

'It's very rare, but it does happen,' I tell her. 'People who suffer with trauma sometimes make themselves forget details about what happened to them. That's what's going on with me, I think.'

'Does it also say that they create lies in place of what happened?' Annie asks — and you can hear the emphasis on the word 'lies' as much as I can, I'm sure.

I swallow. 'That's not really covered, no.' I clear my throat. 'But it would make sense, I think. Seeing what was happening to the old boy in the other car and my . . . my reaction to it. I can imagine my brain would probably want something nicer to remember than that.'

I don't want my voice to waver as I say this. I don't want Annie to think I'm playing for sympathy. But I just can't help it. Now the memory has resurfaced, I'm having a very hard time processing it.

I didn't sleep any better last night for finally knowing the damned truth. And now I have a waking nightmare to go along with the ones I have when I do get to sleep.

The coldness in Annie's eyes falters, and her hand reaches out to touch my arm.

I've created a horrible conflict for my girlfriend. On the one hand, she can see I am traumatised, but on the other, I lied to her about it. And now I'm claiming I didn't know I had.

What the hell is she supposed to believe?

Her hand feels warm and lovely on my arm.

Annie looks at me with tears in her eyes. 'Please call the doctor, Charlie,' she says.

I pull my arm away.

'I don't need to do that. I'm totally . . .'

The look in his eyes. The desperate *look in his eyes as he sat there dying, and I did nothing. I did nothing. I just*

'. . . fine.'

What's a doctor going to do, eh?

Prescribe me a pill? Tell me everything is going to be alright? Dig into my brain and remove the entire memory of the crash, so I don't have to suffer with it anymore?

I know what happened now. I know what I went through. I know why I've been so out of sorts. I don't need a doctor to go poking around! I don't need to sit there and tell a man in a white coat how much of a useless lump I am, before he hands me over a prescription for happy pills, and sends me on my way.

Annie should know how I feel by now. We've had this conversation too many times recently. She put it in a bloody comedy routine, for crying out loud.

I rise from the kitchen table, leaving my tea undrunk.

'I think I'll go have a shower, if that's okay with you,' I tell Annie, not looking at her as I say it.

I don't wait for her to reply. I'm too mad to speak to her anymore right now.

Can't she see how humiliating this is for me?

Weren't the tears last night enough?

Was the three-hour conversation not enough to convince her?

No. Of course not. Because now she thinks I'm a stone-cold liar who will weave a magnificent tale of bullshit, just to avoid telling her about how pathetic I truly am.

But thanks very much, Annie!

Suggesting I go see a doctor for the *thousandth time* is sure to make me feel even more pathetic, so mission accomplished there!

I hope this all gives you some lovely new material for the show. Five minutes on how I can straight up lie to your face should get them rolling in the aisles!

I stomp up the stairs, absolutely incensed at her lack of awareness over my situation.

I need her to believe me, not foist me off onto a complete stranger!

I need her to know that I did not lie to her. That I would *never* lie to her.

That's just not who Charlie King is!

And I am Charlie King, aren't I?

Yes.

I am definitely Charlie King.

And Charlie King doesn't need to see a doctor, because, despite everything that's happened, he is tota

◆ ◆ ◆

'Fancy lunch with a pint?' Jacks says, in an upbeat tone I am floored by.

'You want to go out with me?' I reply, staring at the phone, and completely taken aback.

'Yeah. Of course we do.'

'Even after what happened last week?'

'Yes, Charlie. Even after what happened last week. Leo and I have talked about it, and we . . . we know you meant well. You're just bloody insane, that's all.'

I can't really fault that accusation. I did arrange at great expense to have my two best friends kidnapped in the worst attempt at desensitisation therapy ever committed.

I am truly humbled and grateful that they would want to have anything to do with me after that.

'Meet you in an hour at The Miner's?' Jack says.

'Er . . . yeah, sure,' I agree.

Getting out will do me the world of good. And it'll give me a chance to connect with two people I thought would want absolutely nothing more to do with me, after what I did.

My friends are very special people.

And very tolerant.

The pub is only half an hour's walk from my house, so I take it as a good opportunity to clear my head a little. I also construct what I think is a decent apology speech to deliver to Jack and Leo. I was babbling a bit on the journey back in the limousine, and I doubt I made much sense. I don't think they wanted to hear much of what I had to say anyway.

It's great that I'm going to get a second chance at it.

I'm walking up the steps to The Miner's Arms when my phone rings. My heart leaps into my mouth. Oh God! It'll be Annie! I haven't seen her for three days, and she'll be checking up on me. I don't want to talk about all of it now!

I whip the phone out of my pocket to see that it is, in fact, an unknown number. I feel an unwelcome wave of relief pass over me. It's probably a cold call.

But then it could be something to do with work, couldn't it? I do still have the remnants of a bloody job, after all. Maybe this could be a new client? Maybe the dust has settled enough for people to be coming back?

I stand at the doors to the pub with the phone visibly shaking in my hand.

I should answer it. I should.

No. I *shouldn't*.

Why the hell should I?

I don't need to answer it. I don't *want* to answer it.

I stare at the screen telling me an unknown caller is desperate to make my acquaintance, my hand continuing to tremble as I do so.

For some reason this sparks off another one of my hideous flashbacks.

The dark circles around his eyes. The look of fear on his face. The hitching gasps of breath . . .

The edges of a panic attack are now so familiar to me that I recognise them instantly.

I ram the phone back into my pocket, allowing it to continue ringing.

I then take a shaky step forward and open the pub door. The waft of combined beer and chips that greets me does a great job of grounding me back in the reality of the moment. The Miner's Arms is to posh lunchtime eating what it also is to haute couture fashion – which suits me just fine. I need the down-to-earth, simple familiarity of it today, perhaps more than ever before.

And I need to see my two best friends as well.

Who, if I'm lucky, I will find sat in our favourite booth by the window that looks out onto the beer garden.

And there they are. Both already with pints in front of them, and a third one in the spot I usually sit in.

A sigh of relief blooms in my chest and suffuses my entire being.

There is a great deal to be said for normality. People underrate it greatly, in my opinion.

Also, my phone has stopped ringing in my pocket, thank God.

The idea of answering it right now, when I just want a beer and a burger with chips, fills me with an unreasonable amount of horror and anxiety.

'Afternoon,' Jack says as I arrive at the booth and take my seat.

'Afternoon,' I repeat with a smile.

I notice that Leo looks a little nervous, but I just put that down to Leo being Leo. I can almost guarantee this meet-up was Jack's idea.

'How are you doing?' Leo says, eyeing me up and down.

'I'm tota— I'm okay,' I tell him as I take off my jacket. 'And I want to apologise to the two of you for what happened – again. I think my heart was in the right place, but I went completely overboard.' I take a sip of my pint. It's lovely. 'It won't happen again.'

Jack nods in appreciation. 'Well, thanks for that. It was . . . a bit much.'

Leo looks like he wants to be sick.

'I really am sorry,' I repeat. 'I understand now that you can't just force these things. Your agoraphobia and Leo's fear of violence aren't going to be solved by big, silly confrontations like that.'

'No,' Leo says, his eyes hooded. 'And neither is your PTSD.'

I stare at him for a second. 'PTSD?'

'Yes,' Leo says flatly. 'That's what you've got.'

Jack holds out his hands. 'Now, now. Let's not get into any of that right now. I wanted us to just enjoy a nice lunch. All that stuff doesn't matter for the minute.'

I smile again. 'You're absolutely right.' I then raise my pint. 'To a nice pub lunch and no

gasping for breath needing help dying in front of me

'worrying about things we can't do anything about right at the moment.'

Jack returns the smile and raises his pint as well. It takes Leo a moment to follow suit.

I take a long draught of my beer. 'That can all come later. I'm sure there's a much better way we can get to the bottom of what's going on with all three of us.'

Both Jack and Leo's pints stop in mid-air.

'You what?' Jack says.

I wipe my mouth. 'Like I said . . . trying to force things was stupid. Next time, we'll take it much easier. We'll go slower.'

'Next time?' Leo repeats, voice very low.

I nod. 'Yeah. I'm sure we can come up with something much better.'

'There isn't going to be a next time, Charlie,' Jack tells me. 'We're not trying any more hare-brained schemes.'

'Absolutely not,' agrees Leo.

'We had three goes at it, and all of them ended badly,' Jack continues. 'Me and Leo don't need any more interventions. No more *Shenanigans*.'

'That's right, we don't.'

I take on an apologetic expression. 'Okay, okay. I get it. You're both done.'

'Yes, we are,' Jack reiterates.

'That's fine. That's honestly fine,' I say. 'Like we said, let's just enjoy lunch and forget about all that stuff.'

This mollifies the both of them, which I'm very pleased about.

Of course I'm not going to suggest any more 'hare-brained schemes', as Jack puts it.

. . . the next thing we try will be much more thought out, and I won't bring it up for a good long while. Not until they are ready again.

But I have no doubt I can convince them to try something else. Eventually.

I deliberately move the conversation topic on to something a lot more bland and unlikely to rile my friends up. I know how to handle them.

And the next two hours or so are rather fabulous. We consume a couple of pints each, eat the finest burger and chips The Miner's Arms can come up with (which would get a resolute 5 or 6 out of 10 in any restaurant review), and generally have the kind of good old-fashioned time of it we have had on so many occasions in here in the past.

I am gently riding on a wave of contentment as the afternoon wears on. I don't drink that much these days, so two pints is enough to give me a pleasant, fuzzy feeling, which co-ordinates well with the full stomach I now have.

In fact, my mood is such that I feel I can go home and call Annie to see if she wants to come over.

Jack insists all three of us get an Uber together when we leave. He even offers to pay for it, which is both surprising and gratifying. He even springs for one of the big, posh UberXLs.

I don't quite know why he feels we need such a big vehicle, but I'm not complaining. The idea of walking home for half an hour on my full stomach is not one that fills me with much joy. The giant Uber is much more preferable.

Once we're inside, with Leo sat opposite Jack and me, facing us, the Uber drives away from The Miner's Arms.

In completely the opposite direction to my house.

'Er . . . we're going the wrong way!' I call out to the Uber driver, who is a friendly-looking Asian chap with a clipped beard.

'No, no,' Jack remarks. 'It's fine. Carry on, mate!' he calls out to the driver.

'Oh . . . are we dropping Leo off first?' I ask him. That doesn't make any sense, though. Leo lives much further out than me.

'No, no,' Jack says. 'We're just taking a little detour somewhere.'

My ears go flat.

Well, they don't . . . because only dog's ears can do that. But rest assured, if I was a dog, my ears would be going flat. I might also be looking for the nearest ankle to bite . . .

'What's going on here?' I ask suspiciously.

'Nothing, nothing,' Jack says, in the breeziest voice imaginable. 'We just thought we'd . . . go somewhere else before dropping you off at your place.'

'Where?'

'Somewhere nice,' Leo tells me. 'Somewhere we think you need to see.'

'What kind of somewhere?' My contented buzz has completely disappeared.

Jack rests a hand on my shoulder. 'Somewhere where you can . . . you know . . . have a nice chat with someone.'

'What kind of someone?'

'Well . . . you know . . . a doctor type of person.'

Oh, my God!

'Oh, my God!' I exclaim angrily. 'Oi! Driver! Stop the bloody car, I'm getting out!'

'Don't stop!' commands Jack. 'Keep going and I'll add twenty quid to your fee!'

'You bastard!' I snarl at him.

'Calm down, mate. We're just worried about you. We're all worried about you.'

'All?'

'Yes,' says Leo, shifting back in his seat slightly. 'Annie called Jack this morning and—'

'Oh, for crying out loud!'

I am incensed.

How dare they do this?

How bloody dare my two best friends try to force me into doing something I don't want to do! And how dare Annie put them up to it!

'I don't need to see a bloody doctor!' I snap, and try to get out of the seat, my hand reaching for the sliding car door.

Jack pushes me back down. *Hard.*

Now . . .

It should be noted here that Jack easily outweighs me by two stone, and is a good three inches taller. I have never actually had cause to get into a fight with him, but I have a sneaking suspicion, if I did, I would lose. Jack was once a heavy metaller, and would think nothing of spending an evening in a mosh pit surrounded by like-minded individuals, beating seven shades of tar out of one another for the purposes of enjoyment.

I also know that Jack once beat the crap out of a bloke who assaulted his little sister in a nightclub.

But I don't want to go to a bloody doctor!

I try to rise again, but this time it's *Leo* who pushes me back. Now . . .

I'm fairly sure I could have Leo in a fight, but what would that do to him? He's terrified of violence as it is. I doubt one of his best friends giving him a clock around the ear would improve matters.

I'm trapped.

212

Bloody hellfire and buckets. I'm *trapped.*

'I don't *want* to see a bloody doctor,' I hiss, looking daggers at them both.

'Well, I didn't want to get pushed out of a limo on Dartmoor,' Jack explains, 'but sometimes these things happen to us, and we just have to put up with them.'

'Oh, I see. This is about revenge!'

'No,' Leo snaps. 'It's about you clearly having a very serious problem that you don't want to face properly, and the people who love you most in the world trying to do something about it!'

I point an angry finger at him. 'Don't you do that!'

'Do what?'

'Try to appeal to my emotional side! It won't work!'

'Won't it?'

'No! I want to get out of this bloody taxi!' I lean forward again. 'Driver! Pull over! I want to get out!'

The guy snaps his head round to see what the hell is going on.

'Ignore him!' Jack shouts. 'We're doing this for his own good!'

'No, you're not!' I exclaim, and try to get up again.

This time, both of my so called 'friends' jump up to stop me from escaping. Jack grabs me in a bear hug, and pushes me back into the seat, while Leo somewhat inexplicably goes for my legs, wrapping them both tight in his arms.

'Aaaargh! Let me go, you bastards!' I screech, now completely pinned.

'No! This is for your own good!' Leo says, trying to avoid my flailing knees.

'We want what's best for you!' Jack agrees.

'What's best for me?!' I snap. 'You're restraining me!'

'Damn right we are!'

'Is he going to poo himself?!'

The three of us all freeze and turn our heads to look at the Uber driver, who is now frantically looking at us in the rearview mirror.

'Is he going to what?' Jack asks, incredulous.

'Poo himself!' the driver repeats, flicking his eyes back and forth between the road and our reflection. 'Only, I've just had the seats dry-cleaned because somebody else pooed themselves, and I don't want to have to do that again.'

I lift my arse up from the seat. 'Oh God!' I wail, now fully aware that I am being restrained on a seat that someone has had a poo on.

'How did the poo get on the seat?' Leo asks. 'Weren't they wearing any pants or trousers?'

'This is hardly the time for questions like that!' I screech at him.

'She was very drunk!' the driver says, by way of horrifying explanation. His face takes on a look of abject misery. 'Please do not let your friend poo on my seat. It is hell to get out of the stitching!'

'Oh, for the love of God!' I snap. 'This is ridiculous! You don't have to do this, you bloody muppets!'

Jack's grip grows a little firmer again, now we've established more details than any of us would have liked about how poo got on the seat I'm currently trapped on. 'Yes, we do!' he says. 'If for no other reason than we want to stop you trying to "help" us again.'

'I can't take any more help, Charlie!' Leo pipes up. 'My nerves and bowels can't take it!'

'Please do not poo yourself!' our panicked driver cries.

'Nobody is going to poo themselves!' Jack snaps. 'Just keep driving! I said I'll throw in an extra twenty!'

'Make it forty.'

'Alright!'

This mollifies the guy somewhat, but he still continues to flick his eyes back at our reflection, his eyes wild.

'I'm not going to try to help you anymore!' I protest.

'Yes, you bloody are!' Jack growls. 'I know you, Charlie! We all know you very well! And I'd rather give you a black eye today so that we get you to a doctor if I have to, than find myself upside down in a vat of yoghurt, or something similar!'

'I can't take a vat of yoghurt!' Leo cries in horror. 'I'm lactose intolerant!'

'There's no vat of yoghurt!' I squeal.

'No, but there will be bloody *something*!' Jack says – and in my heart of hearts, I know he's right. I just can't let a problem go once I've got my teeth into it. I *have* to sort it out. I *have* to take control!

I need to take control of this situation right now.

Time for some grotesque theatrics.

'Oh no!' I wail at the top of my voice. 'I think I'm going to poo myself!'

This has the desired effect. The driver's eyes turn into saucers. 'No! No! Please, no!' he cries in a panic. 'You get out of here now! The address you want is just up the road! Do not poo! Do not POO!'

The Uber comes to a screeching halt, throwing the three of us forward. This loosens the grip my two friends have on me, allowing me to wriggle free.

Sort of.

Jack's grip actually loosens more than Leo's, thanks to the fact he bangs painfully into the glass partition between us and our terrified driver. This appears to knock him silly for a moment.

This allows me to pull myself towards the sliding car door, and wrench it open.

Unfortunately, Leo has an absolute death grip on my lower half.

This means that I fall out of the car headfirst, narrowly avoiding a nasty crack on the top of the head by mere centimetres.

'You're not going anywhere!' Leo roars.

'Yes, I bloody am!' I counter.

And then, out of the corner of my eye, I see a figure hurrying towards us down the pavement.

It's Annie.

Annie is here to help usher me into a doctor's office, along with my two treacherous mates.

God damn it all to hell!

'No! No!' I howl, and push myself back against the sides of the car, trying to break free of the surprisingly strong grip Leo has on my legs.

This works. My legs start to come free!

Sadly, my jeans do not.

Oh shit.

I should probably just cave in here and let the inevitable happen. The world does not need to see my SpongeBob SquarePants boxer shorts.

Don't look at me like that.

The washing hasn't been done yet, which meant I had no decent boxers to put on this morning. I had to resort to one of the novelty Christmas pairs I keep getting bought every year, and it was either SpongeBob or the elephant posing pouch.

To hell with it!

I push back against the car even harder, and feel fresh air on my legs as my jeans slither off completely, taking my Adidas trainers with them. I think Leo is one part boa constrictor, given how hard his grip is.

But I'm free of it now, with my SpongeBob exposed to the bloody world.

'Charlie! Stop!' Annie exclaims.

'Don't be an idiot!' Jacks says, pulling himself forward out of the car.

Leo is still gripping on to my jeans for dear life, for some reason.

Bugger all of this for a game of soldiers. 'I'm not going to see a bloody doctor! I don't want to see a sodding doctor!'

And with that, I'm off.

Slapping down the pavement in my Primark socks, with SpongeBob blowing in the wind.

Thankfully, I know exactly where I am. Our local doctor's surgery is sat on the edge of Planter's Park. I can lose my pursuers in there, I have no doubt about it.

Planter's Park is something of an overgrown mess in many places, thanks to the unique and special way the council is funded. The last time it had a good cut back, SpongeBob SquarePants was probably a brand-new TV show.

I hang a left and run straight through the wrought-iron gates. My socks are now soaking wet thanks to the rain that fell this morning, so I slap down the steps beyond the gates, and sprint right towards the big collection of bushes and trees that runs down almost the entire left-hand side of the park.

That'll do nicely.

I've got enough of a lead on my pursuers to be able to jump into the bushy mass before they have chance to see where I've gone.

Paying no heed to potential splinters in my feet, I push my way between two wildly overgrown shrubs and make for a hiding place deeper in the thicket.

Aha! Behind that stubby oak tree will do very nicely!

I squat behind the tree, and try to remain as silent as I possibly can.

With any luck, my evil pursuers will search in vain for me for a while, before giving up on their hunt, and leaving me the hell alone. Then I can—

Then I can do what, exactly? Carve a new life out for myself behind this stubby oak tree? Become the mad old man of Planter's

Park, who occasionally jumps out to scare the children by showing them his SpongeBob?

No matter. What's important is not being forced to go to the doctor today. Anything else is immaterial right now. I must just stay here quietly.

I must remain hidden.

I must—

'What the actual fuck are you doing?' I hear Jack say from behind me.

I whirl around in horror – to discover that my super-secret hiding place behind the stubby oak tree is actually about four feet from the park's iron fence, and that I am completely exposed to the road beyond it.

'Go away!' I hiss, waving my hands about in a hectic fashion. 'Leave me alone! Get away from me!' I'm still crouched down behind the tree, and am now covered in leaves, dirt and small sticks. If you've ever wondered what Gollum would look like in SpongeBob SquarePants novelty Christmas boxer shorts, you now have your answer.

'No,' Jack says. 'You've clearly lost your bloody mind.'

Jack is joined by Leo, who is still clutching my jeans. He sees me amongst the undergrowth and his eyes go wide. He then drops my jeans, and slowly reaches into his pocket for his mobile phone. With a continued look of horrified fascination on his face, he brings the phone up, and I hear the digital click of the camera go off.

Bastard.

'Enough of that, Annie's coming,' Jack tells Leo. 'You'd better bloody send me that later, though,' he adds.

'For God's sakes, Charlie, what are you doing?!' Annie cries as she reaches the fence and grips on to it.

Now it feels like I'm a caged animal in a zoo, being watched by fascinated tourists.

Maybe I'll start flinging my poo at the three of them.

'Just leave me alone!' I snap at her. This is clearly all her fault. My two idiot mates would have had to be put up to this.

'No! You need to come with us!' she orders. 'You're going to catch your death.'

'I'm not going to a bloody doctor!' I roar.

'Why?!' the three of them all bark at me at exactly the same time.

I don't think this is rehearsed. It's just a natural coincidence, but its impact is enormous.

I stare at the three of them in silence for a moment, before my lip starts to tremble. 'I don't bloody know!' I confess, with a rage and frustration that comes from somewhere deep inside me.

Behind Annie, Jack and Leo, the Uber cab screeches to a halt, and the driver leans out of the window. He sees me crouching behind my tree and his eyes go wide again.

'Has he pooed himself yet?' he asks, staring at me like I'm a firework about to go off.

The Uber guy – whose name is Majad, by the way. Very nice chap, it turns out – agrees to drive us all home, on the proviso I am fully clothed and sitting on two plastic bags.

There's not much talking done in the back of the car.

I doubt any of them know what to say to me. I have clearly gone completely off the bloody rails. Nothing else could be the case, given that I've just run down a high street in my boxer shorts, just to avoid a doctor's appointment.

I have no idea why it's got this bad.

I cannot comprehend why I am still so adamant that I don't want to seek out the help of a professional.

219

But I *am* adamant. Still. Even after this idiotic escapade.

It just feels . . . wrong.

Every fibre of my being is telling me that to capitulate to what my two best friends and my girlfriend want would be a very bad idea. It would make things worse, not better.

They might think they have my best interests at heart, but pushing me into doing something I am so dead set against would only be a bad thing.

I do forgive them for trying to physically force me into doing it – after all, I'm not above forcing people into doing things myself, but if I'm willing to show my SpongeBob to the entire world to avoid a confrontation that fills me with dread, then surely that has to be an end to it.

Surely?

That's why it's so quiet in the cab. You can tell one of them dearly wants to ask me why I'm being so obstinate, but doesn't want to risk it, for fear of me jumping out of the window, and running off to hide in the nearest skip.

Besides, I have no idea what I'd say my reasons are. I don't know. I just know it's the *wrong thing*.

But that begs the question – what the hell is the *right thing*?

What does Charlie King do now?

Chapter Ten

STILL WALLS

Stare at a blank computer screen.

That's what he does.

For several minutes, until he gets a headache.

Because I have nothing else to do.

I have absolutely no work. Not a single new email sits in my account. Not one. It's empty – save for Ocado telling me I desperately need to start ordering my online shopping from them again, and someone in Delhi pretending to be B&Q, telling me I've won a lawnmower. I just have to give them my address, bank details, inner thigh measurements and hopes and dreams about the future to claim it.

Other than those very important emails, though, there's nothing. No work emails at all. All my existing contracts have come to their conclusion, and there's nothing else. I'm done. I'm bereft.

I am *unemployed*.

This makes me want to throw up.

Which is unfortunate, as it's lunchtime, and I really should eat something. I don't remember having anything for breakfast. So I probably should be hungry. But I'm not really.

Because my business email account is empty, and I watched a man die in a car crash.

I continue to stare at the computer screen a little while longer, until my brain makes a demand of me, in a desperate attempt to get me off my arse and back out into the real world.

'Coffee,' I say out loud to my lounge.

My lounge, being a room of approximately two hundred square feet, and not blessed with a mouth or sentience, does not respond.

'I will drink coffee,' I tell it anyway, just in case.

Coffee will do me some good. I'm sure of it. It might wake me up a little, if nothing else.

Rising from my office chair, my legs shake a little. I really have been sat staring at that computer screen for far too long.

The blood is pumping back around them okay by the time I go out to my kitchen, and spend a few minutes staring at the coffee machine.

This does not have any work emails on it, either.

I make one of the worst coffees I have ever produced (though still not nearly as bad as Jack's best attempt) with my rather lovely bean-to-cup machine, and drink the foul concoction while I stare out of the window.

There are no work emails out there, that's for sure.

'What the hell am I going to do?' I ask my kitchen, which is no more sentient than my lounge, unfortunately.

Ring ring.

I look down, my heart racing at the sudden noise. My iPhone is in my hand. I don't remember picking it up.

It's an unknown number. I should probably answer it. Could be work. Could be someone wanting my services. Could be—

I press the red button to cancel the call, and throw the phone onto the counter, next to the coffee machine. I instantly feel relief as I do this.

Back to staring out of the window, I think.

That's probably the best thing for me.

I don't know how long I continue to do this.

What I do know is that by the time I hear my phone ring again, my legs have gone numb, and a dull ache has settled into my lower back.

I still don't want to answer it, but when I see Annie's name pop up on the screen, I know I have to.

'Hi Annie,' I say to my girlfriend.

'Hi Charlie. Are you busy?'

'Not really, no.'

'Okay. Could you . . . Could you come over to my place? I . . . I think we need to talk.'

I close my eyes and stop thinking about emails for the first time today.

Annie wants to talk.

Of course she does.

I should never have picked up the phone.

I should have just carried on staring out of the window.

I walk over to Annie's instead of driving. It takes half an hour, but that's an extra thirty minutes I can put off the confrontation for.

But this is an inevitable conversation. One that's been coming for some time now, and one I truly do not want to have.

Once I'm in Annie's flat and sat down, I am – at least to start with – the one who listens. Annie has things she wants to get off her chest. Which is more than fair enough.

And none of it is stuff I couldn't have predicted.

She's worried about me. She's worried about our relationship.

I sit at Annie's kitchen table while she remonstrates with me about the current state of affairs, nodding along and agreeing to everything she says, more or less. At least to begin with. She has every right to be saying all of these things to me – and many more besides.

And I want to give her some sort of response. I want to make her feel better.

But I can't because my email account is empty, and I saw a man die.

I only really come out of my enforced stupor when she says the following:

'You won't accept any help, Charlie. You just ignore everything I say.'

'I don't ignore everything you say,' I tell her, my voice now somewhat petulant.

She affects a mock look of surprise. 'Oh! Oh really, Charlie? You don't?' Her eyes narrow. 'What's the one thing I've been asking you to do for months now, including on bloody stage in front of hundreds of people, that you just completely ignore?'

'I don't ignore you!'

'You ignore *my advice*, though, don't you? You ignore *my feelings*. You ignore anything that inconveniences *you*.'

'That's not true, Annie,' I counter. 'I've explained how I feel about going to the doctor.'

'No, you haven't. You've told me you're not going to do it – but have offered no real reason why.' Annie folds her arms, leans back in the chair and looks at me. 'Would you like to have a go at it now?'

I regard her for a moment, my lips pursed. I could continue to escalate this, but where would that get me?

'I've told you,' I say, in as calm a voice as possible. 'I don't think it would do any good, and I'd find the whole experience very embarrassing.'

'As opposed to running down the road in your underpants?'

I knew she'd counter with that the second the excuse was out of my lips. 'It wouldn't do me any good,' I repeat sullenly.

'You don't know that.'

'Yes, I do.'

'No, you don't.'

'Yes, I do.'

'No, Charlie, you don't!'

'Yes, I—'

Oh, what's the point? This has turned into a dreadful adaptation of that old Monty Python sketch, where Michael Palin goes in to ask for an argument. Annie should produce a dead parrot and the Holy Grail. The scene would then be complete.

The Holy Grail of my life right now would be a decent night's sleep, and a work email or two.

'Just please leave it,' I say in a weary tone, and rub my eyes.

Annie sees that I don't have much of a fight in me, and her own body language relaxes. 'I can't, Charlie,' she says, in a far gentler tone. 'I need to know what's going on with you. I need to understand why you've changed so much. Why this is—'

We both jump as my bloody phone starts to ring again.

You bastard. You absolute bastard. I don't want to hear you! Especially now! I don't care about whoever is on the other end!

I jump to my feet, pull the phone out of my pocket, stab the cancel button and throw the damn thing down onto Annie's kitchen counter – in an unpleasant echo of the same thing I did earlier in my own kitchen. How I haven't broken the thing again yet is beyond me.

'Sorry,' I say.

'It's okay . . .' Annie says, sighing.

'I know you only want to help me,' I tell her, trying to get back to that more conciliatory tone to the conversation. 'But I honestly don't think it's by laying bare all of my problems to a stranger.'

Annie shakes her head. 'Then what, Charlie? What do we do about you? Because I don't think I can . . . I can take much more of this.'

And there it is. The last thing I want to hear in the world, and the one thing that I could have predicted I would hear in this conversation more than any other.

'I know,' I reply, my voice dull. 'I get how you feel. I totally understand. I don't want this to go on any more than—'

The phone rings again.

'Just answer it, Charlie,' Annie tells me.

NO.

'No, I want to talk to you,' I say, and once again hit the cancel button.

'Okay. You were saying?'

I clear my throat. 'I was saying that I don't want this to continue any more than you do. And I honestly don't know why seeing someone about it fills me with such dread. I've tried to handle it. I've tried to find solutions.'

'You're not the one who can solve it, Charlie.' Annie's voice is laced with sympathy. 'And you can't solve your friends' problems, either.'

I don't know how to respond to that.

'But you can solve *my* problem,' she goes on. 'You can do what I ask . . . even if you don't think it'll do you any good.' Her eyes fill with tears. 'For me?'

'It's not that simple, Annie. It's not that easy to jus—'

Ring ring.

Oh, for the love of fucking Christ!

'Answer your phone, Charlie.'

'NO! I don't want to!' The sudden, inexplicable rage seizes me in a vice-like grip. I grab the phone, and throw it against the kitchen wall as hard as I possibly can. The violence and energy I impart is high enough for the phone to actually shatter, showering

226

Annie in tiny pieces of broken plastic and metal. The main body of the phone ricochets off the wall and narrowly misses my girlfriend's head. It instead flies back past her and clatters into the sink.

'Bloody hell!' Annie screams in terror.

The look on her face.

The look on her sweet, gorgeous, wonderful face.

'Annie,' I wail, taking one step forward.

She pushes herself back in her chair, hitting the wall. Annie has never pushed herself away from me. And she's certainly never looked at me with that kind of fear in her eyes.

Oh God. Oh Christ.

I do not know my own mind.

Am I . . .

Am I . . . *dangerous?*

'I'm so, so sorry,' I babble. 'I don't know what came over me.'

'What the hell is wrong with you, Charlie?' Annie cries, one arm held up to ward me off.

'I don't know!' I wail. 'I don't bloody know!' I go over to the sink and pick up my battered phone. 'It's this bloody thing! Why does it have to keep bloody ringing when I'm trying to do something?!'

Annie looks at me, utterly dumbfounded. And no wonder. I've almost killed her with a ballistic phone, just because it was doing its job. 'You just answer the stupid thing, Charlie!'

'No!' I snap, and toss the phone back into the sink. 'I can't answer it! I shouldn't answer it!'

'Why, for God's sakes?!' she cries.

I look into her horrified eyes, hoping for some kind of answer to be reflected back at me.

There are still barriers here.

Still walls.

227

Still things to avoid. To run away from. To keep forgetting.

People say the mind is a complex, multi-layered thing. Mine never has been. At least, it's never felt that way to me before.

The *world* is a complex, multi-layered thing. Of that much I am certain. But I've always managed to negotiate it pretty well, because my mind has always felt like a simple thing.

That's not to say I think I'm stupid. But simplicity does not equal stupidity. In fact, some of the most elegant, intelligent, beautiful things that have ever existed are stunning in their simplicity.

The wheel, for instance. The *Mona Lisa*.

The chocolate Hobnob.

No, a simple mind is a mind uncluttered by doubt or indecision. Or *guilt*.

I've never really had much to feel guilty about in my life. Never really done anything all that wrong. I was brought up by parents who instilled a pretty good moral centre, and I've always tried to be a decent guy. Largely because it's just *easier*. Especially in my line of work – which requires communicating with people on a regular basis. It's incredible what a smile can do, if you use it well enough. Being nice just makes life easier. And less stressful.

All things considered, Charlie King has been a good person for most of his life.

A man with a simple mind.

Until . . .

My humps and my lumps.

It's time to peel back the final layer.

Because the mind *is* a complex, multi-layered thing, no matter how much I wish it was not.

It's a delicate thing as well. It needs protecting.

Sometimes from itself.

Ring ring.

Ring ring.

Can you hear it?

Even over the sound of the Black Eyed Peas? Over the sound of my horrendous singing? Over the sound of the road rushing by beneath us?

I can hear it.

It's Maurice from Mega Lanes.

It's always Maurice from Mega Lanes. In the dreams my mind won't let me remember, when I wake screaming from them in the middle of the night. It's always Maurice from Mega Lanes, who wants to chat about Teddy's birthday party.

And I do need to chat to Maurice. I really, really do. Teddy's birthday has to go off without a hitch. Of course it does. Because I'm Charlie King, and I like to make people happy. I have a new girlfriend to impress. One I think I am very probably already head over heels in love with.

But I can't answer him now, can I? Not while I'm driving.

That would be irresponsible of me.

That would be wrong.

That would be against the Highway Code.

And my parents brought me up with a good moral centre. The kind that precludes me from answering my phone while driving.

But I do so want Teddy's birthday party to be *perfect*. For Teddy. For Annie.

And who knows when I'll get chance to speak to Maurice again today?

I'm so busy, you see. With the meeting at Zenith Games, and then Howling at the Moon, and then Elaine . . .

I'll just see what he wants.

Very quickly.

Shouldn't be a problem.

Shouldn't cause any issues.

Simple.

Easy.

I turn down the Black Eyed Peas on the radio, and answer my phone.

The world is a complex, multi-layered thing.

And it throws things at you.

Vicious, horrible things that you can't avoid.

Everything explodes.

Including my preconceived notions about how simple my mind is.

I stare into Annie's eyes as the horror of it overwhelms me.

Not just the final revelation, but that I still – STILL – have a brain that can hide things from me so damned easily.

So *simply*.

'I w-w-was on the phone!' I stammer. I feel my knees go out from under me, and I end up collapsed forward into Annie's lap. The strength has drained completely from my body.

'What?! Charlie, what's the matter?!'

She grips my shoulders as I shudder uncontrollably.

'I was on the damned phone!' I scream into her lap.

'What?!'

I look up into her eyes.

Probably – no, very *definitely* – for the last time, because after this she won't want to be anywhere near me. She won't want anything to do with me.

My life ends here, because I ended a life.

'The crash! It was . . . It was . . .'

SAY IT.

'It was my fault.'

It was my fault. I was on the phone. Not paying enough attention to the road. Too worried about a stupid bloody birthday party. Too concerned with my plans and my events. Too concerned with being Charlie King.

'What do you mean, Charlie?' Annie asks – but she already knows. The breathless tone, and the look in her eyes tell me so. Her wonderful, expressive eyes . . . realising for the first time that she's been with a monster this entire time.

'I killed him,' I say. 'The old man in the car. I was on my phone, and I wasn't paying attention. I crashed into him.' I fall back from Annie's lap, pushing myself up against the kitchen cabinet. Above me, broken and useless in the kitchen sink, is my mobile phone.

'I killed him,' I repeat, staring into both the distance and the past.

No wonder my mind tried to protect me. No wonder it built all those walls.

I essentially murdered another human being, due to my recklessness.

'Charlie, that can't be right,' Annie says, trying to disagree. But her *eyes* agree. They agree 100 per cent.

She knows I'm telling her the truth now, doesn't she? Even though she desperately doesn't want to. She knows.

'It doesn't make any sense,' she continues.

'It makes perfect sense,' I say in a dull voice. 'It's the only thing that makes sense.'

'You were on your phone?'

I nod. 'Oh yes. Busy, busy Charlie King. Couldn't wait until it was safe to talk to bloody Maurice.'

Annie's eyes go wide. 'From the bowling alley?'

I nod again. 'Had to talk to him, didn't I? Had to make sure everything *was going to plan.*' I put a heavy and disgusted emphasis on the last few words. 'I had to answer the call, because everything had to be perfect. What a bastard.'

'Charlie! Stop it,' Annie says. 'You're not . . . not a bastard.'

Oh, but the hesitation in your voice says different.

I laugh. There's zero humour in it. 'No bloody wonder I've been so screwed up. I'm the guy who likes to help people. Loves to put a smile on their faces. Make their lives better. And look at what I really am. A murderer.'

Annie balks. 'You're not a murderer, Charlie! It wasn't . . . something you did deliberately.'

I look at her with a level of disgust she most certainly doesn't deserve. It's not meant for her, but I'm so brimming over with self-loathing that some of it is spilling out into places it shouldn't. 'I'm sure that'll be great solace to whoever the poor old bastard left behind after his death. I'm sure as he was sat there clutching his chest and breathing his last, he was thinking about how it wasn't something I did deliberately, so it's not all that bad, after all.'

'That's not what I meant!'

'I know, but it doesn't matter, Annie. I killed a man, and there's nothing you can say or do that will change that.'

The look of confusion crosses her face again. 'But the police . . . the paramedics . . . If you'd have done that, then . . .'

'Then what? Like you just said, I never did it deliberately. Just an accident. I doubt they spent much time on it. Just another poor old fart killed on the road by a reckless idiot.'

'But they would have—'

'Enough!' I snap, making her jump. 'You're not going to help, Annie! I did this, and there's nothing that can take that away!'

I scramble to my feet. I don't know why, but I do. I feel like I have to move. Keep moving. *Run.* Run away from all of this. Run away from myself.

'Please, Charlie, don't be angry with me!' she says, the look of hurt almost unbearable.

No.

This is good.

Get her away from you.

'Then stop trying to help, Annie!' I snap. I hate myself. I despise myself. Even more. 'Just stop! Unless you're going to tell me to go to the police and confess my sins! You seem keen on me seeing someone in authority. Why not them? Why not serve a punishment for my crime?'

She stares at me for moment. 'I think you need to see a doctor more than ever before, Charlie.' Her voice is raspy, low. As if she's saying something that causes physical pain, and can't manage to get it out any louder, because it hurts too much.

'Why should I?!' I rage. 'Why should I get to be fixed up and made good again? He didn't get that! Your bloody medical experts worked on him as hard as they could, and he still died! I saw it, Annie! I saw it all happen, right in front of me!'

My eyes sting with tears.

'I don't *deserve* to feel better!' I rant, spittle flying from my lips. 'I don't deserve . . .' I trail off, unable to articulate a truth I have been hiding in a very dark and horrible part of me.

I don't deserve *you*, Annie.

I don't deserve anything other than panic attacks and sleepless nights.

'I have to get out,' I say instead, rubbing my face in my hands.

'No, you can't go anywhere, Charlie. We need to sort this out. We need to get to the bottom of what happened!' Annie rises from her chair, coming towards me.

'I know what happened! God almighty, Annie. We know what happened now!' The worst thing I will ever say then falls from my lips. 'Are you happy now?' I snarl it, like a dog. Like a wounded, angry dog who's backed into a corner by something large, brutish and ugly.

The truth. Delta's fucking *truth* . . . finally here.

Annie looks as if I've slapped her. Worse even than when she recoiled from the flying mobile phone.

Ring ring.

Ring ring.

I killed a man.

I storm out of the kitchen, leaving what will very soon be my ex-girlfriend to reel from my harsh and horrible words.

She'll recover.

She'll get better.

Because I won't be around.

I'm out of her front door before she has another chance to call me back.

Run.

Get away.

But get away from what? I can't get away from my memories. Can't get away from that ugly, brutish truth.

I stumble along the pavement, reliving. Remembering.

The police. Did they question me? Yes, I think they probably did – but I was too far out of it with shock and guilt to recall much now. But I must have lied to them, eh? Must have spun them another one of Charlie King's epic tales that absolve him from any blame or wrongdoing.

Chalk that up as another crime to go down in my already full ledger. Lying to the police.

That moral centre is getting smaller and smaller by the second.

Or maybe the fiction had glossed itself over my mind by then. Maybe my subconscious was already well on the road to protecting Charlie King from his role in the death of an innocent old man.

He came out of nowhere, officer! I would have told them, utterly believable. Utterly convincing.

I was driving so incredibly safely, listening to my marvellous lady lumps on the radio, and then bam*! . . . that's all I remember.*

Yeah. That sounds like Charlie King. Innocent of all blame. Responsible. A good man.

Ha!

Maybe I should walk to the nearest station and hand myself in.

My heart hammers in my chest.

No. I can't do that. Can't take that. I can't . . .

. . . *do the time.*

How many years in prison do you get for killing someone for dangerous driving?

Just keep walking. Just keep going.

Go home.

No! Not home! That's where my empty email account is! That's where the bed I can't sleep in is!

And they'll find me there! They'll find me, and they'll drag me away!

I feel in my pocket. My wallet is there. My credit cards are there. I can just leave. Run away. Go somewhere nice.

Be a . . . *fugitive.*

Hi Mum! Hi Dad! I know you think you raised me with a good moral centre, but I'm a killer, a liar and a fugitive now! Hope that's okay. Am I coming to you for Christmas this year?

Good grief.

A hotel, then. That's easier. That's better. I'll have time to think. Time to get things straight. Time to decide what the hell to do next.

Next.

Is there even a *next* now?

Now the great lie has been uncovered at last. Now the truth has finally come to light. Now the book of *Totally Fine*, written by the great and powerful Charlie King, has ended with the absolute worst last chapter imaginable.

What even is next . . .

. . . other than the epilogue?

Epilogue

The banging outside somewhere is loud.

But it doesn't matter.

It's not for me.

Nobody knows I'm here, you see.

Apart from Lionel.

Good old Lionel. Proprietor of The Crooked Hat pub and bed and breakfast.

I've never been here before. Why would I? It's only an hour's walk from my house, along the old Moore Road. Driven past it a thousand times. No reason to stay here.

Until now. Until the day I needed somewhere to hide.

From myself as much as anyone.

Can't tell you how lovely it was to have a chat with good old Lionel as he checked me in to the bed and breakfast on his antique-looking PC.

I was Charlie King again for a brief moment. Confident. Happy-go-lucky. In control.

Lovely.

The room I've been in for the past fourteen hours is *not* lovely. It is old. It is threadbare. It is far too expensive for a bed and breakfast on the old Moore Road.

It's also got paper-thin walls.

I didn't sleep much last night in the hard bed Lionel has provided for me (no surprises there. I never sleep these days. I don't deserve such nice things), so I got to hear exactly what my fellow Crooked Hat guests were up to.

Sex, in the case of the couple right next door. The kind of muffled sex you have when you know you're somewhere with paper-thin walls.

Maybe that's them doing the banging now. Could well be. They sounded quite young. I'm sure the turnaround is pretty swift.

I don't care. The banging has nothing to do with me, whatever it is.

I can just lie here on this uncomfortable bed, watching the fly bounce around on the Artex ceiling, for as long as I like.

I'll have to get some sort of food at some point, just to keep myself going.

And then I'll have to make a decision about what I'm going to do.

No decisions.

No plans.

Not yet.

That's fine, brain. I'm more than happy to put those kinds of things off for a while longer. I can just lie here and exist in Lionel's Crooked Hat. Maybe until I die.

That's not much of an ending to this story, but it might well be an appropriate one.

A life for a life – like they used to say in those old spaghetti westerns.

I consider my disturbing current train of thought as I watch the fly bounce around on the ceiling, and conclude that, when all is said and done, I very much am not Totally Fine.

Haven't been for quite a while.

Still. That has nothing to do with The Crooked Hat, or Lionel. Or the fly. Or this strange moment I find myself in.

I do wish they'd stop banging next door, though. It's getting annoying.

'Charlie?!' a muffled and very familiar voice says, floating through the paper-thin walls.

My soul freezes.

'Oh God, we're so sorry,' another familiar voice says. 'Wrong room.'

'Try the next one,' a third, stronger, but equally familiar voice intones.

I have a horrible feeling the next room is going to be me.

Quick! Under the duvet!

What?

Under the duvet! Hide! Lionel will protect us! His duvet will keep us safe!

I'm not sure duvets quite have the power to do that.

Do it anyway!

Bang goes my door. Four times in quick succession.

'Charlie?!' Annie's voice is hectic. Laced with extreme anxiety.

Keep quiet!

I pull the duvet over my head.

'You in there, Charlie?' Jack says.

'It must be this one,' Leo remarks. 'It's the last room in the building.'

The door bangs another couple of times. 'Come on, Charlie, open up!'

Go away, Jack! Go away, Leo too!

And Annie?

'Please, Charlie, you need to speak to us,' she says, her voice trembling.

I almost answer her. Every fibre of my stupid being wants to answer her. But I don't.

'You sure this is the last one?' Jack asks Leo, when he realises I'm not going to open up lines of communication.

'Yes, absolutely,' Leo tells him.

'Right, I'll have to put the door in, then.'

You can see him pushing up his sleeves, can't you? That tone of voice has sleeves pushed up to the elbows written all over it.

Jack is about to ruin Lionel's lovely little bed and breakfast. I can't allow that to happen. Lionel likes Charlie King. Lionel doesn't know who Charlie King really is. I want it kept that way.

'Stop!' I cry out, and immediately regret it.

'Charlie! Oh, thank God!' Annie exclaims.

'You gonna open this door, or do I have to?' Jack growls.

I roll my eyes. Jack loves an opportunity to be macho when he gets half a chance. I think that's why I was so delighted to get him into that mankini.

'I'll open it,' I say, and get up from the bed.

With massive, *massive* reluctance, I go over and unlock the door.

Leo gives me a look up and down. 'If I can go the rest of my life without having to see you in SpongeBob SquarePants boxer shorts, I will be a happy man.'

I look down at myself. Oh yes. That's right. I'm virtually naked. Who cares at this point, really?

'How the hell did you find me?' I ask them, consciously barring the door. I don't want them in here. They might bother the fly.

'I . . . I followed you,' Annie explains. 'From my place. I stayed back, because you . . . *scared me*, Charlie. But I wanted to know where you were going. I wanted to know you were safe.' She looks at Jack. 'And then I knew I had to go and get your friends to help me, so you wouldn't . . .'

'Hurt you?' I say, my voice cracking as I remember how hard I threw that phone against the wall.

Annie doesn't answer. She just swallows and breaks eye contact. Oh *God*.

'What do you want?' I say to her. 'Why are you even here?'

'To make sure that you . . . you get help, Charlie. I'm not so sure I can be around for it anymore, but I want to you to get the help you need to make you feel . . . better.'

'No. You shouldn't be around. You're right about that,' I reply, in as cold a voice as I can muster.

Push her away.

Keep her away.

She doesn't deserve you.

I should feel deeply ashamed of my behaviour, but for some reason, I don't. I think I've swum through the rivers of shame and self-recrimination, and into a lagoon of not really caring about the consequences anymore.

That's probably why I can stand here, nearly naked, and why I can look at that expression on Annie's face and know it's the right one for me to be looking at. It's for the best. I can handle Annie. I can push her away.

Jack, not so much . . .

'Right, that's enough of that,' he says, pushing past me and into the room. I could try to put up more of a fight, but no good would come of it. I'll let him have his rant and then I'll get all three of them to leave.

I don't think they realise how far gone I am at this point. But I do.

'Get your stuff, you're leaving this smelly little hole,' he says, looking around with visible signs of distaste. How dare he be so cruel to poor Lionel! All this place needs is a little spruce up, and a special evening, where Lionel and I can invite the local press and

240

council dignitaries to enjoy the delights of The Crooked Hat for themselves. That should get business cooking.

I can send everyone home with a fly each, as a nice pet.

'I'm not going anywhere,' I tell Jack. 'Not yet anyway. I haven't decided what I'm going to do yet.'

'What you're going to do is go home, and get your skinny arse to a doctor tomorrow. No more arguments.'

'No, Jack. I won't be doing either of those things. I killed a nice old man. This is the place for me. This is where I should be.'

'Don't be so ridiculous.'

'Annie's told you about what happened with the phone, I suppose?'

Jack nods, folding his arms. 'Yes. So what?'

'So what? You can look me in the face and say *so what*?' I step closer to him. 'Tell me, what did you think when she told you about how I was on the phone when the crash happened? That it was all my fault?'

Annie tries to step in herself. 'Don't do this, Charlie.'

I ignore her. I have to ignore her. 'Come on, Jack . . . what did you think?'

Jack's cheek twitches involuntarily.

Yep. There it is. The same disgust in his eyes I saw in Annie's. Brief, but very definitely there. 'That doesn't matter,' he says. 'What matters is getting you the help you need.'

'No. What matters to you is doing what Annie asked of you,' I tell him. 'She needed your help with me. I know you well enough to know you wouldn't be here if it was just you.'

The cheek twitches again.

'Jack?' Annie says, looking up at him.

He looks back at her. 'He's not having it, Annie. I'm sorry. I don't think we can talk him around. Not yet anyway.'

Ha!

There we have it.

If it were up to Jack, he'd let me fester here for as long as I wanted. He's done with me. His old friend Charlie King is gone. All that's left is a killer, and a waste of space.

'That's it, is it? You're just going to give up?'

The three of us all turn to look at Leo, who is still stood in the doorway, a look of consternation on his face.

'Sorry?' I say, taken aback.

'You're just giving up? You're just going to sit here and do nothing?' Leo repeats, stepping more into the room.

'Well . . . I . . .'

'That's not *you*, Charlie. That's not you at all,' he says.

'It is now,' I counter.

'You haven't even *tried* to make amends, have you? You haven't even worked out who he was. You always come up with a plan of action, you always *try* to fix things. You always know the facts, the details, and right now, you don't have a clue and you're not even *bothered*.'

'Leo . . .' Annie sounds more than a little perturbed by Leo's tone.

'What? I'm right, aren't I?' Leo insists. 'Charlie's sat here wallowing in guilt about a man he knows nothing about.'

Bloody hell.

Leo is absolutely right. I've been so wrapped up in my own guilt trip that I haven't even tried to find out who my victim was.

Charlie King wouldn't have done that. He'd have been on Google. Searching for any information he could find. This useless lump did nothing, though.

'Does it matter?' Jack asks Leo.

'Of course it matters!' Leo snaps. I don't think I've ever heard him snap at Jack before. 'Who people *are* matter! Who they shared their life with *matters*!' He looks back at me. 'Don't you think you should find out who he was, instead of wallowing in misery, and doing nothing, like you are? Trust me. Doing that will get you absolutely *nowhere*.'

Leo's words are like a cold, hard slap to the face. He is absolutely right that I should find out more about my victim.

About who he was and . . . who he left behind.

I swallow.

'Could you all please leave?' I ask them.

I need to be alone.

But not because I want to lie on the bed and look at the fly anymore.

'Charlie, I don't think that's a good idea,' Annie protests.

'He's right,' Leo counters. 'Charlie does need to be alone. We should leave.' He doesn't take his eyes off me as he says this. 'He needs to do some research. He needs to do *something*.'

I . . . I think I'm slightly scared of Leo right now. Which is not how things are supposed to work in our relationship.

'Ah . . . yeah,' Jack says, also looking at our friend in something of a new light. 'I think we should do what Leo says, and leave Charlie alone for a while.' He looks at Annie with no small degree of consternation, but then cocks his head towards the door.

Annie's lips purse for a moment.

'Trust me,' Leo says, looking straight past me and at her.

She looks down at the threadbare carpet for a moment.

Does she trust Leo? He's known me far longer than she has. But nowhere near as intimately – for obvious reasons. She's scared, and worried, and frustrated.

Annie chews on her lip for a moment longer, before looking up at me. 'Do what you need to, Charlie,' she tells me. 'You don't need me around to tell you what to do.'

Good. That's fine. You're better off without me.

Annie stares at me for a moment longer . . . before she crosses to the door and walks out of sight without looking back. That's probably the last time I will ever see her.

Good.

Good for her.

Jack watches her go before puffing out his cheeks and pointing down at my SpongeBobbed penis. 'Put that thing away properly, before it hurts someone,' he tells me, and follows Annie out.

Leo stares at me in that disconcerting manner again. 'Don't lose who you are to the person you *think* you are, Charlie. Find out the *facts.*'

He doesn't wait for me to reply. He's gone before I can draw another breath.

And therefore, once again, I am alone.

But the door is open. And that's probably a change for the better, all things considered.

I'm going to do what Leo has told me to do.

Find out.

. . . which is surely a better option than a sad little epilogue here in this bed and breakfast, isn't it? Charlie King's book of *Totally Fine* wouldn't end well with a fly bumping around on the ceiling like that. Nor with whatever that stain is on the wall, over by the dresser.

No. This would be a terrible place for this story to end.

There's a better epilogue to it. One that involves me doing something proactive.

Like Charlie King used to do.

You remember him, right?

I'm going to have a shower, get dressed and go and find Lionel. I was very nice to him yesterday, so I'm sure he'll let me use his antique PC. I just hope it has an internet connection.

Chapter Eleven

MARGARET

It does.

Not a fast one, unsurprisingly.

If I wanted to watch a YouTube video, I'd have to wait a good half an hour for it to download.

But the connection is just about fast enough to let me do a little light browsing. Whether I want to or not.

His name was Anthony.

Anthony Silver.

The name of the man I killed was Anthony Silver.

'You alright there?' Lionel asks, from where he's hovering over my right shoulder. 'Only, your hand's gone very tight on that mouse, and I can't really afford to buy another one.'

You probably should, though, Lionel. This still has a ball in it.

'I'm fine,' I say through a tight smile. 'Just seen . . . something that took me by surprise.'

Which I suppose is the truth. My victim had to have a name, after all. But I wasn't sure I would actually find out what it is so quickly.

The local newspaper has done its job for once, though. The report on the accident is short, abrupt and to the point. But it lists the fact that there was one fatality, and, luckily for me, the name of the deceased.

From that, I spend the next ten minutes or so finding out everything I need to know about Anthony Silver.

He was very popular at the sailing club, for one thing. And took great pride in coming fifth at the regatta in the summer of 1995.

I don't find any evidence of children.

But he certainly had a wife.

Her name is Margaret.

Margaret Silver.

The woman I made a widow.

'Honestly, can you not grip it so tight? I can hear the plastic starting to crack,' Lionel says in a tremulous voice.

I force myself to relax a little.

I also force myself to research Margaret, and there's a fair bit more about her on the web than there is her husband.

She's the bird lady, you see . . .

No.

Sorry.

That should be The Bird Lady. With capitals. Because it seems like it's an official title – of sorts. The various news stories I find about her from down through the years certainly all call her it. She's famous. For having birds. Lots of birds. Of all different shapes and sizes. Ones that have won awards. Ones that have been used in TV commercials and movies.

I'm frankly amazed I've never crossed paths with her for my job. It must be some kind of miracle that I've never thought of having a nice colourful selection of parrots and budgies at my events. If I ever had, then surely Margaret Silver would have been the person

I would have gone to for those birds. She's the only person in the area offering such a unique service.

Forty years she's been The Bird Lady.

And for a good twenty of those years, she's also run a pet shop on Carnegie Street. The bird-hiring business must not pay quite enough to sustain itself, I guess.

I can quite easily grab an Uber to Carnegie Street. It'll take me maybe forty minutes to get there. If that.

My mouth has suddenly gone very dry.

Because it's one thing to find out about your victim. It's quite another to go and apologise to someone they were married to for killing them.

But that's what I'm going to do, isn't it?

Leo was absolutely right. Who people are does matter. I've spent so much of my time trapped in my own head over this that it didn't occur to me for a second to think about the other people involved.

I have to go and speak to Margaret. I have to apologise. I have to . . . I don't know what . . . seek forgiveness? Prostrate myself at her feet? Will that do any good? Will it make any difference?

'Oops. That's done it, you're going to have to buy me a new mouse now,' Lionel says, wincing at the poor, old broken thing in my hands.

It was a thirty-three-minute Uber journey, to be exact. Time enough for me to make something of a plan in my head. About what the hell I'm going to say to this poor woman, and how the hell I'm going to say it.

I've gone through multiple scenarios in my head about Margaret's reaction. Will there be floods of tears? Extreme anger? An immediate call to the local constabulary to come and take me away?

She doesn't need to worry about that.

They will be my next port of call after I've done this.

'Are you getting out, mate?' the Uber driver says, looking in the rearview mirror. He hasn't once asked me if I'm going to poo myself. Which is ironic, because I'm far closer to doing it now than I ever was in Majad's vehicle.

I look out of the window at Silver's Pets and Supplies and try to take a breath.

'Only I've got another pick-up due in five minutes,' my driver continues, his voice laced with the kind of muted impatience that you'd expect from anyone who wants to get to his next ride – but would still like a healthy tip from this one.

'Sorry, sorry,' I tell him, and get out of the car. He speeds off to whoever he's picking up next. I envy him. He's been able to happily drive himself out of this situation without a backward glance.

Silver's Pets and Supplies sounds about as old school as it looks. It's the only shop I can see on this entire street, closed in on both sides by terraced houses. Its broad glass frontage is home to a wide selection of bird cages and other avian ephemera. Beyond that, I can see even more bird cages inside – these ones containing birds of various species and sizes.

A sign in the window promises 10 per cent off for anyone who lives locally, which is a nice gesture.

There's a sign on the door that tells me the shop is open for business. This is unfortunate. Because now I'm here I really, really don't want to be . . . and if the shop was closed it would give me a good excuse to run away. And possibly never come back.

I take a breath, and step towards the door.

No bolt of vengeful lightning from the gods on high strikes me down.

You can't rely on cloud-borne deities to do anything right, can you?

My hand shakes as I push the door open. There is a light tinkling of bells as I do, announcing my arrival.

RUN!

No.

It's okay. This is something I have to do.

Inside, the world is full of cages. Which, if I was of a more literary persuasion, I might see as some kind of clever metaphor for my current situation.

I walk up the aisle between the shelves, setting off quite a few of the birds as I do so. It's more than a little unnerving to have every footstep you take be accompanied by squawking, and the ruffling of very many feathers. The beady little eyes don't help much, either. They have an accusing quality to them.

The small counter at the end of the shop is currently unmanned, but a dark, richly stained wooden door behind it now opens and I can feel the darkness closing in on me.

Not *now*.

No bloody panic attacks now, *please*.

I have to do this.

From the doorway emerges . . . clearly not Margaret Silver. Unless Margaret Silver has discovered the fountain of eternal youth. And a very effective sex-change clinic.

'Good morning,' the lad says, his voice reedy.

He looks nothing like the teenager in the third car. But he is also *exactly the same as him in every way, shape and form*.

One day I hope my brain stops making these connections between complete strangers.

I guess it'll find it a little hard to, once I'm safely ensconced behind prison bars.

'Morning,' I reply, barely able to form the words. 'Is . . . Is Margaret Silver available?'

The lad gives me a look of sudden concern. 'Well, she kind of is. I mean, she's here. Out the back.' He jerks one thumb over his shoulder. 'Only, she's . . . er . . . dealing with some things. Might be a little . . . indisposed.'

Oh God.

She's back there crying, isn't she?

Every day since her poor Anthony was taken away from her, she's tried her hardest to maintain the businesses that she's loved all her life, but it's just become too hard. So, she sits out the back and cries her eyes out, while Not Teenage Car Driver deals with the customers out front.

'Oh dear,' is about all I can manage in reply. 'I came to see if I could talk to her.'

The lad shrugs. 'I'll just see how she is,' he says, and pushes the door behind him open again.

'*Wank!*'

'I'm . . . I'm sorry?' I stammer.

The lad looks at me with deepest embarrassment. 'Please excuse the noise.'

'*Wank!*'

His lips didn't move. But I definitely heard the word?

'*Wank!*'

Yes. That's the one.

Can somebody please explain what's going on here? I might very well be losing my mind.

'Now, you stop that!' another voice then says, clearly coming from somewhere at the back of the shop.

'*Wank!*'

Whoever is doing the actual swearing is back there too. It's definitely not the lad in front of me, who continues to look mortified as he goes through the doorway, leaving me briefly alone once again in the shop.

I spend the next couple of moments in a staring contest with a small, blue budgie, who thoughtfully chews upon some seeds, while giving me a look that speaks absolute volumes.

He knows.

He knows who I am and why I'm here.

Budgerigar is Aboriginal for 'The Harsh Judgement of Nature', I believe.

The door to the back office then swings open again.

'*Wank!*'

The woman who emerges is wincing for all she's worth. Tall and quite stately of appearance, Margaret Silver is someone you'd definitely run towards if you were five years old and had a skinned knee.

Her grey hair is tied back in a bun, and she wears a sensible black pair of slacks, with a jumper that's covered in seeds and bird feathers.

'Good . . .'

'*Wank!*'

'. . . morning,' she says, continuing to wince.

'Hello,' I reply. I have to confess my deep sense of guilt, self-loathing and terror has taken something of a back seat to

'*Wank!*'

Yes, that.

Margaret affects a look of deepest apology. Which is completely the wrong way around for this conversation. I'm the one who's supposed to be looking apologetic here.

'I'm so sorry – we're having a little trouble with a new arrival in the shop,' Margaret explains. 'He only came in last night from a lovely couple, who weren't expecting a bird with such a—'

'*Wank!*'

'. . . limited vocabulary.'

Oh.

I see.

Or rather I don't, because the bird in question is fully hidden from view – if not from hearing.

'African grey, you understand,' Margaret further explains. 'They are very intelligent,'

'*Wank!*'

She winces again. 'And rather loud.'

Needless to say, in all my imagined scenarios in the thirty-three minutes in the Uber on the way over here, this was most definitely not one of them.

If it had been, I'd have had myself immediately committed.

'That's . . . That's okay,' I say. 'It's fine. I'm not bothered.'

Margaret gives me a grateful smile.

Which is soul-destroying, considering what I'm about to say.

'What can I help you with?' she asks me, thinking I'm a customer.

Just ask her if you can buy Wank the Parrot, and get out of here!

'I . . . I came to talk to you,' I tell Margaret, not quite able to meet her gaze.

She looks vaguely surprised. 'Oh? What about?'

I stare at her for a minute.

The budgie. Ask if you can buy the blue budgie. You can take it home and it can damn you with its judgement for the rest of eternity.

'Your . . . Your husband, Anthony.'

Margaret's expression immediately changes. Because of course it does. Wank the Parrot may be a serious problem, but it takes a back seat straight away.

'Oh? What about him?' she asks, her eyes doing a very good job of not filling with tears.

I stare at her again. 'I honestly don't know how to say this,' I mumble.

'Say what?'

'I was . . . I was in the accident.'

'Oh.'

Now my eyes are filling with tears, and I don't have Margaret's evident self-control, because I can't do anything to stop it.

'I was . . . in the other car. The one that crashed into Anthony.'

'You were?'

No, Margaret! Do *not* look concerned for me! I do not deserve that!

'Yes.' I swallow, the Sahara Desert filling my lungs. 'I'm afraid . . . I'm afraid I was the one that caused the crash.'

The darkness is coming in again. From all sides.

And, much like the tears, there's nothing I can do to stop it.

My heart feels like it's about to burst.

The feeling of doom washes over me.

Everything turns to cold.

I try my hardest to look at Margaret from the end of an ever-lengthening tunnel. 'I'm the reason your husband is dead,' I push out of my mouth, with the last of my strength.

And then, everything is gone.

'*Wank!*'

I force my eyes to open. They are not happy about it.

I am lying on a lilac couch. It has seen better days. There are what I can only assume are peck marks all over it.

The room I am in is small. And made to feel even smaller by the empty bird cages piled high around me. There is a desk sat across the room from me that features a PC Lionel from The Crooked Hat would think was out of date.

At the end of the couch is a large, ornate metal perch. Upon the perch is a parrot.

What I can only assume is an African grey.

'*Wank!*' Wank the Parrot says to me, and it's frankly quite nice to be able to put a face to the utterance. Because it is a friendly face – if parrots can ever be said to have friendly faces.

The parrot's beak curves up in such a way as to suggest a permanent, good-natured smile. None of the judgementalness present in the budgie out the front.

The parrot is looking down at me with curiosity.

I look back at him with confusion.

I guess I fainted again. How very *embarrassing*. Only this time it was in front of the woman I came to issue grovelling apologies to.

I am obviously terrible at grovelling apologies.

'*Wank!*'

I completely agree, my little grey friend.

The door to the office opens, and Margaret comes in, holding a glass of water. 'Oh my!' she says. 'You're awake!'

'Yes, thank you, I'm fine,' I tell her, sitting up.

Totally Fine.

Yes! Yes! That's me!

'*Wank!*'

No argument here, parrot. No argument here . . .

'Will was just about to call the ambulance for you,' Margaret continues, coming fully into the room and handing me the glass of water.

'No!' I say a little too sharply. I take a breath. 'No. That's fine. I'm fine. He doesn't need to do that.'

'I don't?' Will asks, having poked his head around the doorframe.

'No,' I tell him. 'I'm honestly okay. This . . . This isn't the first time this has happened.'

He nods. 'If you're sure?'

'I'm sure. Very sure.'

'It's okay, Will. Go and mind the shop,' Margaret tells him.

She sits herself down slowly on the edge of her desk, and winces. This is the first indication I've seen of her age troubling her in any way.

She rubs her left hip briefly, in what seems like a very familiar action.

Then she fixes me with a look that makes me wish I was still unconscious. 'If you are feeling better – which I truly hope you are, because poor Will struggled to get you in here. I don't think he could manage to move you again.'

'No, honestly, I'm not going to faint again,' I assure her.

She nods curtly. 'Good. In that case, as you are feeling better, could you please explain what you meant before you fainted? What on earth did you mean by saying you're the reason my husband is dead?'

I blink at her matter-of-fact turn of phrase. This is obviously not a person who beats around the bush.

I sit up slowly and take a rather large gulp of water.

With my head down and my eyes firmly fixed on the floor, I begin to recite the speech I constructed in the thirty-three minutes it took to get me here.

It takes me barely thirty-three seconds to say it in the end.

So much weight, in so little time. It shouldn't be possible.

'I should have never taken that call,' I finish, feeling comprehensively exhausted the second the words are all out of my mouth.

I can't bring myself to look up at her.

There will be rage. There will be sorrow. There will be hate.

Here sits the monster who destroyed her life.

I *force* myself to look up at her. Force myself to confront my guilt face on. I have to. This is how this has to end.

Margaret looks . . . confused.

Oh God. Did I not explain myself properly? Was I not clear? I'm pretty sure I was. I'm fairly certain I got all the awful, salient details out. But maybe my brain got in the way again? Maybe it's still trying to protect me, and in reality, I just came out with a load of nonsensical babble?

'Did you . . . Did you understand me?' I ask in a terrified voice. I honestly don't think I can go through that again.

'You think . . . you were responsible for the crash?' Margaret says. 'Because you were on your phone?'

I nod. 'Yes, yes. That's what happened.' I shift forward on the couch. If I didn't think it would be too much, I'd drop to my knees. 'I'm so, so sorry! I should never have done it! I should never have been on that call! Once I'm done here, I'll turn myself in. I'll take whatever punishment I deserve!'

Margaret regards me with the tears still very much held back in her own eyes. She then rubs her hip again, clears her throat and comes over to sit down next to me on the couch.

She then rummages around in one pocket of her slacks, and pulls out a cashew nut.

Wank the Parrot immediately jumps down off the perch and onto the arm of the couch. Margaret feeds him the cashew very deliberately, her face thoughtful and considerate.

Oh God.

Is she about to sic Wank the Parrot on me? Is that going to be her revenge? You kill my husband, and I let an African grey savage your face?

I'm prepared to go to jail for my crimes, but I don't particularly want my eyeballs popped out by a sweary parrot. That might be a step too far, even for my level of guilt.

I have to resist the temptation to put my arms up over my face.

'Charlie . . . That was your name, wasn't it?' Margaret asks.

'Yes, that's me.'

Or, it used to be me. I don't quite know who this person is.

Her eyes widen. 'Is that so? Sounds like you've been through a lot.'

Oh Christ! Did I say that last part out loud? I must have! Am I saying this part out loud too?

'Sorry. I'm sorry. Yes, I guess I have.'

'Well, Charlie, what you're saying about you being on the phone may be true.' She fixes me with a stern gaze. 'But you are *not* responsible for my husband's death.'

'Yes, I am,' I insist.

'No. You're not,' she insists right back.

'Um . . . I . . .'

I have no idea what to say. She's in denial, I suppose? This wasn't what I expected at all. She's supposed to be on the phone to the police, or sending Wank the Attack Parrot after me.

But instead, she's *arguing* with me.

'*Wank!*'

You're not helping, pal.

'Charlie . . . my Anthony died of a heart attack,' Margaret tells me. 'His *second* heart attack, to be more precise. The incident report was quite clear. The heart attack had started before the accident itself. There was mention of other people involved, but certainly nothing about any guilt on anyone else's part.'

'But . . . But I was on the phone,' I persist. 'It was my fault.'

She shakes her head slowly. 'No, Charlie. It was nobody's fault.' Her face clouds. 'Except for maybe Anthony's.'

I sit back a little. 'How could it possibly have been his fault?'

Her lips purse in a thin line for a second. 'It was his *second* heart attack, Charlie. He should never have been driving. He was told not to, in no uncertain terms.'

'Then . . . why did he?' I ask, still utterly confounded by what I'm being told.

Margaret then rolls her eyes. 'Because he was the kind of man who always thought he was perfectly okay. Totally recovered from whatever it was that ailed him,' she says. 'Always thought he knew best.'

'What?'

'He was stubborn. Never went to the doctor unless I threatened to leave him.' The loss in her eyes is mixed with a great deal of frustration. 'He should never have been driving that car. But that was Anthony for you. Always insisted he was *totally fine.*'

'Totally fine,' I repeat, in what feels like a dreamlike tone.

Because that's what this has become.

A surreal dream I wish I could wake up from.

'Yes. But he very much *wasn't*, Charlie,' Margaret says, making sure to look me right in the eyes as she says it. 'So whatever guilt you may be feeling about being on your telephone while in the car, you need not think it was the reason why that accident happened. I believe a witness stated that Anthony's car was swerving across the road long before he hit you. The boy in the car behind, I believe. He was the one who saw it all happen.'

'The teenage lad,' I mutter, in disbelief. 'Will doesn't look like him at all.'

Margaret looks confused again. And no wonder. 'Perhaps you should drink a little more water?' she suggests.

Perhaps you should drink a little more water, Mr King?

I look at the police officer and nod my head.

'Charlie? Are you alright?' Margaret asks.

I take a sip of the water, and hand the bottle back to the policeman. 'We're almost done here, Mr King,' the policeman says. 'It's a very unfortunate incident, but no one's fault.'

'But I was on the phone,' I say, mostly to myself.

'Yes, I know,' Margaret replies, 'but it definitely didn't cause the accident, Charlie. You don't need to believe that. It wasn't your fault.'

258

I look at her, scarcely believing what I'm hearing. 'It wasn't?'
'No.'

I start to cry then. Proper, gulping sobs. On a beak-pecked lilac couch, in front of a woman who's still mourning her husband's death, with a foul-mouthed parrot looking at me with a good-natured smile on its face.

It's a good job he is here, because otherwise I might be tempted to believe that none of this is really happening.

I do not know my own mind, after all.

But here's the thing . . .

Here's the big, undeniable thing:

My mind – for all its cleverness, for all its ability to mask the truth from me, for all its skill at constructing falsehoods – would never think, in such a fantasy of pure, unadulterated catharsis, to include a fucking parrot called Wank.

Margaret puts an arm around my shoulder. I am equally as mortified by this as I am grateful.

After about a minute, the sobs subside, and I start to feel a little more human again.

A little more Charlie King.

'You must have been carrying this around with you for a very long time,' Margaret remarks with no small amount of sympathy.

'Yes. I have . . . Or, no, I haven't.'

Bloody hell, I'd better go through the whole thing with her, lest she think she's trapped in a room with an absolute nutter.

I don't have to do that. I could just get up and leave this poor woman to her life and her parrot. But I feel like I owe her an explanation. I feel like I owe myself one too.

So, I explain everything to Margaret. The truth – as far as I can define it, or grasp it. It'd probably be easier if I was up a pole.

By the time I'm done, Wank has chewed his way through seven cashew nuts, and I feel a little lighter.

'My God,' Margaret says. 'You've put yourself through the wringer, haven't you?'

'I have.'

Margaret gives Wank a tickle behind one ear. 'Anthony would have liked you.'

'Really?'

'He would, yes. He was one of life's fixers too. Never a problem he thought he couldn't sort out. The hours he spent working on his boats. Getting them working at peak efficiency. If there was a rope that was frayed, or a splinter of wood that needed sanding, he couldn't let it go until it was done. No matter what time of day it was. He was a ball of nerves if things were left outstanding, or not fixed.'

I cringe a little inside. 'Yes, that does sound a bit like me.'

A bit? About the only thing that sounds different is that I don't like boats.

Margaret sighs and then slaps her hands on her thighs. 'Then I get to do something I never got to with him. Something I've wished I'd done before that day, a million times since his death.'

'What's that?'

I don't think it's to sic a parrot on me. That danger has passed.

'I can tell you that you are *wrong*, Charlie King.'

I blink a couple of times. 'Wrong?'

'Yes, *wrong*.' She takes my hand in hers. It feels dry and soft. But the grip is still strong for a woman of her age. 'You cannot *fix* everything. You do not *know* everything. You cannot control everything. And you cannot ignore what others are telling you. Or your own body, for that matter.'

I try to pull away from her, but her grip grows even tighter.

'Don't be as foolish as my poor, sweet Anthony, Charlie.' Margaret is allowing herself to cry a little now. 'Listen to Annie.

Listen to your friends. *Trust them.* And stop trying to make your world into something it's not.'

'What am I trying to make it?'

Her grip loosens, and she pats my hand fondly. '*Perfect*, Charlie King. That's what you're doing. That's what Anthony did too.' She lets out a long, slow breath. 'And it killed him. Because he couldn't cope with the fact it *wasn't* perfect. That there was something wrong with it. Something wrong with him. That he wasn't . . .'

'Totally fine,' I finish.

She pats my hand again. 'Exactly.' Then she smiles. 'If it was a perfect place, my Anthony would still be here, and I wouldn't be dealing with a parrot that I'll never be able to sell because—'

'*Wank!*'

Unbelievably, I begin to laugh.

Slightly more unbelievably Margaret starts to laugh with me.

It goes on for longer than the crying.

I am now standing at another door.

One I am far more familiar with than the one leading to Silver's Pets and Supplies.

But I'm finding it even harder to knock on this one.

So, I just stand here. Unsure of what to do next.

My conversation with Margaret has left me more than a little adrift at sea, you understand. I had plans before it. Plans that would have seen me potentially incarcerated. But those plans have gone completely out of the window, because I finally know the truth.

And I mean it this time . . .

No more surprises are in store.

I know my own mind again. Or, I'm starting to. The pieces of the jigsaw are slotting back into place now, and I don't think any of them are still missing. I hope not, anyway.

The very last piece – the one that only came to me as the last of my laughter tapered off while sat on Margaret's lilac couch – was about how the phone call actually happened in the car on the day of the crash. But I'll get to that.

First is something much more important.

I have to knock on this door.

Because I *need* her. Because I *love* her. Because if I can't be with her then *none of this really matters anyway*.

My hand shakes as I bang the door knocker, partly due to fear, and partly because I'm holding something quite heavy in the other hand, and haven't eaten properly all day.

A few moments pass before the front door swings open.

'Charlie?' Annie says, a very perplexed look on her face. The perplexity turns to confusion as she regards what I'm holding. She can't help but let the slightest hint of a smile cross her lips at the strangeness of it all.

Her smile, no matter how awkward or slight, is like the sun coming up.

'Charlie, what . . . what's going on?' she asks.

'Hi Annie,' I say to her, in as light a voice as possible. 'How are you? Can we . . . Can we talk, please?'

'I . . . well . . . er . . .'

'*Wank!*'

The parrot looks out at us from his cage, which I have temporarily placed on the kitchen table.

I have purchased a parrot.

Wank will have a home again. With me.

I felt it was somehow appropriate.

Annie isn't sure she agrees.

'You've bought a parrot, Charlie. Was that wise . . . you know . . . considering how things are with you?'

'I think so.'

'Parrots can be tricky things, Charlie. Especially ones that keeps saying—'

'*Wank!*

'Margaret says I can train him out of it,' I assure her.

'Does she?'

'Yes.

'*Wank!*

Annie folds her arms. 'Charlie, I need you to do an extremely good job of explaining what the hell is going on, and I need you to do it right now. Last time I saw you, it looked like you were on the verge of self-destructing – and now you are smiling, and have a parrot.'

'I know. I'm sorry.'

Here we go, then. Another apology. This one will be a lot easier, but it will also be far more important. 'I did what Leo told me to do. I found out more about the man who died in the accident. The man, it turns out, I did not actually kill.'

I then go on to detail my entire conversation with Margaret Silver, with constant accompaniment from Wank. Much like the way Margaret fed him cashews while she was talking to me, I do the same now. It's a strangely therapeutic process. I can see why she did it.

Wank is more than happy with it as well, of course. He's going to be a fat parrot, if I'm not very careful.

'You can't call him that,' Annie says.

'I would very much like to.'

'If you have to keep him, he's going to need a better name than that.'

'Okay. Any ideas?'

She studies the bird carefully. 'He kind of reminds me of my grandad, the way he smiles like that.'

'What was your grandad's name?'

'Wayne.'

'Wayne?'

'Yep.'

'Wayne the Parrot?'

'It's still pretty close to what you call him,' she points out, quite accurately.

My nose wrinkles. 'Not sure about that one.'

Annie takes a cashew from my hand and leans forward. 'What do you think, Wayne? You'd like to be called Wayne, wouldn't you?'

'*Wank!*'

'Close enough.' She watches him for a moment while he chews the cashew. 'It would be fun to have a parrot,' she eventually says. 'Maybe we can take him for walks.'

My heart speeds up a bit. 'We?'

She looks back at me, her mouth opening as if to speak. But then no words come out.

It's not her that needs to do the talking here.

I reach out a hand and take hers. She doesn't try to stop me. 'I'm sorry for all of this,' I tell her. 'I'm sorry for being so stubborn, and stupid. I'm sorry I didn't listen to you. Everything you said was right. *You* were right.'

She faces me fully now, leaving Wayne to his munching. 'And what about now? Do you think you can listen to me now? Because if there's anything left between us, Charlie, then I need you to—'

'I booked the appointment with the doctor before I got here,' I quickly tell her. 'There was a brief hairy moment when the parrot interrupted me with his favourite catchphrase, but I smoothed it over with the receptionist.' I smile. 'I'm going in tomorrow. No more excuses. No more avoidance. I'm going to tell them everything. I'm going to get help.'

The look of relief that washes across Annie's face makes me feel both elated and sad at the same time. It should never have come to this. It should never have got this bad. I was on the edge of an abyss I walked myself up to for no good reason.

'Perfect,' she says with a smile.

No, Annie. Not perfect. I learned from a very clever person today that the world is never perfect. And that's something I will remember for the rest of *my* days – because I never want to go through anything like this again.

One thing is still perfect in this world, though. The smile on Annie's face.

There's no doubt about that.

The fact I get to see it again is something of a miracle – and one I won't ever take for granted.

And so — finally — here is the truth. The actual *truth. It's been a long time coming, hasn't it?*

'My humps! It's my humps! You should come and see my humps!' I sing, completely out of tune, and only getting some of the lyrics right. This is very silly song, but it's a hard one not to sing along to.

It will soon become the stuff of my nightmares, but right now, it's just a silly pop song, with some very silly lyrics that I'm getting only about half of right.

'My humps! It's my humps! Get a load of my humps!'

Ring ring.

I look down at my phone.

It's Maurice from the bowling alley. He must be calling about Teddy's birthday party.

Damn.

I know I shouldn't answer the phone while I'm driving, but I do need to speak to him, and I'm not sure when I'll get another chance.

I look down at my phone . . . and then press the button on the steering wheel to answer it.

'Hello?' I say, turning the radio down as I do.

'Hello? Is that Charlie?' Maurice's voice booms around the cabin of my car.

Because of course I answered the call using the Bluetooth hands-free connection.

That's the kind of thing Charlie King does. He's sensible . . . with a good moral centre.

Sadly, the kind of thing Charlie King also does is construct a web of subconscious lies around himself, for no reason whatsoever, other than his inability to accept that the world does not always function in the way he wants it to.

You cannot stop a car veering across the road in front of you because the old man driving it is having a heart attack.

You cannot stop feeling helpless and useless in the face of events you have no control over.

You cannot pretend that everything is totally fine, when it is most definitely not.

And you cannot get through it on your own.

No matter how much you think you can.

Everything explodes.

It has been exploding for several months now.

When the cars come to rest, I see the teenage boy with the cut on his forehead, and I see the old Datsun Cherry Anthony Silver is driving.

I see him gasping for his last breath, when I try to walk over.

I see the other people – including the teenage boy – trying to help him as I sit on the side of the road, gripped by an extreme level of shock and panic I have no capacity to deal with. It will be the shame of this complete inaction that will force my brain to punish me with all the lies it tells.

267

I watch as the paramedics try and fail to save Anthony's life. Try and fail to control the situation. Try and fail.

And in those dreadful cold, lifeless moments, when the world spirals so out of control that I feel like I might just die here on the side of the road along with Anthony, I make up another world.

A better world.

One where things are just a little more . . . perfect.

One where I am not sat on the sidelines, unable to cope. One where I am the Charlie King I think I should be. One where I haven't seen horror and death.

One where I am tota—

. . . oh, you know by now.

It's time I stopped saying it so much.

Chapter Twelve

THE RIGHT ROAD

'I think that's very wise,' Monica says, her pen gently tapping on her notepad as she considers my words.

'You do?'

I know this isn't meant to be about saying the right thing, but I still feel good when I think Monica approves.

'Yes, I think so. You're acknowledging that the mindset is not a healthy one, and – without wanting to descend into too much cliché – acknowledging a problem is often the first step to overcoming it.'

I smile.

I am pleased.

. . . even though I probably shouldn't be. Because none of this is meant to be about saying the right thing, only what needs to be said.

But I'm Charlie King, and I like to make people happy, don't I?

'Of course, that's only the first step,' Monica continues, as if she's read my mind.

'Yeah, I know,' I agree, looking a little sheepish.

There are lots of things that need unpicking in my head, that's for certain. This is my fifth session with Monica, and we've done a good job of realising together that there is quite a lot to unpick.

It's amazing what two hours a week in a shed in someone's garden will do for you.

Calling it a shed is doing Monica's office space a deep disservice, of course. It's actually a rather lovely summer house at the bottom of her garden. But any building in a garden made of wood is a shed to me.

I started this 'adventure' sat in someone's garden shed, and it seems like I will be ending it in one too.

Only this shed isn't in the shape of a wigwam, and I'm not at the end of a journey at all. I'm at the start of one.

Monica specialises in PTSD.

And I definitely have PTSD.

This should come as a surprise to absolutely no one who's been paying attention.

The false memories, the amnesia, the panic attacks – all of them are symptoms of a brain trying its level best to get as far away from cruel hard reality as possible.

Like Monica says, acknowledging what's wrong is the first step in getting over it.

Annie was 100 per cent correct to order to me to go and see a doctor.

But you knew that already. You've been screaming it at me this entire time.

And the doctor immediately put me in touch with Monica. Officially, he put in a referral for a mental health assessment with the NHS, but knowing that would take until the heat death of the universe to get sorted out, he also advised me to seek the help from a professional therapist who specialises in trauma.

Which I did.

And while Monica is mainly helping me deal with the PTSD, she's also working through some of my other issues, which include the obsessive need to people please. Every ridiculous scheme I tried with Jack and Leo wasn't just about their problems, it was about mine too – and my complete inability to accept that I can't please everyone all of the time. I can't help everyone. I can't make everything better.

'You are a problem solver, Charlie,' Monica said to me at the end of our first session. 'But the *real* problem is that sometimes there are problems you just *can't solve*. Like the things your friends Jack and Leo have been through, for instance. You avoided your own trauma by trying to fix theirs, but that only made things worse.'

'For all three of us,' I say glumly.

Monica didn't try to convince me otherwise. It's not her job to make me feel better.

. . . well, it is, of course. But not by soft-pedalling some of the mad stuff I've done in the past few months.

'You can't help your friends in the way you'd like, no matter how hard it is to hear that,' she told me. 'You can't solve their problems for them, Charlie.'

Which sounds so damned horrible, when it's put in such a matter-of-fact way.

Every fibre of my being rails against it.

Things should be solvable!

I should be able to solve them!

Damn it!

. . . you see what I mean about it being the start of a journey, rather than the end of one?

'What are you thinking about?' Monica asks, noting the expression on my face, and bringing me back to the present.

I tell her.

It's very easy to do that.

She nods. 'Yes, that's very true. You are at the start of this journey. Nothing about the human mind is easy or simple, Charlie. It is as complex, weird and wonderful as everything else in this world. It always takes time to pick through what's causing your trauma. That begins with the inciting incident, and often goes back further than that, into the life of the person concerned.'

My face clouds a little.

Monica puts up a hand. 'I know that's the kind of thing you don't want to hear, but the very fact you don't want to hear it is one of the reasons why we're here.'

'Yeah, yeah,' I reply, knowing that she's right, but still not comfortable with it.

She then points a finger skyward. 'But . . . the important thing is that you are on the right road now. These things take time, but with that time comes a better understanding of ourselves, and a measure of peace.'

Well, that sounds marvellous, doesn't it?

A measure of peace.

'I'm on the right road,' I echo.

'You are.'

'Funny . . . when I think of roads, I don't think of good things these days . . .' I mumble.

I can still go back there. When I close my eyes at night, I can go back to that day as easy as if you handed me the keys to a time machine. And I still see Anthony gasping for his last breath. I'm afraid I may see that until the day I'm the one doing the gasping.

'That will change, Charlie,' Monica says, pulling me out of the memory again. 'I promise that will change. The important thing is to keep moving forward, which you're now doing.'

'On the right road,' I repeat.

'Exactly.'

Annie picks me up from Monica's house half an hour later. We've agreed it's best I don't drive myself there. Not for the time being, anyway.

'How did it go?' she asks, face full as much of anxiety as hope.

'It went well,' I then tell her – *honestly*. The days of me pretending to be fine in front of Annie are long gone. If things are going well, I'll tell her that. And if they're going badly, the same applies. Today feels like things went well.

'That's good.'

'Monica says that it will get better.' I tap the side of my head. 'Up here.'

Annie smiles. 'I'm sure it will.'

I look off into the middle distance. 'There are problems I can't solve,' I say, almost to myself.

Annie's eyes fill with sympathy. 'No. You can't,' she says, one hand squeezing my shoulder gently.

'But I'm on the right road,' I say, this time in a stronger voice.

I think this may be one of those things that requires you to keep saying it until you believe it.

I sigh gently, and then look into Annie's eyes. 'Thank you,' I tell her.

'For what?'

'For being here. For *still* being here, I mean.'

Annie gives my cheek a gentle stroke. 'No problem at all, Charlie.'

My brain then does something it's developed a disconcerting habit of doing over the past few months – it sends me on another flashback. Not to the crash this time, though, but instead to me, stood by another car.

In a dark car park, after a stand-up gig, not knowing what the hell to do. Being stuck. Being scared. Confused about everything.

I'm not confused anymore . . . but I think I'm still afraid right now, if I'm being honest with myself (which I'm trying to do as much as possible these days).

But I'm hoping that very soon I won't be scared anymore.

Very soon, I will be brave again.

Because I'm on the right road . . . and Annie is still here, on it with me.

◆ ◆ ◆

So . . . you'd like to think I've completely changed, wouldn't you?

I know that's meant to be the *ending*.

I know that's where Charlie King's epic story *Totally Fine* is meant to draw to a close.

But things are always . . . *messier* than that.

In the real world.

Beyond the stories we tell ourselves, and other people.

And I am still Charlie King. The people pleaser. The one who always wants to help. The one who doesn't know how to stop.

And I have two friends who are *still* avoiding their own demons, while I finally face mine. I haven't forgotten about them. I could *never* forget about them.

And I am on the right road, but I am still *me*.

So . . . fourth time's a charm, eh?

I find Jack working on Gormley, on the hard standing where the mobile home has sat for so long now. Far *too* long, it has to be said. Gormley is very much a beige and dark-brown symbol of my friend's struggles.

Jack is sanding down one of the side panels near the door, and for a moment I stand in the road and just watch him as he does this.

There's a firm gusto about the way he goes at the sanding which is Jack to a tee. He never does anything by halves.

In the past, I've always thought that energy came from a positive place, but now I'm not so sure. Having your own insecurities and anxieties peeled back can certainly give you a better sense of other people's. There's frustration in every scrape he makes alongside Gormley with that sandpaper. Frustration and fear. I never did a good job of seeing these signs in the past. Too wrapped up in my own issues.

'Morning,' I eventually say as I walk up to him.

'Blimey,' Jack replies, genuinely surprised to see me. No wonder. It's been a few weeks. I've been busy with therapy sessions, trying to rebuild my work, and training a parrot not to say *wank*.

The work rebuilding has been going slightly better than the parrot training, it has to be said. I have two new contracts. One of them is with Eloise and Conrad again, if you can believe that. It turns out the influencer world is even stranger than I gave it credit for. Would you believe that the amount of viral attention my massive cock-up generated actually brought them more followers than anything else? They made more cash off it than any of their travel videos.

Conrad sounded rather sheepish about the whole thing when he phoned me. I was fine with that. The fact they wanted to work with me again was all I cared about. I wasn't about to berate the poor chap for highlighting my stupidity across the internet.

I've agreed to help them launch Eloise's new perfume range, which is called Scentimental. This is an awful name, and it smells like something's died in there, as far as I'm concerned . . . but taking on the job means that King Promotions has a chance to rise phoenix-like from the flames, and that's what's important to me.

Conrad and Eloise wanted to see me today, in fact. *Urgently.* Wanted to discuss the plans for the launch *again*. For the sixth time. I can hardly blame them for this, given what happened the last time we worked together, but seven times going over the same thing is a little much – even for someone who got their baby's gender wrong.

I told them *no*.

Can you believe that?

I told my clients that no, I could not see them today, because I had something else I needed to do.

I never say no. Especially not to the people who pay my wages.

But I did.

With my heart racing and shame flushing my face, I said *no*.

And *it didn't bother them.*

Not in the slightest.

Can you believe that as well?

I couldn't.

I was dumbfounded.

It was only a small victory – among many others I'm achieving these days. But the small victories are often the most important ones, because they all add up.

'Hello, mate, how are you?' I say to Jack as I approach him.

'Yeah, great!' he replies.

Yeah, Great would be the name of Jack's story, the same way mine was *Totally Fine.*

'That's good to hear.'

Careful now, Charlie. You can see the look in his eyes. The look that says *Yeah, Great* is a lie. You know that look well.

Be. Careful.

'Giving Gormley a going-over, then,' I say, patting the side of the vehicle affectionately. I'm not altogether sure whether I am all that affectionate about Gormley, but it'll help things along if Jack thinks I am.

'Yeah. I figured he needed a good seeing-to.' He pops the sandpaper down, and briskly claps his hands together, before turning his full attention to me. 'So how are you doing, then? How's the . . . therapy going?' I almost smile at the awkwardness with which he says this.

'It's going pretty well, actually.'

And not just awkwardness. There's some tension here, isn't there? Quite a lot of it, in fact.

Not all that surprising. The last time we were in a room together, we nearly came to blows over me killing someone. The fact I haven't been in touch since probably sits very badly with my friend.

'I'm sorry I haven't been around,' I tell him. 'It's been a weird few weeks. I've been . . .' What have I been exactly? '. . . *resetting*.'

Jack nods in acknowledgement. 'Fair enough.'

'It's helped, though,' I continue. 'Put me on a better path. The right road.'

I pat Gormley again. It seems appropriate at this moment.

'That's good to hear,' Jack says. This is the most stilted conversation I think I've ever had with him.

It's because he thinks he doesn't know me anymore.

And it's because men don't generally do well when their friends are undergoing serious difficulties. Not because they don't care. Quite the opposite, in fact. They do indeed care – it's just that caring comes with empathy, and empathy can sometimes highlight your own problems.

Women see other women as reflections. Men see other men as mirrors. It's an idiotically subtle distinction, but it's definitely there.

Jack probably looks at me and wonders how far away he is from the same kind of breakdown I had.

Not as far as he'd like. The fear in his eyes when he had to get out of that limo will be scored on my heart for the rest of my days.

I *must* do something about that.

'Oh, you're both here already,' Leo says from behind me.

I must do something about this as well.

I have hurt my two best friends in the world. And regardless of any other considerations, I cannot let that stand.

. . . I can hear you sucking in your breath.

Don't worry. This is not going to go the way you think it is.

The real world is very different from the storybooks.

It's *messier*.

'What are you doing here?' Jack says to Leo, though not in an unpleasant way. There's none of the tension between them that exists between Jack and me. Let's see if there's any with Leo, shall we?

'He's here because I asked him to come along,' I tell Jack, before turning to my other friend. 'How are you, mate?' I ask him.

He rocks his head back and forth. 'Not too bad, I guess. Been better. Been worse.'

Nope. There's no tension there . . . but when Leo says things could be worse, that means things are actually awful. I know him very well.

I know them both very well.

That's why this is going to work.

'What about you? How are you and Annie doing now?' Leo asks me.

I smile. He doesn't ask about the therapy. He doesn't need to. He can get all the answers he needs by asking me if my relationship with the woman I love is still on track. 'We're fine,' I tell him. 'It's been a bit bumpy here and there, but we're going to get through it.' I pause, thinking for a moment. 'And when we are through it, I'm going to ask her to marry me.'

This is the first time I've said this out loud to anyone, and it makes my heart jump into my mouth – in the absolute best way possible.

I'm not asking yet, though.

Not yet.

'Good. Pleased to hear it,' Jack says. This would usually come with a smile and a slap on the back, but that tension is still there. The walls are there.

And I need to drive through them.

'Can we go sit in Gormley?' I ask the both of them.

'Oh God. You haven't got mushrooms in your pocket, have you?' Leo says, face stricken.

'No. Nothing like that. I just want to have a chat with you both.'

Jack immediately looks deeply suspicious. As well he might. I have form.

I hold up my hands. 'No mushrooms. No poles. No Fellowships. No plans. Nothing but the three of us, I promise.'

And all of that is the truth. I promise you.

I don't have anything up my sleeve. I don't have any grand master plan I've cooked up using Google and far too much of my brain.

I am flying by the seat of my pants, with no clue what I'm doing.

Because it's messier.

Because it isn't perfect.

It's both terrifying . . . and quite liberating, to be honest.

I don't know what I'm doing.

Which is far better sentence to tell yourself than *I don't know my own mind.*

We're way past where the epilogue to this story should have been, and the road we're on now is as unknown to me as I stand here as it is to you.

'Come on, for old times' sake?' I say to my friends, gesturing towards Gormley's door.

Jack's eyes are still narrowed, but he can't resist the pull of thirty years of friendship. That has an undeniable weight which really can't be resisted. 'Come on, then. You've obviously got something to get off your chest.'

Actually, Jack, I don't think I do, mate – and that's even more liberating.

I have a strong feeling of déjà vu as Jack opens the door in Gormley's side and ushers us both in. Not just back to the night of the mushrooms, but back to all the times we hustled into Gormley together at the start of a new adventure. New Shenanigans.

Aah . . .

Something is forming in my mind.

An *idea*.

A messy idea.

Jack throws the keys onto the little Formica table, and sits himself back down in his customary spot. Leo and I follow suit. This takes us approximately thirty-eight minutes, because Gormley's table space hasn't got any bigger since the last time we were in here.

They both look at me expectantly.

If I had a mirror, I'd be looking back at myself expectantly too, because I have no idea what I'm going to do, or what I'm going to say.

'Well, go on, then . . .' Jack encourages. 'You've probably got a speech rehearsed for us, haven't you?'

'It'll be a long one. He's got that kind of look on his face,' Leo agrees.

Jack nods. 'He's going to try his hardest to sound wise, isn't he?'

'Absolutely.'

'He's had a few therapy sessions, and probably had a make-up shag with his missus, and now feels ready to impart his wisdom upon his poor, troubled friends,' Jack remarks, folding his arms and staring at me.

'Without a doubt,' Leo says. 'There's probably some kind of prop he's thinking of employing as well. Maybe that bottle of rum from last time. That sounds like the kind of thing he'd do.'

I am quite happy to let them get all this banter out of the way, as it's giving me time to think. My friends think they know me well enough to predict what my next move is, but if I do anything they are expecting, this won't work.

'Oh yes,' Jack continues. 'That'd be about right. A nice, symbolic callback he can employ to underline his point.' Jack leans towards Leo. 'The problem is, I threw the bottle out last week, so he's going to have to come up with something else.'

Leo nods sagely. 'That won't please him. He likes his plans to go according to . . . well, *plan.*'

I continue to stare at them both and remain silent.

My heart has started pounding, though, because I've just decided what I am going to do.

And it's *insane.*

Completely unplanned, and completely insane.

But Jack is right about one thing, though.

I do like a bit of symbolism.

And a good callback.

I swiftly lean forward and grab Gormley's keys up from the table.

Before either of my friends has a chance to stop me, I lurch towards the front of the vehicle and jump into the driver's seat.

Leo being Leo just stares at what I'm doing with a look of supreme shock on his face. Jack tries to extricate himself from Gormley's Formica table trap as fast as he can, but the mobile home is clearly on my side today, as it's not letting him out without a fight.

'What the bloody hell are you doing?!' Jack roars.

'Improvising!' I shout back at him. I have to resist the urge not to giggle.

I never improvise.

Charlie King does not improvise.

Fuck it.

He bloody does *now*.

I fire the engine up, slam the gear stick in reverse and wave a triumphant fist in the air.

'Wank!' I shout at the top of my voice, and gun the throttle.

Gormley speeds off Jack's drive and onto the road. I then swiftly turn the wheel to back us into the road proper. When I slam the brakes on, Jack flies back into his seat again. 'Stop it, you bloody madman!' he wails.

Leo is giggling.

He looks terrified, but he's also giggling.

'Wank!' I repeat, this time doing my absolute level best to copy Wayne the Parrot's screechy bird voice.

I slam Gormley into first gear, and speed off down the road. 'We're going on an adventure!' I exclaim to my two friends, channelling Bilbo Baggins for all I'm worth.

Jack has now – finally – managed to get himself up, and he staggers along the tiny aisle towards me. 'Pull Gormley over right now!' he orders.

'I can't!' I tell him. 'I have to keep driving!'

'Why?!' he barks.

'Because it's messier this way!' I say, and laugh. From behind Jack, Leo laughs too.

'What the hell has got into you both?' Jack snaps.

'I have no idea, mate!' I tell him. 'But I know this is the right thing to do!'

'Why?!' he repeats, clinging on to the cupboards on either side of the little aisle for dear life as I take a right turn.

'Because I have no idea why I'm doing it! Because I haven't planned anything! Because I don't know what road we're on!'

282

Ah yes, I do love a bit of symbolism. My friends know me so well.

'Just let him do it,' Leo says to Jack, grabbing him by one shoulder. 'I think he needs this.'

Yes, you're right, Leo. I do need this. I don't know why, but I most certainly *do*.

Jack looks at Leo for a moment, and then back down at me. He points a finger. 'You stick to the speed limit,' he demands.

'I will!' I promise.

'Don't put a scratch on him!' he further orders.

'I won't!'

'I have no idea how far you're going to get. I haven't filled him with petrol for months.'

'We'll see, eh?'

Yes, yes. We'll see. We'll just see where we end up.

I take a left, still with no idea of where I'm going. I do this sensibly, at the speed limit as Jack has ordered, but I still do it with a freedom and a lack of forethought I didn't know was possible for a person like me.

'Let's go and sit down,' Leo tells Jack. 'Let's just trust him.'

Jack gives him a look of utter disbelief. 'Are you serious? After everything he's put us through? After all of his plans that went horribly wrong on us?'

Leo looks down at my smiling, hectic face. 'That's the thing this time, though. He doesn't have anything planned, Jack.' His eyes go wide. 'And maybe that's for the best.'

'You're mad,' Jack retorts. 'You're both mad.' He scratches his chin. 'But then I did once go up a mountain in a mankini, so I guess I must be mad too.' He points the finger of doom at me again. 'Not a bloody scratch, King. Not a bloody *scratch*.'

I snap off a salute, and let my friends go and sit down at the back of Gormley.

So . . . what exactly are we doing here, Charlie? Where exactly are we going?

I don't know.

Yes, you do.

Do I?

Yep. The place you refused to go. The place they need to go.

They won't like that.

No. Probably not.

We won't get in, either. Not today.

No. But it'll be . . . symbolic.

Oh yes. Yes, it will, won't it? And I think in this case, symbolic might well be enough. Because I know my two best friends very well, and they know me.

But maybe not quite as well as they think they do.

. . . not yet.

Time to change that.

It takes me about ten minutes to arrive at the same doctor's surgery they were trying to bundle me into a few weeks ago. I park Gormley right outside it, in a no-parking zone. It has to be right outside the building or the symbolism will be lost.

Turning off the engine, I slide out of the driver's seat and turn to walk back down the aisle. Jack's face is like a thunder cloud. Leo's face is now like the accompanying rainstorm. Both of them are somewhat terrified of me right at this moment.

Quickly now. Before whatever weird friendship magic you've caught here dribbles away . . .

I look at my friends, and in that moment, I know exactly what I need to say.

'I love you both,' I tell them in as blunt and honest a tone as I can muster. Jack's eyes go a little wide. Leo's soften. 'I have put you both through hell, because I love you both. And I wanted to . . . fix you. Like you were . . . I don't know . . . frayed ropes on a boat.'

'Charlie, you don't have to—' Leo begins.

'Yes, I do,' I interrupt. 'Please, just let me say this. I really don't have any of this planned, and I don't want it to . . . slip away.' I try to clear the lump in my throat. 'I wanted to help you both, because you both do need help. The same way I did . . . I mean, *do*. But it can't be me that does it. I can't force you do anything. I can't make you take care of yourselves. All I can do is tell you that I love you, I support you, and I want you to feel better.'

'We're fine, Charlie,' Jack says in a quiet voice, but he doesn't believe it.

I shake my head. 'No, you're not. But you can be. The same way I can. So please . . . because I love you both, and you've done nothing but support me, I want to do the same for you. If you just do the one thing I refused to do for so long because I was scared and embarrassed, I promise I will be there to make sure it's not as scary or as embarrassing for you.'

It's not the best speech in the world. I'm sure with a few more edits and a bit of thought put into it, it could be much better. But it's all I have right now. And it's messy, and imperfect, but it's all true.

'Okay, Charlie,' Leo says. 'I promise I'll see someone about what's scaring me so much. If you're there with me?'

'Of course. I will be there right alongside you, whenever you need it,' I tell him.

I can't read the look in Jack's face. I don't think I've ever seen it before. There's reluctance in there. There's doubt. And there's fear.

He gets up from the little Formica table. It takes him about eighty-seven minutes, but that's fine. I can wait.

Jack then very slowly puts his arms around me, and gives me possibly the best hug I've ever had in my life. 'I love you too,' he tells me in a gruff voice.

The hug goes on for another couple of moments, before he releases it, and stands back.

'Dickhead,' he says with a smile.

And then he turns, pushes Gormley's side door open, and exits the mobile home, headed straight for the entrance to the surgery.

'It was only supposed to be symbolic,' I say, watching him go, somewhat perplexed.

'Charlie, Jack couldn't do symbolic if you put a gun to his head,' Leo tells me, quite accurately. 'Go and park Gormley properly,' he adds, before following Jack out of the door.

Do you know something . . . I'm not sure Gormley's tired beige and brown interior is exactly what you'd call the perfect place to end this story, any more than the confines of The Crooked Hat were.

But it'll have to do.

After all . . . the world isn't perfect.

And neither are we.

The Actual Epilogue

The road is busy.

I say that both as a metaphor about my life and as a description of the road we're being driven along. I'm finding I'm getting quite good at metaphors. And symbolism. Maybe there's a novel in me, after all.

Cars whip by on my right-hand side as I gaze out of the window.

The weather has been remarkably similar to the way it was that day.

Cool, but sunny.

Calm.

The kind of English weather you can really get behind.

The perfect kind of weather for a wedding.

I look away from the road, and down at my left hand, on which there now sits a brand-new ring on the third finger. The hand is clasped in my wife's.

My wife, Annie.

The term still gives me a little bit of vertigo . . . in the best possible way.

Her hand tightens on mine. A little reassuring gesture that is very much appreciated.

Because being on this road is . . . difficult.

Coming back along here is something I've wanted to do for quite some time now, but have been very afraid to actually commit to.

Because it stirs things inside me that I would rather stayed decidedly unstirred.

And on any other day, I would avoid it. I very much doubt I will ever drive down this road again, once I've done what I've come here to do.

But today, I had to do it. I had *to come here.*

On the day I made my vows to my new wife about our future, I felt I had to mark the past properly. Draw something of a line under it. Travel along this road for the final time.

The wreath sits at my feet.

Its dark-green leaves feel deeply incongruous, when set against the bright cream of the limousine's interior, and the even brighter white of Annie's wedding dress.

It also feels odd because it's a symbol of bad things, *on a day that – so far – has been full of very* good things. *Friends. Family. Vows. Cake. Alcohol. More cake. A lot more alcohol.*

Annie wasn't sure about doing this on our wedding day. But I explained my reasons and my feelings, and she understood where I was coming from immediately.

I'm getting a lot better at explaining my reasons, and my feelings. The many, many sessions I've had with Monica over the months have made that possible.

Margaret was very touched when I told her what I was planning to do. It was lovely to see her at the wedding, as well. She did a very good job of wrangling Wayne the Parrot – who enjoyed the entire ceremony . . . largely because he was fed a constant supply of cashew nuts.

Having a parrot as the third of your best men may sound crazy, but Wayne has become an integral part of my life, and I don't apologise for his inclusion. I did apologise to Leo when the parrot pooped on his shoulder, though. Jack's laughter echoed around the church.

'Here!' I say to the driver. We have reached a point on this road that nobody else would pay any heed to whatsoever, but for me, it's burned into my soul.

The driver nods, having been told way ahead of time what my plans were, and knowing exactly what to do at this moment.

Because Charlie King is always the man with the plan.

Well. Mostly.

These days I find it a lot easier to do things by the seat of my pants, when I'm in the mood for it. Nothing wrong with mixing things up a little, every now and again.

The limo slows, pulls over to the side of the road, and into the lay-by that was once full of the remains of my old MG.

'Do you want me to come with you?' Annie asks, giving my hand another squeeze.

I shake my head. 'No. This will only take a minute, I promise.'

It's something I feel I have to do alone.

I want to do alone.

I pick up the wreath and climb out of the limo. Cars continue to hurry past as I walk back along the road a little way. I probably won't be able to put it down at the exact spot – but right here, where it's safe, will be more than adequate.

I lay the wreath against the hedgerow that runs along the side of the road.

'I'm sorry,' I say in a quiet voice, to nobody but myself.

I then allow the tears to fall, because that's a perfectly natural thing. No point in trying to control nature. It'll only bite you on the arse if you do.

With that small but necessary gesture over with, I turn and start to walk back to the car.

And I know that by the time I get back into the limo with my new wife, the tears will have dried, and the smile will be back on my face.

Because I have a lot to look forward to.

. . . a life with the best person I know.

And a parrot.

'Are you okay?' Annie asks me as the limo drives away from a place I will never visit again for as long as I live.

'Yes, I'm fine,' I tell her with a smile.

And that is the truth.

Totally.

ACKNOWLEDGEMENTS

Writing a book could be a traumatic experience for me . . . were it not for all the people who help me turn the contents of my brain into something you can actually read. They are: my agent Ariella, her assistant Amber, my editors Sophie and Sammia, the entire hardworking team at Amazon Publishing, and my lovely wife, Gemma. With all of them, my books tend to come out . . . Totally Fine.

ABOUT THE AUTHOR

Photo © 2023 Nick Spalding

Nick Spalding is the bestselling author of nineteen novels, two novellas and two memoirs. Nick worked in media and marketing for most of his life before turning his energy to his genre-spanning humorous writing. He lives in the south of England with his wife. Find out more about Nick and his books at www.nickspalding.com.

Follow the Author on Amazon

If you enjoyed this book, follow Nick Spalding on Amazon to be notified when the author releases a new book!
To do this, please follow these instructions:

Desktop:

1) Search for the author's name on Amazon or in the Amazon App.
2) Click on the author's name to arrive on their Amazon page.
3) Click the 'Follow' button.

Mobile and Tablet:

1) Search for the author's name on Amazon or in the Amazon App.
2) Click on one of the author's books.
3) Click on the author's name to arrive on their Amazon page.
4) Click the 'Follow' button.

Kindle eReader and Kindle App:

If you enjoyed this book on a Kindle eReader or in the Kindle App, you will find the author 'Follow' button after the last page.

Printed in Dunstable, United Kingdom